DEVIL'S BRIGADE

DEVIL'S BRIGADE

TRACKDOWN III

MICHAEL A. BLACK

Devil's Brigade

Paperback Edition
Copyright © 2021 Michael A. Black

Wolfpack Publishing
6032 Wheat Penny Avenue
Las Vegas, NV 89122

wolfpackpublishing.com

All rights reserved. No part of this book may be reproduced by any means without the prior written consent of the publisher, other than brief quotes for reviews.

This book is a work of fiction. Any references to historical events, real people or real places are used fictitiously. Other names, characters, places and events are products of the author's imagination, and any resemblance to actual events, places or persons, living or dead, is entirely coincidental.

Paperback ISBN 978-1-64734-235-7
eBook ISBN 978-1-64734-234-0

DEDICATION

To all my brothers and sisters in law enforcement who are under fire in these troubled times—Stay safe, stay strong.

My mind is troubled, like a fountain stirred;
And I myself see not the bottom of it.

Troilus and Cressida
William Shakespeare

CHAPTER 1

Phoenix, Arizona

Every time Wolf replayed the scene in his mind it turned out the same way, marred by death and the staccato blasts from automatic weapon fire and the explosions. It all came down to those missing eight minutes.

Today was no different.

On this early morning run, the velvety blackness had given way first to an encroaching orange glow and then a brilliant yellow as the orb edged its way over the eastern mountain range. Wolf had started out earlier than usual this morning to beat the heat of the day and also due to the special job that he and Mac had planned. But that didn't mean he had to make it easy. Instead, he carried a five-pound weight in each hand and was feeling the burn in his shoulders, forearms, and right down to his fingertips. Work the hands, his boxing coach had told him long ago. Build them up so you can deliver the power. Wolf had done the same run for so many mornings over the past few weeks and his body knew the route by rote. His thoughts raced along those familiar pathways as well, going back four years ago to replay the incident in his mind once more. And still, the missing section remained cloudy in his thoughts, hidden by mocking shadows thicker than the fires that had erupted around him and his squad on that dusty Baghdad street.

Every time, it ends the same way, he thought. Every damn time.

It all came down to those missing eight minutes and today was no different.

Iraq ... His last mission as an Army Ranger. A bogus mission set up by Lieutenant Jack Cummins, Military Intelligence. Meeting up with a PMC, the Vipers, led by a transplanted big cowboy named Eagan. Their simple objective: to assist in an interview of some locals.

Yeah, right. Simple was the word for it. Until the shit hit the fan and the lights went out.

He'd awoken to a haze of violence, betrayal, and death.

And the critical explanations were covered by a shroud of darkness. It was a translucent shroud, allowing certain facts and images to gradually reveal themselves, but overall, his complete recollection was indistinct. Like a jigsaw puzzle with some crucial pieces missing.

So, once again, it all came down to those missing eight minutes.

How many times had he asked himself, what had actually happened in that stinking, worthless shack on that Baghdad street?

And every time the answer was still the same: He didn't know.

Or rather, he didn't remember. That was more accurate. He knew that two Iraqi civilians had ended up dead and he'd gotten the blame for it. And one of his squad members, Spec-four Julio Martinez, had died, too, and another, Jeff Thompson, was severely injured by an IED blast. In his dreams, Wolf still saw their faces almost every night. It wasn't the first time he'd seen members of his squad get hit but he felt doubly responsible for this one. It was tied to the shame of his dishonorable discharge and loss of rank and benefits, the court martial and subsequent prison term, and all the rest of it. He hadn't even been able to mount a decent defense, all because of those missing eight minutes.

Now over four years and a host of dead bodies later, the circumstances still dogged him. Someone had set him up then and they continued to come after him now and he had nothing to go on except some persistently elusive memories, a few names remembered, and a cheap looking plaster bandito from south of the border that was somehow the key to everything. Exactly how or why the bandito fit into the equation was another mystery.

It was like having a key and not knowing what lock it fitted into.

Why was it so valuable that men would kill to possess it? And who was behind this serpentine conspiracy? What the hell did it all mean?

He wondered if he'd ever figure it out.

As Wolf reached the half-way point, the road marker that indicated the hiking trail up the mountain, he swung his body around to return to the ranch. That would give him a good four miles instead of the usual six. There was simply too much to do this morning.

And too much on his mind.

He'd gone about a mile or so on the way back when he saw another figure running toward him. From the size and lopsided gait he knew it was Mac. He'd been joining Wolf periodically on some of the morning runs although never for the full six or even the four-mile distances but that was okay. Not only was Mac a generation older than Wolf, he'd sustained more hits than any ten men put together and had enough shrapnel imbedded in his skin to set off an airport metal detector if he got within three feet of it. Plus, when their bounty hunting business took them down to Mexico a few months ago, Mac had taken a through-and-through and was still technically in the recovery stage, although he'd be the last to admit it.

No doubt about it, Wolf thought, Mac's the toughest man I've ever known.

And the best one, too, he added mentally.

Slowing his pace to a near-stop Wolf held out his fist and McNamara brought his up and gave him a bump before pivoting and heading back toward the ranch.

"Figured I'd join you on the last leg," McNamara said. "Hope I don't slow you down too much."

"It'll probably be the other way around," Wolf said, grinning.

McNamara grinned too. The two of them glanced in unison over their left shoulders to check the roadway, before crossing the asphalt so they could face any oncoming traffic.

"You feeling ready?" McNamara asked.

"More or less."

McNamara snorted, then spat.

"Now what kind of statement is that?" he asked. "Tomorrow night you're gonna be getting into the ring with a guy who's hoping to tear your head off if he gets the chance."

"Then I'll have to make sure I don't give him one," Wolf said and threw a couple of punches. "And they call it an octagon, not a ring."

"Right. But that don't lessen the danger none." McNamara took three long strides before adding, "You sure you want to go through with this thing?"

"You talking about the MMA match or the B and E we've got planned this morning?"

McNamara laughed but Wolf could tell he was breathing harder than usual. Perhaps it was time to slow the pace a bit more.

"Let's do this last mile as a walk," Wolf said.

"The hell you say." McNamara elevated the speed of his shuffling steps. "Remember, you were just a Ranger while I was Special Forces."

Just a Ranger, Wolf thought. But not anymore.

He adjusted his pace to catch McNamara, then slowed down again, hoping Mac would leave his pride behind them and modify his steps.

"The match," McNamara said. "It's not all holy-hell important, you know."

"The money will put us back in the black, won't it?"

McNamara nodded quickly but said nothing. The sweat was pouring off him now.

"And as far as the B and E," Wolf said. "It's long overdue. We should have done it right away."

"Yeah." McNamara's word came out like he'd spat out a brick.

Wolf backed off on his speed a little more. "So let's quit talking about it and do it."

McNamara nodded. His slick face was looking pale

in the early morning light.

"And one more thing," Wolf said.

"What's that?"

The gravel road that bisected the highway was only about fifty yards away now.

"Let's do a cool-down and walk the rest of the way," Wolf said as he slowed to a walk. "Since I was only *just* a Ranger."

Mac smirked and fell into step beside him.

"One of these days," he said, the words coming out between gasps for breath. "You'll be able to keep up with me."

***

Piccolo Mobile Home Park
Phoenix, Arizona

Jack Cummins studied his new image in the mobile home's bathroom mirror. The mustache and goatee were filling in nicely and seemed to complement his shaved head. With the extended-wear contact lenses replacing his rather thick glasses, he looked suddenly more formidable, despite his actual lack of much substantial muscle tone and any substantive toughness. And despite the ten pounds he'd lost in the past week or so, his body was still on the borderline of morbid obesity. At least the constant dyspepsia and diarrhea had subsided a little. That was a good thing, too, because spending the time in the rather limited confines of this overrated mobile home, inaptly named The Majestic Model and getting up suddenly to rush to the narrow confines of the bathroom remained highly problematic. Adding to the discomfort was the presence of his two roommates, Roger D. and Cherrie. But that couldn't be avoided either. They shared the main sleeping quarters which left him to bunk on the secondary room. It was less comfortable and commodious than the officer's billets he'd stayed in during his brief deployment in Iraq but at least he felt safe—safe from the predators in the County Jail, and temporarily out of reach for Fallotti and Von Dien. He was convinced that they were going to kill him which was why he had to figure out an exit plan, a permanent one, and also why he had to stay in the good graces of Roger D. Smith.

It was one of those chance meetings that had turned out to be mutually beneficial for both of them. Cummins had been alone, white, and defenseless when the four blacks had approached him in the bullpen of the county jail. Up until the bond hearing, his brief incarceration had been an uneventful overnight stay in a small, one-man cell. He'd been charged with fleeing and eluding and a weapons violation—the loaded .38 that he'd discarded inside the car at the last minute. Both were misdemeanor charges which assured a low bond. And he'd stuffed his pockets with all the cash he could from the stash that his now deceased partner in crime, Zerbe, had kept in the van. Bonding out was not going to be a problem, of that he was certain, and he'd remained relatively confident until it happened.

The police transport van he was in pulled into the lower basement area of the courthouse. He'd been handcuffed and crammed into it along with six other prisoners, of whom he paid little attention. His goal was to post bond as quickly as he could before they connected him to whatever had happened at the McNamara Ranch. He assumed that either Zerbe and his South African friends had killed Wolf and the others or that Wolf had beaten the odds once again. All the prisoners had been unhandcuffed and herded into the huge fenced in area in the lower portion of the courthouse. The guards called it a bullpen and it was more reminiscent of a cattle pen. There were perhaps twenty-five or thirty men in there, most of them Hispanic or black. Cummins was suddenly aware that he was in the distinct minority and he wasn't liking it one bit.

"Hey, white boy," one of the blacks said. "You look like you got titties. How'd you like to be my girlfriend when we get down to the County?"

The other prisoner was a lean looking black guy. The whiteness of his smile was marred by a missing front tooth. Three others immediately filled in next to him and Cummins found himself being shuffled to the back of the big pen. Bodies seemed to coagulate in front of him forming a human wall of sorts. A hand reached out and slapped his face. He jerked back, raising his hands, but knowing it was obvious he knew next to nothing about fighting. Another hand pushed him closer to the rear wall, this time coming from a large black man. His face was a set mask of menace. More of them moved in, punching his sides and forcing him down to his knees.

Voices mumbled in harsh whispers about the things they were going to do to him and someone tore his glasses from his face. He heard the plastic frame bounce on the hard concrete floor. He fell forward, curling into a fetal position as they began to kick him. His hand sought and luckily closed around his fallen glasses.

Just when he thought the worst was inevitable, a strong voice broke through the cacophony of jeers.

"Leave him alone, you black-ass motherfuckers," the voice said. It had a Southern twang to it.

A figure pushed through the crowd, chopping and punching, and Cummins looked up to see a widespread pair of legs in front of him. His savior was a muscular white man with a buzz cut. The man's fists were balled up and there was a tattoo of a triangle with a circle of stars on his right forearm. The outer edge of the triangle was framed in red and blue.

"Who you?" one of the tormentors started to say.

The white man's foot shot upward so quickly that Cummins barely could discern the snapping kick that caught the underside of the other man's chin. A flurry of punches and kicks followed, the motion so rapid that Cummins was barely able to follow it in the blur of his myopic gaze. Suddenly, the human wall dissolved leaving the four men lying on the floor oozing blood from torn lips and ruptured nostrils. Another black man rushed the white guy from behind just as Cummins was struggling to his feet. He collided with the on-rusher and the man bounced off. It sent Cummins sprawling onto his side again. The white guy whirled and smashed his fist against the stunned black man's jaw, dropping him.

Cummins felt strong fingers grab his arm and lift him to his feet, the savior's face showing a grin as he said, "Thanks, brother. But we better get to the front before the guards see us." As they shuffled through the now parting crowd, the man whispered, "Name's Smith. Roger D. Smith."

"Jack Cummins."

And so the friendship began.

Cummins had enough cash in his personal property to post bond for both himself and Smith, who was in for attempted grand larceny.

They were picked up outside the courthouse by a cigarette smoking woman named Cherrie Engel whose peroxided hair showed substantial black roots, in a beat-up Chevy Malibu that belched out an effluvium of haze every time she stepped on the gas.

"Honey-pot," Smith said. "This is my friend, Jack. He posted bond for me. Me and him got into a fight with a bunch of niggers in the lockup. He's gonna be staying with us for a few days."

"Pleased to meet cha," Cherrie said popping her gum.

Ordinarily, these were the kind of people Cummins would walk across the street to avoid but the accidental circumstances being what they were, he began to see the possibility of an opportunity. They both obviously had room temperature IQ's so manipulating them would be no problem. And their mundane banality could prove to be an asset.

Being on the lam myself now, or at least planning to be, Cummins thought, who'd think to look for me with these two?

Some knuckles rapped on the wooden door of the toilet area.

"You almost done in there?" Cherrie's whiny voice asked. "I gotta pee and do number two, too."

Cummins felt a wave of revulsion at the thought of that as he opened the door. She stood there in a flimsy nightgown that was so translucent he could tell she was naked beneath it. Although her armpits had noticeable stubble and he could discern a dark pubic thatch through the diaphanous material, the sight of her like this did kind of arouse him. He had to admit that her body wasn't half-bad.

He averted his eyes immediately. He didn't want to think of what might happen if Smith caught him sneaking a peek. From the way her lips curled back into a smile, he could tell she'd enjoyed giving him the show.

"Sorry," he said, turning sideways and edging past her. "Rog around?"

"He's outside doing his kung fu shit." She took a drag on her cigarette as she slid the door closed.

Cummins went to the door and down the steps to the outside.

The Majestic Model mobile home, he thought. It's anything but that.

There was a small cement porch with stairs affixed to the doorway and the damn trailer itself was mounted on some kind of foundation. He doubted whether it ever had wheels.

The air was already hot even though it wasn't yet mid-morning. He saw Smith doing push-ups on the small section of cement that separated this trailer from the one next to it. The beat-up Malibu was parked about twenty feet away and in front of it was a portable grill. The man's upper torso was shirtless and the sweat glistened over taut, rippling muscles. Smith canted his body to one side and began doing one-armed push-ups, effortlessly knocking off ten with his right arm before switching to his left. With his set finished, Smith jumped to his feet and gestured to Cummins.

"Hold them focus pads for me," Smith said brushing the dust off his hands. "So's I can finish up my workout."

Cummins went to the aluminum lawn chair next to door and picked up the two big mitts. He'd held them for Smith before and it was a jarring task he didn't particularly relish. The other man went through a series of punches and then kicks, and then a combination of both, lasting about twenty minutes and leaving Cummins sweating and winded just from trying to keep his arms elevated.

Finally, Smith signaled that he was finished and went for a dirty, once-white towel on the back of the chair. He wiped at his face, chest, and then under each arm. The man's body odor was so pungent that it was noticeable from three feet away. Cummins knew from experience that neither Smith nor Cherrie were super-conscientious about their personal hygiene but of course, he had been slipping in that department a little as well, given the small shower space in the trailer. Cummins was sweating, too, and Smith flipped him the same towel he'd been using.

Not wanting to offend his benefactor, Cummins took the towel and daintily dabbed at his face.

"I like you, Jack," Smith said, watching him. "The way you threw yourself against that nigger that was trying to jump me back in the lock-up. You got salt."

Although that hadn't actually been the case, Cummins shook his head.

"Nothing compared to yours," he said.

One side of Smith's mouth twitched into a half smile.

"We gotta look out for each other," he said. He regarded Cummins for several seconds more, then asked, "You ever think about making a new start?"

"All the time," Cummins said.

And he did. He definitely needed to figure out a game plan to get out of this current situation. It was one thing to lie low until he figured out his next move but this was extending into something more than he'd intended. But of course, Smith did have the right connections and had helped Cummins obtain a new set of IDs as well as a fake passport. The framework of an escape plan was germinating in Cummins's mind. Perhaps it was time to call Fallotti again. The first call he'd made, soon after the debacle at McNamara's ranch that night, had gone directly to voice mail. Cummins was certain that Fallotti and company were ignoring him. They still hadn't called him back and the anonymous credit and debit cards that had been in the safe at the hotel room all went as dead as his cell phone. Luckily, he still had the burner phones he and Zerbe had been using. And he had a substantial amount of cold, hard cash, too.

After bonding himself and Smith out, Cherrie had driven them to the hotel where Cummins had luckily been able to retrieve as much as he could. Both of them had stayed in the car making out, which gave Cummins a free rein to clean out both his and Zerbe's rooms. That included a substantial amount of money in the safe that Zerbe had been holding to pay off his South African mercs and other expenses. And since they were no longer a concern, Cummins found himself with enough operational capital to fly under the radar, at least for the time being. While it wasn't enough for a permanent retirement, it gave him enough to be comfortable and concealed for the moment and also to stay in the good graces of his new hosts by paying their monthly rental fee for their Majestic Model and buying them enough food, liquor, cigarettes, and groceries for a month. He'd also been successful at keeping the two hillbillies from finding out exactly how much money there was thanks to the money belt that had also been stuffed in the safe in the room. Although it didn't exactly fit around Cummins's expansive waist, he'd managed to secret it inside his doubled-over neoprene back-brace, which he now wore constantly, even to bed.

For once, he thought, being a fat man has its benefits.

Smith seemed about to say something more as they approached the trailer, but the door flew open and Cherrie stood there completely nude this time and holding a towel around herself and not too well. Cummins caught another glimpse of her dark pubic hair.

"You gonna empty the fucking black water soon?" she said pausing to bring a cigarette to her lips. "The toilet don't flush good."

Smith sighed and said, "I'll take a look," as he ascended the steps. "Now go get yourself dressed, dammit."

She frowned at him and turned, giving both of them a clear view of the bottom of her ass.

Smith rolled his eyes.

Cummins laid back a few steps, continuing to use the towel to wipe his hands, not bothering with the sweat that had collected on his forehead and cheeks. Then he tossed the towel onto the chair and felt for the burner phone in his pocket.

"I'll stay out here for a little bit," he said. "Give her a chance to get dressed."

Smith said nothing as he entered the trailer.

Cummins took a deep breath. He now had a few private minutes alone but he'd have to hurry. Smith had told him that they had some important business to attend to this morning, whatever that was. He turned on the phone and watched it boot-up. As the screen came into focus he saw he had one call, a Manhattan exchange.

Fallotti's number.

He checked his voice messages but there was none.

The prick had called but not left any message.

Typical.

I'm just another one of those loose ends they're always so worried about, he thought. But this time, I'm going to turn the tables on them.

He licked his lips and stepped to the front of the RV so as to eliminate the possibility of being overheard and then hit the redial button.

***

The Von Dien Winter Estate South Belize

Richard Soraces stood on the finely tiled outdoor patio that overlooked the spacious side yard next to the reddish brick mansion and took a sip from the iced glass that the pretty brown girl in the white maid's uniform had given him. She appeared to be about nineteen or twenty with an alluring look that seemed to say that, should the opportunity arise, she could give him all that he could handle.

He'd said something to her in Spanish and she'd giggled as she slipped back through the French doors leading back inside. Her dark eyes had flashed a message of availability, should he require another drink.

Or something along those lines.

Soraces smiled at her as she left.

But business before pleasure, he thought, although the layout seemed specifically designed for the latter.

Large, scrupulously maintained gardens filled with all sorts of flowers and vines gave the air a fragrance reminiscent of an African capitol. But here the bougainvillea, wildflowers, and other plants seemed tranquil instead of anticipating the sudden spray of automatic gunfire. It exuded safety and security. The efflorescence spread out from beyond the stone wall and into a subdued forest. Through the thick canopy of trees, Soraces could discern a few trimmed pathways leading to a high, fifteen-foot fence topped with triple strands of barbed wire. He wondered if the fence was electrically charged.

Most likely, he figured. He'd remembered seeing some signs posted on the gate when he'd arrived featuring a skull and the words: *DETENER. PELIGRO. NO TOQUES LA CERCA. NO ENTRADA.*

The gate guard had thrown a series of switches from inside the brick gate shack before the large metal gate opened to allow them entry.

A man's home is his castle, Soraces remembered thinking. Or in this case, his fortress.

He knew virtually nothing about the lawyer, Fallotti, who'd contacted him and even less about this Von Dien character. Soraces only knew that he was rich. Very rich, and since Soraces was now a free agent in the espionage business, having temporarily "retired" from government service with the Agency, being rich was all the qualification the man needed.

So why turn down a free trip down here to Belize? He was between assignments for the Agency, being officially a non-entity and he might as well hear what this rich son of a bitch had to say.

"*Señor* Soraces," a voice said.

This one was distinctly male.

Soraces turned and saw a large Hispanic man dressed in a butler's uniform. His face was clean-shaven but his beard was so dark it looked like he had a five o'clock shadow at eight in the morning. Plus, the bulge under the left armpit of the butler's jacket was unmistakable. Soraces guessed it to be a small caliber semi-auto.

Good for close-up housecleaning, he thought.

He took one last sip from the frosty glass and set it on a table, still not certain of what exactly the drink was. Perhaps later, if things worked out, he'd have the little brown girl make him another and tell him exactly what the components were.

Or perhaps not.

The butler was holding the French doors open and Soraces could feel the chill of the air-conditioning wafting out into the moistly humid air. He was wearing one of those yellow short-sleeve polo shirts and tan slacks. As he strode to the door, he removed his Oakley sunglasses and casually hooked one of the side pieces just above the highest button of his shirt, leaving the rest dangle like a tinted, plastic necktie or adornment giving the effect of casual insouciance.

Perfect to project the confidence and lack of trepidation when dealing with a rich man who had a bunch of local brown folks cow-towing to his every whim.

A slight ping sounded as Soraces stepped through the doorway and the butler held up his hand.

"Excuse me, *señor*, but I must ask you to stop for a moment."

Soraces did so and held up his hands.

"You have any metal in your pockets, *señor?*" the butler asked.

Soraces reached into his right pants pocket and removed the special pen that he'd brought with him. He handed it to the butler who did a cursory examination and set it down on a near-by table. A second man, this one wearing a more formal tan uniform with a patch on the shoulder identifying him as *Seguridad*, stepped next to them and moved a metal detecting wand over Soraces's body. The wand pinged as it passed over his left pants pocket.

"Coins that I might throw to the children," Soraces said still keeping his arms elevated. The other man murmured an apology, stuck his finger into Soraces's pants pocket, and withdrew several Belizean coins. He deposited them next to the pen and continued his sweep with the wand and after finding nothing, bowed slightly and said, "My apologies once again."

"*No problema*," Soraces said and picked up his items.

It pleased him to no end that they didn't discover that the pen was, in fact, a disguised knife with a razor-sharp blade that could be used for slicing or throwing. Soraces was an expert at both and after all his years with the Agency, never went anywhere without it. He considered it his good luck charm.

"If you will come this way, *señor*," the butler said as the wand-master faded into the background.

Soraces smiled as benignly as he could and followed.

It was time for this rich prick to meet the master fixer and show that displays of a bunch of money and pseudo-power over some servants were not intimidating factors when dealing with the man who'd played king-maker in foreign lands, toppled governments, protected corrupt politicians, and changed the course of human events in countless countries around the globe.

No, Soraces thought. Intimidating me is not in the cards.

The inside of the house was as sumptuously furnished as the outside grounds were green. Soraces felt his feet sink into a thick layer of carpet as he walked. The walls were lined with exquisite oil paintings, bronze and marble statues of varying sizes and a glass display of what appeared to be stone figures of some kind. None of it impressed Soraces that much. He'd seen similar displays in the mansions of presidents and dictators all around the world. Men who spent their lives procuring crafted objects of beauty that they felt would elevate them above the masses. One painting in particular on the wall, a Van Gough, caught his eye and Soraces gave it more than a cursory glance. He was certain he'd seen it in an art museum somewhere.

Chicago's Art Institute perhaps?

It was no doubt an original or an excellent forgery and knowing the reputation of this Von Dien, he doubted it was the latter.

The butler opened another door, this one solid looking and gleaming under a heavy sheen of polish. They went inside and the saw the room was a library of sorts. The high windows were stained glass and the sunlight filtered through the ones on the east side affixing a radiant collage of colors in a prismatic display on the opposite wall. There were three men at the far end of the long wooden table, two seated and one standing. Frosty glasses sat on the table in front of the two seated men, the condensation collecting on two curved, wooden coasters.

The standing man was huge, wearing a tight black T-shirt that displayed a set of massive arms laced with a brocade of prominent veins. Seated next to him, in an ornately carved high-backed chair, was a grotesquely fat man. His head was huge even in comparison with the rest of his body, which looked as soft as an inflatable life-raft. There appeared to be a waxy quality to his skin and each breath seemed to be an effort. He had a terry cloth robe draped around his sloping shoulders and from what Soraces could see of his chest, he hadn't been out in the sun for ages. The man's scalp was hairless and looked something like an enormous egg.

The big blonde guy, obviously the bodyguard, shifted his body slightly, lowering his right hand down toward a weapon on his hip. He appeared formidable, very formidable. As he drew closer Soraces assessed the gun. Judging from the front and rear serrations on the stainless-steel slide and the extended beavertail grip, he judged it to be a Walther Q4 Steel Frame semi-auto in a pancake holster. The pistol had red dot sight attached and an extended, suppressor adapter on the front end of the barrel.

The fat man must have an aversion to loud noises, Soraces thought.

A large tanto knife, canted for easy withdrawal, resided on the left side of the bodyguard's belt.

I wouldn't want to go up against that dude in a

dark alley, Soraces thought. Or a lighted one, either.

Across from them was a swarthy guy, who to be looked around fifty, with jet black hair and a well-trimmed mustache, rose to his feet.

That one, Soraces figured, was Anthony M. Fallotti. He looked Italian in his light blue short-sleeve shirt and tan shorts.

Ready for the tennis court, Soraces thought.

Almost, he added mentally as he saw a dribble of ebony hair dye forming an incipient droplet alongside the lawyer's left ear.

Even in the air-conditioning, the truth ekes its way out, Soraces thought, but he said nothing about it to this prospective employer.

After nodding as nonchalantly as he could to the three of them, he redirected his gaze toward the lawyer. He figured that was who would be doing most of the talking.

"Mr. Soraces," the man said. "It's a pleasure to meet you. I'm Anthony Marco Fallotti. I believe we spoke on the phone two days ago."

Soraces nodded and kept the smile on his face.

"Would you care for something to drink?" Fallotti asked.

"Sure," Soraces said. "An iced tea would be great."

Without another word, the man in the butler's uniform turned and left the room.

Fallotti held his hand out toward the chair on the

opposite side of the table. Soraces pulled it out and sat.

"This is Mr. Dexter Von Dien," the lawyer said holding his palm outward toward the fat man. "I'm Mr. Von Dien's personal attorney."

Soraces nodded again, recalling what he'd heard about this Von Dien character. When he'd been at the Agency, they'd kept a file on a lot of people of potential interest and Von Dien had been one of them. This rich billionaire had been born with a silver spoon in his mouth and owned copious amounts of property and businesses all over the country and the world. Obviously, this place in Belize was one of them and Soraces also recalled hearing something about an island estate somewhere in the Caribbean. Old money and as eccentric as hell. Sort of like a rich Buddha.

And then the Buddha spoke: "You don't say much, do you?"

Soraces waited for several beats before answering. "I try to listen more than speak."

One of the dangling bags of fat under the Buddha's eyes twitched a bit. Whether he was put off by the reply or not, Soraces wasn't sure, but he was glad he had his trusty pen knife in his pocket in case the bodyguard was ordered to administer some discipline to a capricious prospective employee.

But instead, the Buddha smirked and fluttered his fingers at the lawyer.

"You come highly recommended," Fallotti said.

"Your resume with the government's quite impressive."

Soraces said nothing. If these two had enough clout to gain access to his highly classified personnel file from Langley, then they obviously knew everything about him.

"I understand you've recently retired," Fallotti continued.

This time Soraces shrugged. "Let's say semi-retired. I like to keep my options open, and, as you know if you've seen my file, I'm good at what I do."

The Buddha spoke again: "And what is it you would say you do best?"

This time Soraces was ready with his set answer. These two wanted something done. Something delicate and illegal, otherwise they wouldn't be approaching him like this. He waited a few more beats to gain their full attention and smiled broadly.

"I'm sure you know the answer to that already," he said. "I do whatever it takes. What have you got in mind?"

CHAPTER 2

The McNamara Ranch
Phoenix, Arizona

Just a little B and E, thought Wolf as he slipped into the white, long-sleeved coveralls. Mac had taken meticulous care to assure that both of the bogus uniforms had matching patches.

Dangerous as all hell, considering they now had both the police and the FBI on their tail. But for once he agreed entirely with Mac. It was absolutely necessary. The last touch was the bandana and baseball cap that he slipped on. He left the bandana looped around his neck for the time being. There was no sense looking like an outlaw before the game began. After picking up his metal tool-case, he headed for the side door. When he emerged from the garage/apartment, McNamara was already waiting for him by a white pickup truck. As Wolf approached, Mac patted the side door, which had an emblem affixed to the driver's door saying, *Acorn Electronics*. A Phoenix area address followed which Wolf assumed was bogus.

"Had these babies specially made up," McNamara said, peeling back the upper edge of the emblem slightly before letting it flip back into place with magnetic alacrity. "Whaddaya think?"

"Pretty slick. Where'd you get the truck?"

McNamara grinned. "Remember our buddy, Lonnie Coats?"

They'd scooped up Coats a few weeks ago on a bench warrant for DUI and McNamara had convinced Manny Sutter to post bond for him once again. Mac had also helped Coats cover his abrupt absence from his job at an auto dealership. Coats had been so grateful he reciprocated by lending them vehicles from time to time.

"Sweet," Wolf said. He saw that McNamara was also clad in his coveralls and had a dangling mask attached to his left ear.

"Got a dummy plate on the back end, too," McNamara said. "Remember that one you found when you were running along the highway?"

"Glad it was put to good use," Wolf said.

McNamara pulled open the door and slipped in behind the wheel. Wolf set the toolbox into the bed of the truck and got in the passenger side. He wasn't looking forward to this morning's task.

"How's Kasey doing?" Wolf asked.

McNamara shrugged. "As good as to be expected, I guess." He heaved a sigh. "You know, I'm feeling pretty low about the way I treated Shemp. I never really gave the poor son of a bitch much of a chance, did I?"

Wolf agreed but said nothing.

"I guess I was just scared she'd get involved with the wrong guy again," McNamara said. "Which reminds me, we gotta get back as soon as we can. The asshole's coming by to pick up Chad for his two weeks of custody."

Chad was Mac's grandson by his daughter, Kasey. The asshole was Charles Riley, Kasey's ex-husband. Wolf had never met the man even after having lived at Mac's in the apartment above the garage for the past six months or so and from what he'd heard, he wasn't looking forward to the meeting. He hoped he could keep Mac out of trouble because he'd become even more protective of his daughter and grandson of late.

"I wish I would've been around to tell her not to marry that asshole in the first place," McNamara said. He heaved a sigh. "Story of my life. Always off fighting somebody else's wars, solving somebody else's problems, never realizing I was missing out on my little girl growing up."

"What time's he coming?" Wolf asked.

"High noon." McNamara said. "Just like that old movie."

Let's hope it doesn't turn out like that, Wolf thought.

They rode the rest of the way to the downtown address in silence.

***

Office of Emmanuel Sutter
Bail Bondsman
Phoenix, Arizona

The day was turning to shit fast and when Cummins saw where they'd pulled into the run-down strip mall, he almost choked. There it was, sandwiched between a game shop and a laundromat, the yellow sign in the front window spelling out *BAIL BONDSMAN* in big black letters.

Manny Sutter's place, he thought. What if he recognizes me?

His dyspepsia flared up immediately and as soon as the beat-up old Malibu stopped moving, he pushed open the rear door. After regurgitating the meager breakfast that Cherrie had prepared for the three of them onto the asphalt, he spat twice and wiped his mouth.

"Shit, I didn't think my cooking was *that* bad," she said from her perch in the front seat.

"It's my stomach condition," Cummins managed to say. His mouth still had that sour taste stuck in it. "It's delicate."

"You ought to get that looked at," Cherrie said. "But then again, you could stand to drop a few pounds anyway."

The remark irritated Cummins but he knew better than to show it.

Smith popped open the driver's door and got out, cocking his head to indicate they do the same.

Cherrie pulled out a package of gum from her bra and offered him a stick. Smith took one and jabbed his thumb at Cummins. She popped her own gum, took the second to last stick, tore it in half, and then handed it to Cummins. "Here, have one. It's Juicy Fruit."

Cummins reached out and accepted it with a measure of reluctance. He couldn't afford to do anything that might offend these two hillbillies but he felt his revulsion grow as his fingers sensed the sweaty dampness on the wrapper. Anyway, that was the least of his problems. First, he'd gotten another no-answer from that damn Fallotti. Once again, his call had gone straight to voice mail. Cummins had left a cryptic, "Call me at this number," and hung up. And now, Smith had pulled up in front of the same bail bondsman that Cummins had met before in Las Vegas setting up the fiasco in Mexico. If the bail bondsman remembered him and made the right connections, it could be disastrous. This son of a bitch was one of Wolf's buddies.

But we only met that one time, Cummins thought. And that was months ago. I look different now ... the hair, the beard, the contacts ... I've even lost a little weight.

After unwrapping the half-stick and tossing the papers down onto the ground, Cummins slipped the gum into his mouth and pulled himself out of the vehicle. He was careful not to step in the puddle of vomit and this seemed to amuse Cherrie to no end.

"Come on," Smith said. "Shake a leg, both of you. I want to get him bonded out so's we can go get his car next."

"And then what?" Cherrie asked. "Ain't we all going out for beer and ice cream?"

The thought of that combination made Cummins's stomach tighten once again but this time the upward flood of bile only reached the base of his throat.

"Later, sweetie pie," Smith said. "I told you we got things to do this morning."

Cummins slowed his pace, still concerned about the possibility of being recognized. If that happened and this guy told Wolf ...

"Hey," he said. "Aren't we supposed to be wearing masks, or something."

"Nobody's paying no attention to all that bullshit," Smith said. "Come on. We got to look respectable."

Respectable, thought Cummins. Fat chance.

Smith had slipped on a short-sleeved tan shirt and a pair of black gym shoes that looked like they'd found their way off the shelf of a second-hand store. He hadn't bothered to shower after his workout and big half-moons of sweat stained the shirt under each arm. And Cherrie wasn't looking all that classy, either. Even though she'd showered, for which Cummins was thankful, she'd slipped on a flimsy tank-top and a pair of blue jeans that were so tight you could see the cigarette lighter and the denominations of some coins in her pockets.

But perhaps that'll act in my favor, Cummins thought. Her figure's pretty good and this bondsman will be more interested in her tits than scrutinizing me.

Smith was holding the door open and scowling. Cherrie sashayed through with all the elegance of a stripper on stage and Cummins trundled in after her. The office itself was cluttered with two desks, three large filing cabinets, several padded chairs, and ubiquitous stacks of paper. The place had a musty smell and a myriad of dust mites floated in the interrupted flow of sunlight through the front window. At least the air-conditioning seemed to be producing a nice steady flow of cool air.

The room's two occupants looked up as the procession entered the office. One was a thin guy who looked to be in his mid-twenties. He had a messy crop of red hair and a pair of thick glasses that sat unevenly on his hooked nose. The other one Cummins recognized as Emanuel Sutter or Manny to his friends and clients. He hadn't changed much since their Las Vegas meeting a month or so ago, although in that one he'd seemed cleaner looking. Now his shaggy, bob-style haircut looked greasier and more unkempt. His upper body was still the size of a barrel and the padded leather chair in which he sat emitted a metallic squeal as he shifted his enormous bulk.

This guy makes me look small, Cummins thought, as he watched the bigger man pop the last piece of a chocolate donut into his mouth. He held out an open palm and indicated that they should seat themselves in the row of four chairs in front of the messy desk.

"Welcome," he said while chewing the donut. "What can I do for you?"

"A friend of ours got himself in a little trouble, sir," Smith said. "We was looking to get him bonded out."

Smith's use of the formality made Cummins wonder if he had military experience. That could explain his physical prowess. It also made Cummins realize he had very little knowledge of Smith's background, not that the issue had been explored or even brought up. Cummins had been just as reluctant to divulge too much about himself to this tough hillbilly.

"What kind of trouble?" Manny asked.

He finished chewing and was rolling his tongue over his teeth now, staring at Cummins with interest.

Oh, God, Cummins thought. Does he remember me?

"Ah," Smith said. "He's in County on a trumped-up charge of grand larceny."

"A felony, I take it?" Manny was licking some chocolate off his fingers now. He shifted backwards a tiny bit and said, "Hey, Sherman, give me another one of them chocolate ones."

"There ain't no more of them," the kid with the red hair said. His mouth twisted in something akin to disgust or hatred. "And the name's Fred, remember?"

Manny pushed his chair back and grabbed a white box with several grease stains from the space between the two desks. He slammed it on top of his own desk and shuffled through the selection of remaining donuts, finally selecting one with an array of colored sprinkles on pink frosting. He bit into it and started to set the box aside, then hesitated and held it forward.

"Care for one?" he said.

Cummins shook his head, as did Smith but Cherrie reached over and grabbed one similar to the one Manny had.

"Don't mind if I do," she said. "I kinda like these ones with the sprinkles, too."

Manny looked almost forlorn as she started eating, then set the box aside.

"What's the bond?" he asked.

"Twenty-five thousand," Smith said. "Ten percent."

Manny took another bite and considered the amount.

"Your friend working?" he asked.

Smith smiled one of those "good old boy" grins as he shook his head.

"Well, he was," he said. "But he got fired."

"How come?"

The good old boy grin was still in place, giving Smith's face an almost innocent cast.

"Well, sir, the place where he worked was where he got caught stealing from."

"And where's that?" Manny asked.

This time the smile dissipated. "Imperial Armored."

"The armored car place?" Manny asked.

"That's right," Smith said.

Manny nodded, masticated some more, and then took another bite.

"What'd he do there?"

"Guard."

Manny was working his tongue over his front teeth again. Cummins noticed that Manny was paying close attention to him.

Shit, he thought. He does recognize me.

"Hey, we met before?" the big bail bondsman

asked, his forehead wrinkling slightly. "You look kinda familiar."

The younger one, Fred, bumped his glasses up on his nose and stared as well.

Cummins felt a bitter flood of bile creeping up his esophagus. "Don't think so," he said, intentionally trying to lower his voice to give it gravelly inflection.

The big bail bondsman stared at him a few moments more, then shrugged and popped the remnants of the partially consumed donut onto his mouth.

"It'll come to me," he said. "I never forget a face."

Oh shit, Cummins thought. He stood. "You mind if I use your bathroom?"

He was still trying to keep his voice low.

Manny pointed to the room off to the side.

Cummins shuffled over and slammed the door. He barely managed to lift the seat in time to deposit the flood of bile into the bowl. He remained there, bent over the porcelain throne for several seconds.

There's no way he totally recognized me, he told himself. No way at all. It was almost two months ago and I don't even look the same now.

He could hear their voices through the closed door. After flushing the toilet, he rinsed his mouth in the adjacent sink and dried his face with a few paper towels. When he opened the door he saw Manny reaching for another donut.

"Don't eat no more, Uncle Manny," the red-haired

kid said. "Remember your sugar."

Manny's hand froze above the box and he smiled.

"Thanks for broadcasting it, Sherman," he said then turned back to Smith. "I think we can do business. What you got for collateral?"

Smith reached into his pants pocket and withdrew an envelope.

"Got the deed to his mobile home." He pronounced it mo-bile. "Worth a whole lot more than twenty-five grand."

Manny's tongue flicked over his lips and he reached over and took the envelope.

Cummins knew that the document was one of the fakes that Smith had obtained from the expert forger they'd used.

This would be a good test to see how much of an expert that guy was.

After perusing the deed, Manny replaced it into the envelope and handed it to his nephew, telling him to put it in the safe.

The bail bondsman's oversized head tilted to one side as he continued to scrutinize Cummins for a few seconds more, then shifted his gaze back to Smith.

"All right," he said. "What's this guy's name you want me to spring?"

Cummins saw Smith's face crack into a wide smile.

"Riley," Smith said. "Charles Riley."

***

The Von Dien Winter Estate South
Belize

"So this guy, Wolf was in prison, eh?" Soraces said pausing to take a drink of his iced tea. So far, the summation they'd given him seemed like it could be easily remedied. The question was why hadn't that been done already?

"He got four years in Leavenworth," Fallotti said. "Courtesy of the little scenario we set up in Iraq."

"And you say there have been three unsuccessful attempts to neutralize him?"

Fallotti and the fat Buddha exchanged glances. Von Dien gave a slight nod of his head, which Soraces took to mean that he was as good as hired.

"Right," Fallotti said.

"Who did you use?"

Again, the two men exchanged a quick glance, then the lawyer said, "In Leavenworth it was the Aryan Brotherhood. A contract thing set up by a mutual client. In Mexico we had employed a PMC known as the Vipers. A man named Eagan headed things up."

"I know him," Soraces said.

"Knew," Fallotti said. "Past tense."

Soraces raised both eyebrows. Eagan had a pretty good rep and he and his team had performed well the times Soraces had used them.

"Disgusting incompetence," Von Dien said. "Vastly overrated as were that second group of cretins. From Africa. Overrated and all bluster. Wolf defeated them all and they purportedly had him outnumbered and blindsided."

Soraces assumed the fat man was referring to the South African group in the third attempt. It seemed this guy, Wolf, was not someone to be taken lightly.

"One of my employees was also involved," Fallotti said. "Jack Cummins. We had planned on jettisoning him but he may be of some use."

"The one you want me to track down?" Soraces said.

"Right. He's still in the Phoenix area but we're not sure about his exact whereabouts at the moment."

"You're sure that Wolf has this *item* that you want?" Soraces said. He still wasn't sure exactly what that was. So far, they'd been dancing around any specifics in that department.

"We believe so," Fallotti said.

"He *has* to have it," Von Dien said. "And we must move quickly before it's lost forever."

"And we're uncertain as to whether or not he's aware of the item's significance?" Soraces asked, purposely using the plural personal pronoun now as a subtle way of establishing himself as already having been hired.

"At this point, we're not sure what he knows," Fallotti said. "When we get hold of Cummins we should know more."

"He's reached out to you by phone?"

Fallotti nodded. "Twice, once just a little while ago. We've got some people checking on things and we know he was arrested. He's apparently out on bond but we know precious little else. We've already scrubbed his association with the firm and his identity but we can't do more until we locate him. He knows way too much and could be a potential problem down the road which is why we need someone on the ground to take charge. Someone capable. Highly capable."

And I do come highly recommended, Soraces thought. He deliberately delayed any response in favor of taking another long drink of the iced tea.

Make 'em wait a little, he thought. Increase my marketability. It's all about the money.

"You know," he said leaning forward and carefully setting the frothy glass back on the wooden coaster. "Maybe you're going about this the wrong way."

The Buddha's mouth twitched and pulled into a puckered frown. He said nothing.

"What do you mean?" the lawyer asked.

"Simple," Soraces said. "Think of this whole thing in terms of a transaction. This guy Wolf's got something he knows you want so what does *he* want? What's his price?"

"His price?" Fallotti said.

"Yeah," Soraces said. "Everybody's got one."

For several seconds neither man spoke then the Buddha looked at the lawyer. "You know, that is a good point. We've never tried to buy him off."

Fallotti's lips tightened. "I don't know. At this point, that may be problematic. He was set up and sent to prison, lost all his military rank and benefits, and he's got to know that we've tried to kill him at least twice."

"So we just sweeten the pie a bit more." Von Dien smiled. "As Mr. Soraces said, everybody has their price."

"It might also let him in on just how valuable the artifact is," Fallotti said.

"Which he might already know, at this point." Von Dien's face twisted into a scowl. "This entire operation has been one failure after another. I hired you to oversee things, Mr. Fallotti, and you seem to have failed miserably. I like Mr. Soraces's suggestion."

The lawyer's face reddened and he said nothing.

This is my cue to take charge, Soraces thought. To put myself in the *numero uno* position.

"If I may," he said affecting a tone of sincere deference that he'd used on the other side of the globe when talking to warlords, foreign dictators, and king-of-the-hill thugs. "Why not let me go out there and do some ground work investigation. I'll get a feel for

Wolf and what he's after. See what his game is. Then I'll figure out a way to get what we want."

"So you propose to approach the man outright?" Fallotti asked.

Soraces shrugged. "Why not? If it seems efficacious."

"And exactly what makes you think he'll talk to you?"

"Among my other qualifications," Soraces said, "I am a member in good standing of the Maryland Bar. It'll be a simply matter of setting myself up in a local law firm out there and approaching him as a lawyer representing an interested party, who wishes to remain anonymous."

"Do you really think he's going to be open to a negotiation after all he's been through?" Fallotti asked.

Soraces flashed a confident, lips-only smile. "Like I said, that depends. But it's one tactic we should consider. From what I've gathered, he doesn't have all the facts, only piecemeal stuff, correct?"

"As far as we know."

"Good." Soraces nodded. "Then there's a distinct possibility we can spoon feed him a story that the other groups were hired as independent contractors to obtain the statue, and all of the resulting unpleasantness, the prison set-up, the attempts on his life, were their work, not ours. We could tell him we didn't know about them nor would we have approved of it and we're willing to offer some generous compensation."

Von Dien sat in silence, his tongue darting out to moisten his pendulous lips.

The Buddha's buying it, Soraces thought. Money means nothing to him.

But then the rich bastard shook his head.

"Even if he can be bought," he said, "this leaves me too wide open for an investigation. The authorities already are nosing around. I can't have any loose ends that lead back to me."

Soraces let his expression appear totally neutral. "Nor will it. We buy him off and get the item. From what I gather, this guy came from dirt, so he'll jump at the chance to get a suitcase full of money. And once he's delivered the item, we can always kill him then."

And I'll take possession of the suitcase full of cash, he thought.

The fat Buddha's eyebrows rose in unison. "Mr. Soraces, I like the way you think."

"All right then," Fallotti said. "When can you start?"

This time Soraces let the hint of a modest smile grace his lips.

"Just let me assemble some of my old wet-work team and I can begin immediately."

***

Phoenix, Arizona
The office building of the late Rodney F. Shemp
Attorney at Law

It was a five-story office building down the street from one of the courthouses. The name Rodney F. Shemp was still on the legend even though the lawyer was recently deceased. The police had initially treated his death as an accidental fall down the stairs at a hospital until the autopsy revealed severe trauma to the back and sides of his neck. Two of his cervical vertebra had been forcefully broken, which was inconsistent with a tumble down a flight of stairs. It took them less than an hour to connect the dots and locate video identifying one of the South Africans who'd been involved in the home invasion at McNamara's place. The lawyer's office was quickly sealed off by yellow crime scene tape as detectives sought a warrant to go through Shemp's files in what was now a homicide investigation. Luckily, the judge balked at giving the police cart blanche to peruse the files of an attorney, albeit a dead one, especially with the alleged perpetrator also being deceased.

"In view of the circumstances, what's the rush?" the judge said and announced that he would select another attorney to act in the capacity of a curio amicus, a friend of the court.

This gave Wolf and McNamara the much-needed

break they needed to cover their tracks. The file that Shemp most likely had in his office regarding their ill-fated Mexican venture would provide the FBI with all the ammunition they'd needed to mount a case against the two of them for lying to the federal authorities. Thus, the little B and E job became an urgent necessity.

McNamara pulled the truck into a loading zone at the back of the building and then he and Wolf hustled around to the front, pulling the cotton masks up over their faces as they walked. Wolf carried the toolbox and Mac had a clipboard with a bunch of papers clipped to it. Being that it was only nine-fifteen, the building wasn't officially open yet, but the lobby was still manned by a security guard. The guy sat in a chair by the elevators looking half asleep. He stirred to life as they tapped on the glass door. Slowly, the guard rose from his seat and ambled over to the door which was still locked.

"Building ain't open yet," he said. "Not till ten."

McNamara held up the clipboard. "We got a fix an outlet up on five," he said. "Keeps blowing the circuit breaker. Bad wiring."

The guard squinted as he looked through the glass at the paper attached to the clipboard.

"Want to make sure it's working by opening," McNamara said, "or the building management will have my ass on a platter. You know how it is, right?"

The guard's head bobbled up and down with agreement, the unwritten code of one working man to another, both united to keep their asses out of the management lawnmower. He flipped open the lock and allowed them entry, staring at the masks they both wore.

"What's with them things?" he asked.

"Regulations," McNamara said. "We gotta wear them now because of that virus bullshit." He punctuated the sentence with a snort.

The guard shook his head.

Both Wolf and McNamara kept their heads canted downward, imposing the extended bills of their ballcaps in what they hoped would be the wide-angel lens of the camera at the far end of the hallway.

"You said five?" the guard asked. "You gotta have a special code to get the elevator to go up there, you know."

"We got it," McNamara said figuring that would make their illicit venture sound more authentic. And they did have the code, too. Kasey had given it to them.

"Well, okay, I guess," the guard said.

Wolf regretted that they hadn't stopped at the Dunkin' Donuts to get the guy some goodies.

Maybe next time, he thought and smiled underneath his mask.

They walked to the elevators, and the guard

stopped.

"Say," McNamara said. "Can you open up the maintenance room down there for us? We gotta check that circuit breaker."

The guard nodded and shuffled through his ring of keys, selecting one as they walked underneath the camera to the solid metal door at the far end of the hall. After opening it, the guard made a slight hissing sound and wiggled his mouth.

"You guys don't need nothing else, do ya?" he asked. "I got to hit the john."

"Don't let us keep you from something that important," McNamara said chuckling to show his camaraderie.

The guard chuckled too and hustled down the hallway.

Wolf watched the man go and glanced at his watch.

Zero-nine-twenty. Plenty of time.

Hopefully ...

He silently hoped the late Rodney Shemp had been a good record-keeper.

He glanced back at McNamara who consulted the printed legend, flipped a switch off, and took out the camera surveillance system. He then closed the metal door but not before slapping a square section of duct tape over the latch so it would appear to be closed and locked, but could be pulled open. They went to the elevators and pressed the UP button. The door slid open and they stepped inside. McNamara punched in the code that Kasey had given them and they felt the car rising. The code was the same as the previous times they'd visited the late Mr. Shemp. Wolf had grown fond of the lawyer who'd been engaged to Mac's daughter. McNamara, however, had held the man in contempt up until the very end and was now feeling a bit of regret for not having treated his daughter's suitor with more respect.

Wolf felt the pangs of regret as well as or perhaps even more so than Mac. Shemp had worked pro bono on revisiting Wolf's court martial case trying to clear his name. Although he hadn't met with very much success, he had given Wolf a lot of free legal advice. And Shemp had also run interference for both Wolf and McNamara when they'd been pulled in for questioning by the FBI regarding the incident in Mexico.

That was the file they needed to find.

The elevator doors opened and Wolf saw the yellow crime scene tape forming a big X across the doorway to Shemp's office. An official-looking notice proclaiming *CRIME SCENE. NO ENTRY* was affixed to the glass door. Both of them had on latex gloves and Wolf opened the toolbox and withdrew a razor-knife.

"You want to do the honors," he asked, "or should I?"

"Lead on, McDuff," McNamara said.

Wolf flipped open the knife and carefully sliced the top portion of the three-inch ribbon of tape. It sagged downward and Wolf sliced the bottom portion. McNamara withdrew a set of keys and slid them into the top and bottom locks on the door. Then he twisted the knob and went inside the waiting room.

Wolf recalled the times he'd been there and the pretty secretary with the auburn hair who'd been manning the desk, seated behind a large computer monitor and a telephone.

It sat empty now, and he wondered for a brief second if the girl had found another job. She'd had a very sexy sounding voice. Wolf moved behind the desk and peered underneath it. The computer pedestal was still there. He set the toolbox onto the desk and opened it, removing a screwdriver and a computer hard-drive. Luckily, Kasey had helped her fiancé set up his office and she'd given Wolf and Mac all the info on what type of hard-drive each computer used.

"I'll check the filing cabinets," McNamara said as he stepped toward the inner office door. Wolf fitted the small, Phillips screwdriver bit into the electric screwdriver and began a quick disassembly of the secretary's pedestal.

I guess they aren't called secretaries anymore, he thought as he removed the screws. Now they're called administrative, office assistants.

McNamara jingled the keys again and unlocked the door to what had been Shemp's inner office

Wolf could feel the sweat trickling down his sides

as he removed the computer hard-drive and slipped a new one in place. After reassembling the pedestal, he replaced it under the desk and dropped everything into the bottom of the toolbox. He then went to the office where McNamara was going through one of the tall, wooden filing cabinets.

Wolf took a moment to recall the last time they'd been in there. It had only been a little over a week. He and Mac had practically strong-armed poor Rodney into accompanying them to the hospital so they could interrogate the burglar that McNamara had shot during a break-in to the Ranch. It hadn't been something they wanted to leave totally to the police but it had turned out to be a tragic waste of time and life. Shemp had been murdered in the hospital by one of the South Africans who'd subsequently taken everyone hostage at the Ranch.

At least we avenged him, Wolf thought as he moved behind the dead lawyer's desk, checked for another computer but found none. This was in accordance with what Kasey had surmised. Shemp had preferred to do his office work on a laptop and a tablet.

"Looks that pretty little gal he had as a secretary was very conscientious about her filing," McNamara said, standing over the open drawer of the cabinet and withdrawing a file. He flipped open the manila folder and thumbed through it.

"Hell, this has transcripts of your whole court

martial in it," he said.

Wolf wondered if they should leave it. It was already common knowledge to the feds that Shemp had been looking over Wolf's case. An absent file might create undue suspicion once the newly installed harddrives were discovered.

"Guess we'll leave that one here," McNamara said, obviously on the same page as Wolf.

"Sounds good to me." Wolf tried the first drawer of the desk but found it locked. Checking the center drawer, he found that secured also. "Let me see those keys."

McNamara replaced the file in the cabinet and tossed the ring of keys to him.

"We'd best shake a leg," he said. "I'd like to be out of here sooner rather than later.

Wolf perused the keys and selected a small one that appeared to match the lock in the center drawer. He tried to insert it but it didn't fit. He tried another. That one didn't work either.

More sweat began trickling down from his armpits and he checked his watch again.

Zero-nine-forty-eight.

"I got mine," McNamara said, as he removed another file and pushed the drawer closed.

"I don't," Wolf said. "None of these keys fit."

"Shit, we gotta find that laptop and tablet." McNamara moved closer to the desk. "We're cutting too close for comfort. Plus, we got restore that damn circuit. Break the motherfucker."

"My sentiments exactly." Wolf removed a large screwdriver from the toolbox and jammed the edge between the drawer and the frame of the desk. He tried wiggling it back and forth to catch the latch and slip it but McNamara placed his hand over Wolf's and pushed down. The wood made a cracking sound and the drawer popped open.

"We ain't got the time for subtlety," he said.

Wolf pulled the top drawer all the way open exposing a neat arrangement of office materials, paperclips, pens, a small calculator, envelopes, and a few other miscellaneous items.

"Looks like poor old Rodney was a little bit Obsessive-Compulsive," McNamara said.

Wolf said nothing but hoped the lawyer had been just as meticulous in storing his other items in one of the three successive side drawers. He pulled open the first.

It had another divider for pens and paperclips, but it also had an old-fashioned rolodex and another plastic container full of flashdrives.

"Better take that, too," McNamara said. "No telling what's on them."

Wolf placed the container in the toolbox, closed the top drawer and opened the second one.

"Shows what kind of slow-ass burglar you'd make,"

McNamara said. "You should've started with the bottom one first. That way you wouldn't waste time closing each one."

"But we struck paydirt," Wolf said pulling out a tablet and a red-colored laptop. He set them on the desk and checked his watch.

Zero-nine-fifty-three.

He looked up at Mac who shook his head.

"Let's just take them with us," he said.

Wolf silently concurred and placed the two computers into the toolbox. He had to rearrange the other items, the two screwdrivers, the roll of duct tape, the purloined hard-drive, the plastic box of flashdrives, and the file that Mac had procured, but eventually managed to get the two metal lids to close around the handle.

They hustled out of the inner office and closed the door behind them.

"You gonna make sure it's locked?" Wolf said with a grin, even though he knew Mac couldn't see it because of his facemask.

"Let's leave that for the curio amicus and the cops to worry about," McNamara said, shaking the ring of keys and moving toward the main door. He cracked it open and peered through the silver of opening. "Clear. Let's go."

He held the door open wider and Wolf slipped under the remaining ribbon of police tape. McNamara followed and took a roll of clear package tape out of his pocket. As he pulled out a small section, Wolf set the toolbox down and held the dangling police tape back in its original position as McNamara affixed the two ends together with the clear tape. They repeated this with the other sliced ribbon and then moved to the elevators. The car was still in place waiting for them and they rode down to the lobby. The security guard was at the main doors now opening the doors. Several people were waiting outside. McNamara went to the maintenance closet, pulled the door open, and removed the swath of duct tape. Then he reached up and flipped the circuit breaker back in place, restoring the camera system.

Wolf followed Mac to the door where they nodded a goodbye to the security guard.

"All set," McNamara said. "Nobody has to worry about nothing now."

Wolf chuckled silently at the intentional double negative.

I hope that turns out as intended, he thought.

***

Police Impound Lot
Phoenix, Arizona

It had taken them less time than Cummins had thought to pick up this guy Riley from the county lock-up once the bail bondsman made the appropriate phone calls and sent his idiot nephew to sign all the paperwork. The police impound lot was another story. It was obviously a contract place run by a private company on the outskirts of town, surrounded by a ten-foot cyclone fence with three strands of barbed wire mounted on cantilevers along the top. The office building was solid brick and everything was transacted through a Plexiglas window just inside the front door. The bored woman on the other side of the wall tapped a few keys on her computer and told them the impound fee was five-hundred dollars.

"How come it's so much?" Riley asked, his lower jaw jutting out in a huff.

The woman shrugged and gave no oral reply.

"Shit," Riley said. "I ain't got that kind of dough."

Cummins had sized the man up when he'd slid into the back seat of the Malibu outside the lockup. He looked to be in his late twenties or early thirties, with a handsome, boyish face. His dark hair was slicked back in an oily pompadour and he looked average in build and height. What was noticeable was a bandage on his left forearm. When he'd gotten into the car and Smith had made the introductions, he'd asked how Riley's arm was doing.

"It's getting better," Riley said, peeling back the bandage to reveal a large swollen and vividly discolored area on the outer aspect of his forearm. "Being in there with all them fucking niggers and Mexicans didn't help none."

His voice had a similar-sounding twang as Smith's—another good old boy.

"You get in any fights with 'em?" Smith asked.

"Had to flatten a few of them before they left me alone," Riley said.

Smith grunted an approval. "I had to do the same. Me and Jack here got into it in the bullpen right before our bond hearings. Handed a bunch of those assholes their heads and knocked one shine's ass up around his fucking neck."

Riley smiled and gave a nod of acknowledgment to Cummins.

As Cummins remembered it, it had been Smith who'd done most, if not all, of the fighting but he said nothing. Let Riley think it had gone down that way. Building a reputation, even an exaggerated one, couldn't hurt with a pair of morons like these two. He did wonder why Smith had attributed any of the action to him, though.

Stealing a look at the infection site on Riley's arm, Cummins was able to discern that the discoloration was partially due to a tattoo. Despite the swelling, he was able to discern that it was the same type that decorated Smith's left forearm: a triangle framed in red and blue with a circle of stars inside.

Riley carefully replaced the bandage and said they

needed to get moving.

"I'm supposed to pick my kid up from my ex's by noon," he said. "And we got that other thing to plan out, too."

Smith slammed the Malibu into gear and they took off, leaving Cummins wondering what the "other thing" was.

Now, as the three of them stood in a huddle by the impound lot's window, Smith and Riley continued to confer about that nebulous topic.

"We're on a time-table as it is," Smith said. "Maybe we should just forget about the damn car."

"I know that," Riley said. "But I can't go showing up at her house in your jalopy. Her old man's a suspicious old coot. And that's the last thing we need when we're about to head—"

"Shut your mouth," Smith said. He pursed his lips as if he were contemplating something, and then turned to Cummins.

"Jack, you good for the five hundred?" he asked. "We can pay you back the day after tomorrow."

Cummins wondered what that meant as well. He certainly had enough money to handle the fee without raiding the special money-belt account but letting Smith know how much he had probably wasn't prudent. But then again, Smith had no doubt already seen that Cummins had a very thick wallet and possibility even knew or suspected about the stash. Besides, he couldn't afford to offend the tough hillbilly. It was still time to keep lying low, flying under the radar, until he heard back from Fallotti or could figure out his next move.

"Yeah," Cummins said. "I think so but it'll pretty much drain me."

That last part was total lie and Cummins watched Smith's face for any signs that he suspected, but there was none.

Room temperature IQs, Cummins thought and pulled out his wallet. He opened it, withdrew five hundred-dollar bills and handed them to Smith.

Both of the hill-rats grinned and Smith slammed the currency onto the small counter by the window slot and said, "There you go, honey. And make sure you give us a receipt."

"And make it snappy," Riley added. "We're in a hurry."

The woman behind the Plexiglas seemed to move with exaggerated slowness.

"Thanks, brother," Smith said.

Riley glanced at him with a questioning look and then to Cummins.

"I appreciate it," he added. "And like my brother says, we'll pay you back tomorrow."

Cummins smiled and gave a slight nod. He felt like he'd suddenly been made an honorary member of the hillbilly brotherhood or something.

Just then, Smith's cell phone rang and he glanced at the screen, then immediately answered it. After a few exchanged words he terminated the call and looked at Riley.

"It's Keller," Smith said. "He's getting close."

Riley nodded and then stole a quick glance at Cummins.

What the hell was this all about?

CHAPTER 3

McNamara Ranch
Phoenix, Arizona

By the time they got back from their little escapade at Shemp's old office and finished dropping off the borrowed pickup truck, Wolf felt like he needed another shower. McNamara had driven his new maroon Escalade back to the ranch at record speed, complaining the whole way that he wanted to get back in time to say goodbye to his grandson.

"I sure don't feel good about letting that shitbird take him for two weeks," he said. "But we got no choice. That's what the damn custody agreement says."

Wolf wondered if that was one of the reasons Mac had been so hard on Rodney Shemp. In addition to being Kasey's fiancé, he'd had also been her lawyer and set up the custody arrangement. Wolf wondered whether Shemp had done a good job with given the situation but that was a moot question, at this point, since Shemp was deceased.

"Maybe we can both find new lawyers," Wolf said and left it at that.

McNamara seldom talked about his ex-son-in-law but did mention that he was ex-military, and Kasey had met him about six years ago. The marriage had been sudden and brief, leaving her with a young son and an absentee husband away on multiple deployments. Mac had reluctantly reached the end of his own military career, reaching mandatory retirement age, and settled in Arizona. He'd been shocked, but not surprised, when his divorced daughter had shown up on his doorstep with her one-year-old son and asked if they could stay with him. That was when he'd found out his ex-wife had been killed in a car crash. Wolf had never met Mac's ex but had inferred that she liked to drink.

And he knew precious little about Charles Riley as well. The few times he'd shown up to take little Chad for a weekend outing, Wolf had taken pains to stay as far away from any interactions as possible. From a distance, Riley looked to be kind of handsome, if you liked the type, but not really outstanding in any other way. One time he'd almost ventured out to intervene when he'd heard Mac threatening to "plant" the guy in the garden. Wolf had rushed down from his garage apartment only to see a tearful Kasey holding her father back as Riley escorted an equally upset, crying Chad to a dilapidated white Dodge Caravan. Wolf remained frozen in the doorway, not knowing what to do. A subsequent angry glance from Kasey convinced him to back off and he didn't mention the incident after that. The relationship between him and Kasey had always been tenuous at best, although things seemed to have been improving a bit recently, the unexpected death of her fiancé had cast another pall over their relationship. Not only was he still inadvertently cast as "the son her father had always wanted," he was now the man responsible for bringing this trouble to their lives and getting Shemp killed.

Wolf knew that wasn't entirely the case, but again, he said nothing.

He felt bad enough about sponging off his mentor for the free room and board, even though he was now starting to hold his own with bringing in the bounties. Things had slowed recently, with the national health concerns, but now were slowly starting to return to normal. And with the money he was scheduled to make for this upcoming MMA fight, he felt confident his purse would put Trackdown, Inc. securely in the black and give him enough money left over to perhaps buy himself a car or maybe a motorcycle. He'd already been able to invest in a used laptop.

McNamara was in the driveway now playing

catch with his grandson. Chad was dressed in a T-shirt, jeans, and gym shoes. His little suitcase sat next to the front door.

Wolf watched them toss the ball back and forth, appreciating the broad grin on both of their faces. Then his eyes caught sight of movement over at the junction of the highway and the macadamized roadway that led to the ranch. Two vehicles had pulled off onto the road, a green Dodge Caravan and a black Chevy Malibu.

Wolf couldn't see the number of occupants but he was sure the Dodge Caravan most likely contained more than one person. The hairs on the back of his neck stood up and he couldn't shake that unmistakable feeling that something bad was about to happen.

He hoped he was wrong but decided to stay close just in case Mac ended up needing him.

This could be trouble coming, he thought.

***

Cummins had been watching in horror as the Dodge Caravan slowed and made the left turn onto the roadway that led to, of all places, McNamara's ranch house.

Christ, this was the same place he'd narrowly escaped from a little over a week ago … The site of the aborted attempt to get Wolf and McNamara to surrender that damn bandito and that had turned into an unmitigated disaster. This meant that going back into the lion's den again and that meant flirting with danger. If Wolf was there, McNamara too, and either one of them saw him, it would be all over. They were most likely armed. Plus, even though he was out on bond, he was still facing charges in court. An incident could get him rearrested. But it was significantly more dangerous than that. Wolf wouldn't stop until he got the answers he wanted and Cummins doubted either Smith or Riley would be able to stop him. Well, maybe Smith might stand a bit of a chance.

No, probably better than that, he thought. But Wolf was like an indomitable force.

He scanned the wide driveway between the ranch house and the big garage and saw three figures standing there.

One of them was a small child but the other two were full-grown men, and one of them looked like Wolf.

Oh, God, no, he thought.

"Hey," he said. "Stop the car and pull over, will ya?"

Smith, who was driving, looked over at him. "What's the matter?"

"I gotta puke," Cummins said.

He was in the front passenger seat and pulled up on the door-handle.

Riley had requested that Cherrie ride with him until he picked up the kid so it would "look better." He'd said that his ex-father-in-law was a real tough bastard and reiterated that any problems, at this point, were the last thing they needed.

"Not with the op coming up," Riley added.

Cummins once again wondered what these two hillbillies were referring to with all these cryptic comments.

But now he had more pressing issues to worry about.

"Stop it, would ya," he yelled as he felt the rise of bile from his stomach.

Smith pulled off to the side of the road and jerked the Malibu to an abrupt halt.

Cummins unfastened his seatbelt and leaned his upper body to the side as the flood of bile and vomit burst forth.

He remained hunched over for several seconds, continuing to retch.

"That's a real nasty habit you got there," Smith said. "But leastways you didn't get none in my car."

He chuckled.

"It ain't a habit," Cummins said. "I told you, it's a medical condition."

"If you say so." Smith's tone was still full of mirth.

Yeah, go ahead and laugh, asshole, Cummins thought, then realized the sudden dyspepsia attack had been a godsend. If they hadn't stopped, Smith would have no doubt pulled into McNamara's driveway leaving them in the full view of Wolf.

Disaster averted, he thought. At least for the moment.

"You done?" Smith asked, his foot still on the brake.

Cummins thought for a moment before answering, and then said, "Maybe, but stay here, will you? I don't want to get too close to anybody."

***

The black Malibu was still stopped about a hundred yards away on the access road. The Dodge Caravan continued to pull into the driveway and Wolf recognized Kasey's ex-husband behind the wheel. Mac and his grandson stopped their game of catch and the little boy smiled.

Looks like he's glad to see his dad, Wolf thought, wishing there was a better lot for the kid.

Every boy deserves a father, he thought, thinking back to his own childhood.

A blonde woman sat in the front passenger seat, a cigarette dangling from her mouth.

"Oh, Jesus, will you look at that," McNamara said walking with his grandson in tow, to Wolf's side.

The woman took an extended drag on the cigarette as she opened the car door and slipped out. She exhaled a plume of smoke and Wolf caught a whiff of it. She appeared to be in her late twenties with blonde hair that came straight out of a bottle. Her figure wasn't half bad and she was dressed to show it off.

Riley descended from the driver's side and strolled over at a slow pace. He was dressed in a dirty white T-shirt, a pair of cut off orange shorts, and army combat boots. There was a bandage around his left forearm, some yellowish discoloration working its way through the white cross-weaving. His eyes darted from Mac to Wolf to his son and his mouth remained in a perpetual sneer.

Finally, he moved his head ever-so-slightly and muttered, "Jim, how you doing?"

McNamara returned the nod but remained silent, his hand still on his grandson's shoulder. The boy apparently knew what was coming and was a bit subdued.

No one spoke for several seconds and then the woman smiled and bent over, giving both Wolf and McNamara a view of her well-stuffed brassiere as the loose-fitting tank top spilled open.

"Is this your son, Charlie?" she asked, clapping her hands together like she was summoning a dog. "Ain't he a little darling?"

"I hope you ain't planning on smoking around my grandson," McNamara said still keeping a firm grip on the boy.

"Wouldn't dream of it, sugarplum," the woman said

and tossed the cigarette away. It landed about ten feet away, still smoldering.

"Where's Kasey?" Riley asked.

"I'm right here," Kasey said from the door of the ranch house. She walked toward them briskly holding a flip-phone. Wolf noticed she had on a light blue blouse, jeans, and sandals, her usual attire for her morning college class.

Going to her son, she knelt beside him and hugged him close, whispering something, then giving him a kiss on the cheek. As she stood, she turned and looked directly at the woman and then to Riley.

"Who's this?" she asked.

"Her name's Cherrie," Riley said. "Not that it's any of your business."

"That's Cherrie with an I E," the woman said.

Kasey frowned. "It's my business who my son's spending time with."

"He's spending time with me. I'm his father."

"And I've got custody," Kasey shot back.

"For now."

That seemed to hit Kasey like a slap in the face and she recoiled. "What's that supposed to mean?'

"You just wait and see," Riley said.

McNamara stepped forward and thrust his finger toward Riley's face. "And you better watch your mouth talking to my daughter like that."

Riley looked ready to yell something back when

the woman named Cherrie smirked and said, "Listen, honey, I grew up in a household with six brothers and I was the oldest, so I know a thing or two about taking care of little boys." She turned to Riley and put a hand on his shoulder, leaning close. "Just calm down, sugar and remember what we got going, okay?"

This seemed to mollify him slightly.

Wolf felt awkward just watching the situation unfold and felt very sorry for Chad.

"Come here, little man," Riley said, holding his hands out. "You ready to spend some time with your daddy?"

The boy looked up at his mother who walked forward with him. His face was a mixture of trepidation and uncertainty.

This is doubly bad, Wolf thought, both for Chad and for Kasey.

He knew that Shemp had been working on limiting the custody visits to supervised sessions only but with his untimely demise, it was anyone's guess how long a change in the agreement would take now.

Kasey held up the phone and showed it to Riley.

"I want this to go with him," she said. "My numbers are programmed into it and I expect him to call me every night. Understood?"

"Is that an honest to goodness flip-phone?" Cherrie asked. "Shit, I ain't seen one of them in a month of Sundays."

Kasey pursed her lips into a frown as she turned toward the woman, then bent over and tucked the flip-phone into Chad's pants pocket. "Honey, this is a phone you can use to call mommy any time. And I want you to call me every night, okay?"

Chad nodded.

Kasey stood and glared at her ex.

"Anything else?" Riley asked with a condescending lilt to his voice.

"Like I said." McNamara took a step forward. "You watch your mouth."

"Or what, old man?' Riley took a step back and half-cocked his right arm.

Wolf stepped forward between the two men and stared into Riley's eyes, giving him one of the "Don't fuck with us" looks that he'd mastered in the prison yard. No words were spoken between them and none was necessary. Riley's lips compressed inward and then his teeth emerged in a mocking smile.

"You got yourself a new fella, huh, Kase?" he said. "Who're you?"

Wolf wanted to say, "I'm the guy that's going to kick your fucking ass up one side of this driveway and down the other," but instead took a breath and said, "Your son doesn't need to see this."

Riley tried to hold Wolf's gaze, then blinked several times. He inched backward a few steps and reached his hand out toward his son.

"I'll make sure he calls you every night," Riley said. "If that's what you want."

"By seven o'clock," Kasey said.

Riley eyed her up and down and then turned his head toward Wolf. After trying to affect a solid stare, he averted his eyes again and gave a curt nod.

Kasey squatted down and gave her son a kiss and another hug, telling him that he was going to spend two weeks with daddy and that if he needed her, all he had to do was press a button on that phone. The little boy nodded, but still looked less than contented.

"Hey, sweetie, y'all got a charger for that thing?" Cherrie asked. "The flip-phone?"

Kasey stood, said she'd be right back, and ran toward the house, leaving the four adults and the child standing in the middle of the driveway in front of the Caravan.

"Mind if I smoke while we wait?" Cherrie asked, smiling at McNamara.

Without waiting for him to answer, she reached into her bra and took out a pack of cigarettes and a plastic lighter. Wolf knew little about cigarettes but noticed the pack had a circular red and blue design, as did the cigarette. He couldn't quite read the label.

Cherrie shook out what must have been the last one, crinkled the pack up, and dropped it down by her foot as she fired one up and the sudden smell of the burning tobacco assailed Wolf's nostrils.

McNamara snorted in obvious irritation.

"Put him in that car seat, would ya?" Riley said to her.

Cherrie nodded and held her hand out for Chad. "Come on, honey."

"Remember what I told you about smoking near my grandson," McNamara repeated.

She wrinkled her nose, blew twin plumes of smoke out each nostril, and took one more copious drag on the cigarette before tossing it away. Chad glanced back at Wolf and his grandfather as he rounded the side of the Dodge. Kasey came walking out with a charger dangling from her fist. As she went by Riley, she thrust it into his hands and went to check on her son. Wolf watched through the front windshield as the two women secured Chad in the car seat. To his surprise, they seemed almost cordial as they secured the boy with the straps. Kasey leaned in and kissed him once more and stepped away from the vehicle. Cherrie opened the passenger door and got in.

"Come on, will ya?" she yelled, cracking open the door and leaning halfway outside. "Get that air-conditioning turned on, for Christ's sake. It's hotter than a Texas whor—ah, hen house in here."

"I'll take good care of him," Riley said as Kasey rejoined her father and Wolf.

"You'd better," McNamara said.

Wolf had no doubt that, despite the age difference,

Mac could pound the other man into the ground.

Riley stared at him and then turned and got into the vehicle. It started up and he said something to Cherrie as he backed it up, pulled forward, and then swung out toward the access road.

Wolf noticed that the black Malibu was still idling over there. It looked like two people were inside but it was difficult to tell with the tinted windows. It did a wide turn and headed back toward the highway. The Caravan turned out of the driveway and followed. A procession of three dark sedans turned off the main highway and passed the two vehicles going the opposite direction. The trio of cars had a distinctly familiar look to them.

"Aw, shit," McNamara said. "Looks like the feds are coming back for that shooting team interview they told us about."

Wolf was thinking the same thing. He looked at Kasey.

"I'm sure Chad will be all right," he said, trying to reassure her. She looked about ready to cry. "Kids are pretty resilient at that age."

She nodded and pressed her lips together.

"And as soon as we find another good lawyer," McNamara said, "we'll do something about this damn custody bullshit."

The dam broke and tears streamed out of Kasey's eyes. She turned and ran toward the house. Mc-

Namara's face twisted into a pained expression.

"Cherrie." McNamara blew out a puff of breath.

"With an I E," Wolf said.

"Hell," McNamara said. "If she's got a cherry she's using it as a taillight."

Wolf smirked. "Could have been worse."

What he didn't mention was his concern about the cut-off shorts that Riley had been wearing. The bright orange color, the absence of pockets, the elastic waistband devoid of belt-loops, no laces in his boots ... It was all familiar.

Too familiar, he thought. Jail or prison pants, hacked off to look like a pair of shorts.

"Better go tell her to stay in her room," Wolf said. "The last thing she needs now is the FBI trying to grill her."

McNamara glanced toward the road, then nodded.

"I got something else I need to talk to you about, too," Wolf said, thinking of the orange-colored cut-off shorts.

"What's that?" McNamara asked.

"It'll keep," Wolf said. "Go tell Kasey to lay low."

McNamara nodded and went into the house. Wolf walked over and stepped on the still-smoldering cigarette. After he'd ground it out, he bent over and picked up the two butts and the crumpled pack, unrolling it in his palm.

UPTOWN BLUES MENTHOL, the label read. *For*

those with sophisticated tastes.

***

"I smell cop," Smith said gunning the Malibu past the three navy-blue sedans. "What you all hunched down for?"

"Those are feds," Cummins said thankful that he'd been able to get the hell out of there before being spotted by Wolf or the FBI.

"How you know that?" Smith asked.

"Believe me, I can tell."

As well he could. Although he'd pulled the baseball cap down on his face and leaned forward as the FBI cars had passed, he managed to catch a glimpse of some of the drivers and passengers. Although he couldn't be sure, Cummins was almost certain it was the same two agents he'd exchanged glances with when he'd escaped from the botched hostage situation here before. The feds had called in the plate on his rental van and he'd been subsequently stopped by Phoenix PD, which had led to his arrest after they'd found the snub-nose he'd tried to conceal under the seat after he'd tried to get away. That it was a totally bogus bust was beside the point. Cummins was confident he could have beaten the case in court. He was, after all, an attorney, and not a half-bad one at that. But he also knew sticking around to face charges and eventually getting sucked into the ongoing investigation of what had happened at McNamara's and Wolf's that night would put him on a one-way trip to the penitentiary.

Ironic, he thought. Me and Fallotti and Eagan had all gone to such elaborate ends to set that son of a bitch, Wolf, up for those murders in Iraq, and afterwards in Mexico. Now, I'm the one sweating it.

And that bastard, Fallotti, wasn't even answering his calls or even calling him back. The prick.

Everything that had happened after the Mexico trip tended to convince Cummins that he, too, had been placed on the "expendable's list." He'd come to suspect that Fallotti had told Zerbe and his South African mercenary band, to exterminate him as soon as he'd verified the artifact. That was all they needed him for at this point. They'd gotten him in so deep, used him, and now were ready to toss him away, like soiled toilet paper. At this point, he owed them nothing.

But they owed him.

The lot of them did. Fallotti, Von Dien, and anybody else associated with them.

If only he could get some leverage on them, figure out some way to gain the upper hand.

He glanced over at Smith, who was chatting with Cherrie on his cell phone. Cummins paid no attention to the superfluous one-sided end to the conversation. Instead, he mentally reassessed his current predicament and situation.

Wolf had something of value, the bandito containing the artifact and that was what old Von Dien wanted more than anything. And he was willing to pay just about anything for it. Wolf may or may not know that, at this point, but either way, he didn't know how to contact Von Dien.

But I do, Cummins thought. And I'm also in possession of something Wolf wants: the truth about Iraq and maybe a way to clear his name.

Cummins placed a hand on his gut and pressed in slightly, trying to settle his stomach a bit. He didn't think he was going to have another attack but couldn't rule it out, either. He went back to his ruminations.

How could he trade what he knew for the artifact? Once he had that, he could advise Fallotti and Von Dien of his possession and name his own price. He didn't want much just a sure-fire way to stay out of jail, to never have to work again, and have plenty of money to spend on wine, women, and more women.

He needed a bargaining chip, something of value.

The artifact obviously was the trump card but how could he obtain it?

And then the idea came to him. The leverage he needed was right there in front of him: the kid.

He was McNamara's grandson and McNamara was Wolf's friend and mentor, letting Wolf live on the ranch, taking him on as a partner in the family business... What better bargaining chip could anyone ask for? Wolf and McNamara would certainly give up the bandito for the safe return of the brat. Now all he had to do was figure out a way to get the kid away from the hillbilly gang. All he'd need would be the right opportunity. Stash the kid in a motel room or even let one of the morons hold him. Once he'd accomplished that, it would be a small matter of contacting Wolf and arranging a trade. Once the bandito was secured, Cummins could re-contact Fallotti and VD and this time he'd be the one calling the shots.

I've got the artifact and it's genuine, he imagined himself saying on the phone to his former employers. *And if you ever want to see it, I'll expect just compensation for all that I've been through.*

The particulars would take a bit of time to work out but at the moment he had a bit of time. Smith seemed in no rush to evict him from his temporary bedroom in The Majestic Model and him paying the impound fee for moron number two would certainly buy him a few more days. Smith had mentioned that Riley lived in the trailer next door, so the kid would no doubt be close by. Cummins knew that all he had to do was befriend the bastard so that the little tike wouldn't throw a hissy-fit when kindly, old honorary Uncle Jack took him for some ice cream or something. There was a slim danger that the kid might recognize him. He had been in McNamara's house, albeit briefly, when Zerbe and his South African goons were holding them all at gunpoint.

But hell, I look different now, he thought. The beard, the contacts, the buzz cut ... I've even lost some weight.

Plus, to a little punk that age, all adults probably look the same.

It would work, kindly "Uncle Jack." He'd have to give the kid a candy bar when they got back to the trailer park or something.

Yeah, that would work.

In the meantime, re-contacting Fallotti could wait. It could wait until the escape plan had been worked out and was ready to go.

***

Wolf watched as the procession of federal vehicles pulled into the driveway spreading out so as to form a blockade. He felt a wave of amusement as he saw they all waited for a command to exit their vehicles so they all got out at the same time, almost in unison. It was obviously designed to instill mild intimidation into the hearts and minds of the regular citizenry but Wolf was unimpressed. After all, he'd forgotten more about tactics and intimidation than this group had ever learned.

Two familiar faces, Special Agents Franker and

Turner, stood by the first car along with a woman dressed in a sharp-looking blue pants-suit. Her hair was dark brown and pulled back into a tight bun behind her head. She carried no purse and Wolf immediately noticed the gold badge affixed to her belt and the conspicuous bulge on her right hip. Both Franker and Turner seemed to be giving her a wide berth. Obviously, she was the boss. Two sets of three men exited the other vehicles. Half of them were wearing the standard Bureau outfits of blue suits and neckties and the other three wearing khaki-colored Royal Robbin, 5.11 cargo pants and blue and yellow FBI nylon Raid Jackets. The guys in khaki pants looked vaguely familiar. They stationed themselves by the other two sedans. One carried a rather large valise and the other a brown briefcase.

Wolf continued to watch them as Franker leaned over to the female agent and whispered something. She gave a slight nod and moved forward, her lips tightening into a lips-only smile as she approached with an extended open palm.

"Mr. Wolf," she said. "I'm Special Agent in Charge, Shelia Rappaport. How are you, sir?"

Wolf accepted her hand, noting that her grip seemed pleasantly strong. He then shook hands with Agents Franker and Turner.

"We're here as part of an FBI Shooting Investigation Team," Agent Rappaport said. "In reference to the incident that took place on—"

"I remember," Wolf said deciding to seize the initiative. "The police have already done all the processing, I think some of your guys were out here the other night, as well. We gave our statements then."

"To the local police," she said. "But not to the Bureau."

Her tone was a bit officious and it set Wolf on edge. It reminded him of trying to explain the intricacies of a mission to a butterbean lieutenant in the army.

"I wasn't aware that this was a Bureau case," he said. "Besides, all the bad guys that hit us are dead and the missing guy that took off got busted by Phoenix PD on a gun charge. I gave you people all the names I recalled."

"And we appreciate that, sir," she said. "Nevertheless, we still have to conduct our investigation."

The six other agents had closed ranks behind her, Franker, and Turner. Their faces had that vacuous expression of automatons on an assembly line.

Mac exited the house and came sauntering up.

"What's this?" he asked. "Are you guys collecting for the FBI charity fund or something?"

Special Agent Rappaport cast a quick glance at Franker, who nodded.

"Ah, you must be Mr. McNamara," she said and introduced herself to him, using her full title once again.

"Just what are you investigating?" McNamara

asked. "It was pretty cut and dried. A bunch of thugs broke in here and threatened us. We took their guns away from them and kicked their asses all the way to hell. The police already investigated it and cleared us."

Special Agent Rappaport's expression reminded Wolf of his sixth-grade teacher listening to a substandard student reciting a lesson.

"Mr. McNamara," she said. "Any time an agent fires his or her weapon, a shooting investigation team is dispatched to do a thorough investigation of the incident."

McNamara raised both eyebrows and cast quick looks at both Franker and Turner.

"You know," he said. "It's funny but I don't recall your two G-men here doing any of the shooting."

"Special Agent Franker had an AD," she said.

Franker blushed.

Mac grinned. "Well, I'm glad he missed his foot."

"Hey," Wolf said. "Let's all take a breath." He turned back to Special Agent Rappaport and smiled. "Listen, Ms. Rappaport, the whole incident was very traumatic for us. Several people died. It's really hard for us to discuss it, at this point. I mean, the police responded and cleared us of any wrongdoing. We were just defending ourselves."

"That's *Special Agent* Rappaport," she said. "And I appreciate that it was a traumatic incident for you. I've read the FD-three-oh-twos—"

"The what?" McNamara said.

"Standard Interview Report Forms," she said. "And I have a few more questions. Additionally, our team needs to take some more pictures and we need to interview all of the victims. Is your daughter home, Mr. McNamara?"

"She's sedated," Mac said. "The whole thing was doubly bad for her. You see, her fiancé was murdered recently."

Rappaport seemed generally unfazed.

"Have you talked to Bonnie Murphy?" Wolf asked, trying to get some information out of the tight-lipped fed. "She's our teenage babysitter or at least she used to be. Poor kid was here when they broke in. Luckily she wasn't hurt."

He happened to know that poor Bonnie had been so traumatized that her parents had forbidden her to do any more babysitting and placed the girl under the care of a therapist. Wolf doubted that she would be answering any questions without her doctor present and what could she say anyway? Kasey had told him and Mac that the girl had totally blocked out recollection of the incident.

Sort of like me and those missing eight minutes, he thought.

"It goes a lot better if we ask the questions, Mr. Wolf," Special Agent Rappaport said.

"Say," McNamara said flashing an ingratiating

grin. "Since you're so into formal titles, maybe you should address him as Staff Sergeant Wolf. You can just call me Sergeant Major if you want. *Command* Sergeant Major."

Rappaport canted her head and her lips parted slightly showing a modicum of irritation.

"I'd be glad to," she said, then directed her gaze at Wolf. "But didn't he get stripped of all rank and privileges after his court martial?"

McNamara's grin faded replaced by an expression of simmering anger.

"Lady, or Special Agent, or whatever the hell you want to be called," he said. "This man here's a combat veteran and he's given more, suffered more, done more than the whole lot of you. And I will not tolerate you coming onto my property and insulting a man who's been there and fought and bled for his country. You all can leave. This interview is finished."

"Mr. McNamara," she said. "Please, we have to file a report regarding this shooting incident. We just need to ask you a few questions."

McNamara frowned and stared directly at her. "Ain't that what you special agents said to General Michael Flynn before you set him up? I'll thank you to get off my property."

He turned and ambled back into the house.

Wolf knew the bluster was more a tactic to get rid of the feds without saying anything specific to them.

Both he and Mac had been comprehensively grilled by Franker and Turner before concerning the incident in Mexico, which was also a Bureau case, and they were both leery about talking to the FBI.

Rappaport turned to Wolf. "Mr. Wolf, ah, sergeant. I meant no offense."

"None taken," Wolf said. "And you don't have to call me sergeant. You're right, I was busted down to an E-one and given a DD."

She compressed her lips and Wolf figured he'd won this round. The fight had gone out of her and she didn't seem to know what to do next. He guessed she wasn't used to people not being intimidated by her rank and position of authority.

"That said, however." He leveled his gaze at her. "I have to agree with my buddy, Mac. Our statements are on the record with the police. We've said all we're going to say about this."

"But—"

"Mac's right," Wolf said, interrupting her. "We've already made a statement and if we happen to not recite something back exactly, we could find ourselves in the trick bag, correct?'

"We don't operate that way, Mr. Wolf."

He smiled and said, "Tell that to General Michael Flynn. Mac served under him, you know."

Rappaport frowned, reached in the pocket of her jacket, took out her card, and handed it to him.

"Would you mind if we took some pictures of the scene?"

Wolf turned sideways and held out his hand. "Take away. I'm sure Special Agent Franker here can give you a blow-by-blow. The police also took a bunch of photos of the inside of the house that night, so you can get those from them."

Rappaport compressed her lips and motioned to the agent carrying the valise. He set it down and unzipped it, taking out a 35mm camera.

"I would like to say thanks to you guys," Wolf said, holding his hand out toward Franker, who looked stunned. "If you two hadn't shown up when you did, who knows what would have happened."

Franker accepted Wolf's hand and they shook. The agent's mouth was slightly agape.

"You've got two brave men here, Special Agent Rappaport," Wolf said, extending his hand toward Turner. "These two guys unknowingly walked into a hornet's nest and no doubt saved our lives. And when the bullets started flying neither one of them flinched. They helped us secure the scene until the police arrived. So AD or no AD, that makes them all right in my book. The kind of troops I'd want next to me if my back was against the wall."

"Thank you for that ringing endorsement," Rappaport said apparently unimpressed by Wolf's accolades. "You have my number on that card. Call me if and when you decide you want to cooperate."

She walked off with the photographer and began dictating into her smart phone.

Wolf started to head toward his apartment across the way to call Mac and tell him about his suspicions regarding Charles Riley's modified jailhouse garment when Franker called out.

"Hey, Wolf."

He stopped and turned.

The FBI man walked over to him.

"I appreciate what you just said." Franker blinked several times. "And …"

His voice cracked slightly and trailed off.

Wolf waited as Franker approached and spoke in subdued voice.

"The truth is, I owe you." The FBI man gestured toward his partner, Turner. "Otis and I both do. If you hadn't shouted out that there was a gun involved, we'd both probably be dead right now. Thanks."

Wolf had been laying the bullshit on pretty heavy to Special Agent in Charge Rappaport, and they both knew it, but Wolf also knew that he'd made an in-road with this man. He wasn't sure if he could consider him an ally but at least he had the feeling that the fed wasn't all that keen on getting him and Mac in his sights anymore.

Not a bad place to be when the FBI was hot on your trail.

CHAPTER 4

The Office of Emanuel Sutter
Bail Bondsman
Phoenix, Arizona

Wolf and McNamara pulled up in front of Manny's office in the new Escalade and Mac jumped out of the vehicle and strode to the door. Wolf followed and thought Mac was going to kick down the door when he found it locked with a sign saying: *Back in 30 minutes* scotch-taped on the inside of the front door window. They got back into the SUV to wait and Wolf ruminated on the path that had brought them here in such a hurry.

Earlier, he'd watched the squad of FBI agents from his upstairs apartment over the garage, narrating their progress to McNamara via cell phone. They snapped numerous pictures of the driveway, the front door, and a scuff mark on the asphalt that Franker pointed out. Wolf assumed it had been where the agent's accidental discharge had struck the ground.

"That son of a bitch didn't even say nothing that night," McNamara said. "I should go out and check for damages. Maybe I can sue their asses."

"I'm sure you could," Wolf said. "But maybe that's not the best thing to do right now. Franker came up to me afterward to say thanks."

"Thanks? For what? Saving his and his partner's sorry asses." McNamara snorted. "Hell, if we hadn't jumped into action, those damn mercs and that fucking Zerbe would've lit those two FBI guys up."

"That's right," Wolf said. "And Franker and his partner both know it. So I think we can assume that they're probably going to close out that Mexico case without too much more fanfare. At least our part in it."

"Shit, I don't know. When have those federal fuckers ever just dropped something?" McNamara laughed. "Plus, it tends to look kind of suspicious. Every time we're in the picture, a whole lot of bad guys end up going down."

"Just the same, let's let it ride." Wolf paused, took a breath, and then said what he'd been dreading. "There's something else. Something more pressing."

McNamara was silent for a second, then said, "What?"

Wolf relayed his concern about the orange cut-offs and Mac was none too pleased.

"Anything about incarceration in the child custody paperwork?" Wolf asked.

"I doubt it," McNamara said. "And unless we know for sure that he's been arrested we're just pissing in the dark."

"Can Kasey check him on the computer?"

"I'm sure she can but I don't want to worry her right now. Meet me down by the Escalade once these fuckers leave."

Which brought them to see Manny in hopes that he could do one of his informal and off-the-record police records check.

McNamara had started the Escalade and fired up the air-conditioning but the idling vehicle sitting in the midday sun was less than a match for the heat. Finally, afraid the Escalade would overheat, McNamara shut the engine off after rolling down the windows.

"I guess we sweat till he gets back," he said and they sat in silence. "Let's just hope that thirty minutes is about up."

Wolf didn't know what the next move should be. One thing was for certain, they needed to find a new lawyer, for Kasey's sake and for their own as well. Maybe Manny could recommend someone.

Just as that thought crossed Wolf's mind, a white Tahoe pulled up and they saw Manny in the passenger seat. His nephew, Freddie, was behind the wheel. Manny was biting into a thick hamburger and holding a grease-laden bag of fries in his left hand. He wiggled his head in a modified wave when he saw Mac.

Both McNamara and Wolf hurriedly exited the Escalade and met the two bail bondsmen at the door to their office.

"Ah," Manny said, his mouth still stuffed with hamburger and fries. "My two favorite bounty hunters. You guys looking for more work? Cause guess what ... I got something. Something real big and it's right up your alley. But you're gonna need some back-up."

"Later," McNamara said. "I need you to do something first."

Freddie unlocked the door and held it open. Manny strode inside holding the two paper bags. The others followed suit.

"What you want? Me to post bond for somebody?" He laughed, expelling bits of chewed food, as his big hand rustled inside the brown paper bag, emerging with another cluster of fries.

Even though it was a few minutes past noon, Wolf felt no hunger pains after seeing that.

At least the office was cool as Freddie closed the door and Manny plopped in the padded leather office chair behind his desk. Wolf and McNamara sat in front.

"I need you to run a check on somebody," McNamara said.

Manny tossed one of the bags to Freddie and spread the unwrapped contents of his own bag on top of the sea of papers on his desk.

"Sherman," Manny said. "You want to take care of that for them?"

Freddie frowned as he grabbed what appeared to be a wrapped hamburger from his bag.

Wolf was aware that Manny mistreated his nephew and took every chance to tease the young man by giving him all the grunt work to do and constantly calling him Sherman, after some old cartoon show character. The kid was far from a Rhode's scholar but Wolf had always gotten along with him. The constant berating rubbed Wolf the wrong way, but there was little he could do about it.

Maybe one day the worm will turn, he thought as he Freddie's mouth pucker with apparent resentment.

"What's the name and DOB?" he asked.

"Last name's Riley," McNamara said. "Charles F."

Before he could recite the date of birth, Freddie turned and blurted it out.

"That's right," McNamara said. "How'd you know?"

Freddie's eyes shot toward his uncle, who had just taken a huge bite of his hamburger.

"What you want with him?" Manny asked.

"That's my business," McNamara said. "You heard

of him?"

"You might say that," Manny said, managing to shift some of the food to the side of his mouth. "I just posted bond for him a couple of hours ago."

***

Piccolo Mobile Home Park
Phoenix, Arizona

Cummins didn't like the looks of this new guy called Keller. He looked too much like one of the band of South African mercenaries he'd just been forced to deal with. The man also had the hard-edged appearance of an ex-con. Blue tattoos decorated his huge neck and probably most of his torso, Cummins imagined. With the dark hair, mustache, and black BDU blouse, the guy could have almost doubled for Sylvester Stallone in one of those old *Expendables* movies except that he was taller. A lot taller. He regarded Cummins with obvious disdain and suspicion. At the moment, the four of them sat at the small kitchen table in Smith's mobile home.

Keller had eyed him suspiciously when he'd first arrived and made some comment about the two of them bringing in an outsider.

"Let's go somewhere private and talk business," he said to Smith and Riley. "Just the three of us."

"Hey, Jack's okay," Smith said. "Me and him met up in the County and fought some niggers together. Been thinking about asking him to join us."

Keller's eyes scanned Cummins.

"He don't look much like Brigade material," Keller said. "In fact, he don't look like much at all."

Cummins took offense at the slight but wasn't too sure what the man had meant. Brigade material? What the hell was that?

But if he wanted to get control of the kid and use him as a bargaining chip with Wolf, he had to stay close. Real close.

He kept his mouth shut and let his hillbilly savior, Smith, do the talking. Posting that bond and the impound fee would hopefully pay off now.

"Like I said," Smith continued. "Me and him's tight. He posted bond for me and got Charlie's Caravan outta impound. Plus, we're gonna need a good wheel man for this, ain't we?"

Keller glared at him momentarily, then rotated his head toward Chad and Cherrie, who were splitting a bag of M&M's.

"Take the kid to the other room," Keller said.

"There ain't no other room," Cherrie said. "Least not one where we ain't gonna be able to hear you, sugar."

Keller's face darkened and Cummins figured the man didn't like being corrected or talked back to by a woman.

Riley stood up and dug in his pocket, coming up with a couple of dollars and the keys to his Caravan. He handed them to Cherrie and said, "Can you take him for some ice cream or something?"

Cherrie glanced at Smith, who nodded.

"Come on, baby," Cherrie said, standing and taking Chad's hand. "Let's go get us a couple of banana splits."

The boy's face lit up and he smiled and got up.

When they'd left, Keller turned back to the group and centered his view on Cummins once more.

"How much you know about the Brigade?" he asked.

Cummins was taken aback, unsure of what to say. From the sound of things, the Brigade was some kind of radical fringe group. Getting involved with them might not be such a good idea. Still, he had limited options, especially if he wanted to try to grab the kid. He decided to play along.

"At the moment, nothing," he said. "But I'd like to know more."

Keller just stared at him, slowly looking him up and down.

"Where you from?" he asked.

"New York originally," Cummins said. "Upstate."

"And what you do for a living?"

"I'm a lawyer. Or at least I was. I haven't been practicing lately."

Keller's eyebrows twittered slightly at the mention

of a law degree, then he squinted.

"So you got money, I take it?" he said.

"Some," Cummins answered. "I got a severance package from the law firm I used to work for."

"A what?"

Cummins couldn't help but frown at this big moron's ignorance.

"A lump sum payoff to tide me over until I find another job," he said trying to keep the condescension out of his tone.

Keller sat in silence for several more beats, then said, "Lemme see your wallet."

"What?" Cummins said.

"Hey, Lou," Smith said. "I told you he was all right. I'll vouch for him."

Keller continued his probing look, then asked, "Can you drive?"

What the hell kind of a question was that?

"Of course," Cummins said.

"Lemme see your wallet," Keller repeated.

Cummins hesitated. He still had around five-hundred dollars in his wallet, not to mention the secreted money belt. But he didn't want the others, least of all this new, big, uncouth lout fingering through it and knowing he had that much.

"Sure, he's got some money," Smith said. "I already told you that, dammit. And he already paid five hundred helping Charlie get his Caravan out."

"Shut up," Keller said.

"Hey," Smith said, his face reddening. "You best watch how you're talking to me in my own house, motherfucker."

"I'll talk to you any god damn way I please," Keller said. "You forgetting our rank structure?"

Smith's mouth curled into a snarl but he said nothing.

"Lou," Riley said, holding his hand out over the table. "We're gonna need more people, ain't we? If we're gonna get enough to start over?"

Keller and Smith continued their stare down. Finally, Keller spoke.

"How do we know he ain't some kind of undercover cop?"

Cummins almost snorted in laughter. Was that what this idiot was raving about? He reached for his wallet and started to remove it when Smith grabbed his arm.

"I told you, we was in lock-up together," he said. "You think they'd leave an undercover cop in a bullpen to get raped by a bunch of niggers?"

Keller shifted his gaze to Smith and then back to Cummins.

"You got any military experience?" Keller asked.

Cummins nodded. "Army. I did a tour in Iraq."

This was stretching things a bit since his tour had been with a reserve unit and was cut short after a few months. Fallotti had managed to use his contacts within the Pentagon to pull a bunch of strings.

"What was your MOS?" Keller asked.

"Military Intelligence," Cummins said, then added, "How about you?"

Cummins hadn't meant for the response to come out as confrontational as it had sounded. He suddenly felt a rush of bile starting to creep upward from his stomach and hoped he hadn't offended this oversized reprobate. He tried softening things with a smile. "I mean, you have the bearing of a military man."

Keller stared at him and then said, "Eleven bravo."

The code number for general infantry.

That figures, Cummins thought. Appropriate for those with the least amount of intelligence.

"Shucks," Smith said grinning that hillbilly simper of his. "We was all eleven bravo. That's how we met."

"You talk too god damn much," Keller said.

Smith shrugged. "I told you, he's all right. We can count on him."

It was making a bit more sense to Cummins now. They were a group of old army buddies who'd been grunts together in the Sandbox. Now they were all getting together again, but for what?

Several more seconds elapsed without anyone speaking again, then Keller lifted his left arm and began folding back the sleeve of his black BDU blouse. His forearm was so massive this proved to be a rather laborious task. Then he thrust his left arm forward so it hovered over the table. He cocked his head toward Smith and Riley, who were both wearing T-shirts. Smith rotated his arm and Riley peeled off the sodden bandage from his.

They all had identical tattoos in exactly the same spot: a triangle enclosing a circle of stars. The outer edge of the triangle was framed in red and blue. The images and lines were clearly defined on Smith and Keller. Riley's was pus-laden and distorted, but still recognizable.

Cummins had seen Smith's tattoo before but gave it little significance. Now, however, he realized it was more than just a decoration. A shiver went up his spine.

"This is the symbol of the Brigade," Keller said. "Of the Freedom Brigade."

Oh shit, Cummins thought. Fanatics.

He lifted his head and saw the intent expression on each of the other men's faces.

"The question is," Keller said. "Are you man enough to join with us?"

"You remember about that new start I was talking to you about, Jack?" Smith asked. "Well, this is it."

Cummins felt a new rush of panic. During his days in MI he'd read bulletins about fanatical groups within the U.S. Usually, they were highly secretive and on the periphery of society. He suddenly got the feeling that declining to join was not an option at the moment. Usually with these highly secret organizations, once you found out about them, it was either join up or die.

"Hey, Charlie," Smith said, gesturing toward the window. "Looks like you got visitors."

All four of them watched as a maroon Escalade pulled up in the parking area next to Riley's trailer. Two men got out and Cummins felt an immediate surge of panic as he saw it was Wolf and McNamara.

"Shit," Riley said. "It's my god damn ex-father-in-law."

"Looks like that older one's packing," Keller said. "He a cop?"

"Huh-un," Riley said. "A bounty hunter."

"Same difference," Keller said, peeling back his blouse and pulling out a large Desert Eagle from a pancake holster on his right side. "Whadda they want?"

Riley shrugged. "Must be about my kid. I'll go see."

He started to get up but Keller shoved him back down.

"We don't need no complications," he said. "Not with the operation so close."

"Shooting them's gonna bring the cops around," Smith said. He stood. "Lemme go get rid of them."

Cummins didn't want that either. Not if he was going to approach Wolf about trading the bandito for the kid. But what was this about some "operation?"

Keller licked his lips and nodded then turned to Cummins and Riley.

"You two go over there and stay out of sight. Telephone your girlfriend to stay away from here till they're gone."

"She's *my* girl," Smith said taking out his phone and scrolling down the lexicon of numbers. He handed the phone to Riley. "Here, call her."

He waited until the other three had moved away from the window and then opened the door and made a slow descent down the steps.

***

Wolf watched the man in the T-shirt and jeans approach from the trailer next door. The guy appeared to be in his late twenties with a buzz cut that was straight out of the 'Stan. The short sleeve on his left shoulder was rolled over containing what appeared to be a cigarette pack. His arms were well-muscled and the guy moved with a lithe gracefulness that reminded Wolf a big jungle cat. Those types were the most dangerous and hardest to fight. But they were looking for Chad, not trouble.

"Can I help you?" the man said. He pronounced "help" like "hep," which seemed to indicate a Southern accent.

This guy was one of those good old boys.

"We're looking for Charlie," McNamara said.

"He ain't home."

"Know when he'll be back?" McNamara asked.

The man shook his head. "Took off a while ago."

"Was he alone?" McNamara asked.

Smith cocked his head to the side.

"As I recall, he had his gal and his little kid with him. Said something about going to the Grand Canyon."

Wolf saw a black Chevy Malibu parked on the other side of the expansive driveway, by the trailer this guy had exited. It was covered with a patina of dust. There was a U-Haul box truck parked on the other side of the Malibu. Something about the Chevy jogged his memory. He'd seen it before. It was the same one that had been parked on the access road by the ranch earlier when Riley had picked up Chad.

And now, here it was, parked close to Riley's trailer, which was hardly a coincidence.

"They say when they'd be back?" McNamara asked.

The man shook his head. "Don't recall that they did." He smiled. It was a good old boy smile, ingratiating, friendly, guileless. "But the Grand Canyon's quite a drive from here. I expect they'll be gone at least overnight."

McNamara's lips compressed in frustration.

"They took that ragged-ass Caravan of his all the way to the Grand Canyon?" Wolf said stepping forward. He wanted to get a closer look at this guy. "Why didn't you loan him your Malibu?"

The man's forehead twitched a bit and he studied Wolf as if contemplating how to reply.

After about fifteen seconds of silence, the man replied, the grin still etched on his face. "That old Dodge runs better than it looks."

"You must know him pretty well," Wolf said.

The man shrugged. "Fair to middlin' is all."

"Know where he works?" Wolf asked.

The good old boy smile drooped a bit. "Why you asking?"

"I'm his father-in-law," McNamara said. "Or at least I was. I need to talk to him about something."

"Something?" The guy lifted his eyebrows. "What's that mean?"

"That's between me and him," McNamara said. "Family business."

The man's head bobbled up and down in a knowing acknowledgment.

"Say," Wolf said. "Would you happen to have his number? Maybe we can just give him a call."

The fatuous grin returned once more as he shook his head.

"Can't say that I do. Sorry. Maybe try information."

Wolf and McNamara exchanged glances.

"I do declare," the man said jutting his head in the direction of the Escalade. "That sure is a fine-looking deluxe ride you got there. That's a mighty pretty color, too."

"Thanks," McNamara said.

As the man walked up the steps to his trailer, he flipped down the rolled-up left sleeve of his T-shirt and removed a cigarette pack with the same red and blue design of the empty one that the woman had dropped on the driveway.

Uptown Blues Menthol, Wolf thought. For those with sophisticated tastes.

"Hey," Wolf called out. "I didn't catch your name."

"I didn't throw it." The man stopped, put a cigarette in his mouth, and lit it. "But it's Smith. Roger D. How about you?"

"Wolf."

Smith replaced the pack and lighter in the fold of his mini-sleeve, blew out a plume of smoke and then asked, "Them jump wings you got there on your arm for real or just for show?"

Wolf had gotten the tattoo of the Airborne insignia on his right forearm shortly after graduating jump school at Fort Benning.

"They're real," Wolf said.

"How far?" Smith asked.

"All the way," Wolf said.

Smith grinned and peeled the right sleeve of his T-shirt displaying a well-developed deltoid with a picture of paratrooper descending and the words *DEATH BEFORE DISHONOR* underneath.

"Thank you for your service," Wolf said.

Smith nodded and said, "Right back at ya. I'll let Charlie know you stopped by if I see him." He pulled open the door and went inside his trailer.

When Wolf and McNamara got back into their Escalade, Wolf could see the worry stretched over Mac's face. He started the SUV and did a slow look at Riley's trailer and then to Smith's as they pulled away.

"You believe him?" McNamara asked.

Wolf shrugged. "Hard to say. He's more than just a concerned neighbor, though. That Malibu was out on the access road this morning when Riley picked up Chad."

"So I noticed," McNamara said. "So they're asshole buddies and that guy Smith might be covering for my not-so-upstanding ex-son-in-law. I wonder if he's a jailbird, too?"

"Birds of a feather."

"Shit." McNamara slammed his open palm against the steering wheel. "And he's got my grandson."

"With this damn custody thing, there's not a whole lot you can do at the moment. The best thing's to try and find a new lawyer for Kasey."

McNamara accelerated down the street, passing cars like they were standing still, then he abruptly slowed down.

"I guess we'd best go back and tell Kase about this," he said.

That was one task Wolf hoped Mac would prefer to do alone.

***

Cummins had been watching as Wolf and McNamara got into their Cadillac and drove off.

Thank God they've gone, he thought.

The flood of bile had risen up to his throat and then luckily subsided. His tonsils still burned, however.

Smith had been standing near the front door smoking and watching. He turned and came back to the kitchen table after the Escalade vanished.

"They gone?" Keller asked.

"Sure enough," Smith said.

"What the hell did they want?" Keller asked.

"Looking for Charlie," Smith said. He took a drag on his cigarette, leaned his head back and puffed out a hazy smoke ring. "I told them y'all'd all gone to the Grand Canyon."

"Shit," Riley said, smirking. "Good thinking."

"Did they buy it?" Keller asked.

Smith shrugged. "They fucking left, didn't they?"

Keller's nostrils flared.

Cummins was wondering about all this. There was a lot more going on here than he'd bargained for ... a whole helluva a lot more.

Keller pointed at Riley. "You go pack your bags.

Best spend the night elsewhere. You and the kid. We can't take the chance of them two coming back and seeing any of you."

Riley nodded, scratching at the bandage on his left arm which was now covering the tattoo again.

"And you both figure out what you want to take to Base Freedom," he said to Smith. "Then come dark, we can load it into the U-Haul."

Base Freedom? Cummins thought. What the hell did that mean?

Smith looked around the trailer and nodded.

Keller turned back to Cummins.

"What you got in your wallet?" he asked.

They were back to that again. Cummins wasn't sure on how to take this question. He didn't answer.

Keller's expression grew more intense. "What you got in your fucking wallet?"

Cummins shrugged, now wishing he'd stashed more of his money in another place. He mulled over his options and came to the conclusion that it was better to fork over the wallet than to have this brute pull out the Desert Eagle again. Plus, there was still the kid to consider. It was all about pretending he was in for the duration until the time was right. And at the moment, he needed to keep floating under their cloak of anonymity.

Smith started to say something but Cummins waved dismissively and took out his wallet. Keller reached over and peeled open the billfold. His big fingers shuffled through the bills, removed all the credit cards and emptied out the scraps of paper and cards. He looked at Cummins's driver's license and the false ID card that he'd had made up.

"What's this for?" Keller asked, his index finger tapping the bogus ID.

"I'm out on bond," Cummins said. "Thought I might need it down the road."

Keller seemed to consider this. After counting and setting the money aside, he went through the credit and debit cards next and finally the other stuff. He stopped and looked at one of Cummins's business cards.

"John H. Cummins," Keller read. "Attorney at law. Guess you really are a lawyer, ain't ya?"

Cummins nodded.

Keller flipped the card over as saw the writing on the back. It contained the phone number he had for reaching Fallotti.

"Fallotti Law Firm," Keller said in a halting tone as he struggled to read the words. "This the place you work at?"

"Used to," Cummins said. "As I told you, I left."

"Why'd you do that?"

Cummins felt he was treading on thin ice here. One wrong answer and the son of a bitch might just pull out that big pistol and that wouldn't be pleasant.

"Actually, the firm went out of business," he managed to say, sticking as close to the truth as he could without divulging too much.

Keller pulled out his cell phone and dialed the number on the card. Cummins was confident that it would come back as "No longer in service," which it did.

Keller's tongue protruded from between his lips, like a big lizard searching for food. Then he hung up and shoved the pile of money, credit cards, and other stuff across the table to Cummins. He began reinserting everything back into the wallet.

"You gonna make a donation to the Brigade, ain't ya?" Keller said. It didn't sound much like a question.

Cummins paused and the other man held out his hand.

Feeling he had little choice, Cummins stripped off one of the hundreds and laid it in Keller's open palm.

Keller didn't move, his hand still extended, his eyes fixed on Cummins.

There were one twenty and two tens but Cummins could see the venal gleam in the big prick's eyes. He wouldn't be satisfied with something small. Cummins put another hundred in the other man's hand but Keller still didn't move.

If I give it all to the prick too easily, Cummins thought, it'll be a tip-off that I have more.

But the thought of provoking this big psycho also

had its risks.

Smith leaned forward and put his hand on Cummins's wallet.

"Charlie and me already owe him," Smith said. "He helped us out."

Keller rotated his head upward and locked eyes with Smith then smirked and crumpled the two hundreds in his hand. He reached over with steady deliberation and grabbed one more century note and tucked the currency in his pants pocket. Standing, he grinned and looked down at Cummins.

"Jack," he said. "Welcome to the Freedom Brigade."

***

Kasey was more than a little upset when they'd broken the news to her. Mac asked Wolf to back him up but Wolf had let him do all the talking. He merely stood and watched. Kasey seemed to crumble under the news, the tears welling up in her eyes and spilling down her cheeks. She immediately called the cell phone she'd given to Chad but it went directly to voice mail. Charlie called her back a few minutes later and claimed that he was on the road and couldn't answer. She flipped the phone on speaker so the three of them could listen.

"Where are you?" she asked.

"Huh? Why?"

Wolf caught the evasiveness in the man's tone but remained silent.

"My dad went over to your trailer," she said. "Chad has some medicine he was supposed to take."

They'd all agreed that it would be best not to mention that they knew of his recent arrest.

"What kind of medicine?" Riley's tone had grown accusatory. "Why didn't you give it to me when I picked him up?"

"Just some vitamins his pediatrician recommended," she said quickly. "They hadn't arrived yet when you came by."

Riley made a huffing sound.

"So your neighbor said something about you going to the Grand Canyon," Kasey said.

"That's right." His tone was still confrontational. "Ain't nothing wrong with me taking my boy on a little trip, is there?"

"Well, it would have been nice if you would've told me."

"It woulda been nice you told me you got some stud muffin staying with you, too. He your new boyfriend?"

Wolf felt a flush of embarrassment. Nothing could be farther from the truth but Riley was revealing himself to be the jealous type who jumped to conclusions.

McNamara's face betrayed no emotion but Wolf knew this was hard on him as well.

Kasey assured her ex that wasn't the case and asked to speak to Chad.

"We just stopped for ice cream," Riley said. "I'll have him call you later. Seven o'clock was what we agreed on, right?"

With that, he hung up.

Kasey looked both furious and concerned. She glanced up at her father.

"Oh, dad, I don't know what to do now."

McNamara placed a hand on her shoulder and told her not to worry.

"At this point," he said, "we got to play it smart. You did good not telling him too much on the phone. The main thing we got to do now is find us another good lawyer and work on getting this custody thing readjusted."

She nodded and Wolf saw that she was close to tears. The situation seemed unsettling to him and he felt that there was more going on than met the eye, so to speak. But given his tenuous and often strained relationship with Mac's daughter, he kept his suspicions to himself.

"If only Rod hadn't gotten killed," she said and then broke down into tears. McNamara put his arms around her and pulled her to his shoulder.

If only, Wolf thought. But he knew, as difficult as it was, there was nothing to do but ride this one out.

For now, anyway.

And he had the feeling it was going to be anything but a pleasant ride.

***

Mixed Martial Arts Fighting Academy
Phoenix, Arizona

An hour later, Wolf was clad in a sweat suit at Reno's huge gym, oblivious to the cacophony of the clatter of lifted weights, the staccato rhythm of the speed-bags being pounded, and the grunting of the other participants smacking punch after punch into the heavy-bags. Even the relentless soundtrack of the heavy rock music barely registered with him. Instead, he remained totally focused on the task at hand, at least to the best of his ability.

Wolf threw a couple more jabs at the focus pads, then followed up with a straight right. He knew his performance was desultory. He'd only been at it for about twenty minutes and already felt spent. Reno Garth smacked his cane against the side of the octagonal cage and yelled.

"Pick it up, Steve," he yelled. "Dammit. You better start showing me something."

Wolf knew he looked bad. His body was here but his head was back at the Ranch worrying about Chad and Mac and, yes, Kasey. He threw another combination that was a little bit faster, then followed up with an uppercut as George Patton, his informal, sometimes trainer, flipped his hand down to give him the target.

"What the hell's wrong with you?" Reno yelled once again. "You're supposed to be on the razor's edge and you're looking like you couldn't break an egg. Put some damn snap into those punches."

Wolf snapped a double jab, followed up with a straight right, and then, as George stepped back, Wolf sent a quick round-house kick to an extended mitt.

"That's better," Reno said. "Now you're looking a little more like contender material."

Contender material, Wolf thought. Ironic.

Two months ago, he and Reno were the bitterest of enemies, poised to go toe-to-toe on the street at any moment. And then Mexico happened, leaving Reno's leg shattered along with his hopes of regaining his lost title. Now it was as if he wanted to regain his former MMA contender status and fulfill his championship dreams through Wolf. The big block letters painted in red, white, and blue on the front window still proclaimed: *RENO GARTH, MMA CHAMPION, TRAINS HERE.*

A 7.62 mm bullet in Mexico had dissolved that dream and forged an unexpected friendship.

Ironic, but understandable, he thought as he delivered another combination to the focus pads.

Wolf had experienced a lot of accidental friendships during his time in the army. Combat makes strange bedfellows sometimes.

"All right," Reno shouted, sounding enthusiastic now as Wolf delivered a quick series of kicks to the pads now.

Finally, Reno signaled it was time for a break and Wolf ceased punching. He felt good and not exceptionally tired despite the new coating of sweat that covered his body. And it was supposed to be an easy-going workout in deference to the match being tomorrow.

George grabbed a towel and began wiping Wolf's arms and shoulders down. Reno pulled open the gate and limped into the octagon.

"How you feeling, man?" he asked.

Wolf gave a quick nod in reply.

Reno nodded back. "You got the look of a man with a lot on his mind. Something bothering you?"

"A lot's bothering me."

Reno stood in silence for several seconds, then nodded again. "I wish you'da come in earlier," he said. "I had a couple more sparring partners lined up to go over some more shoot techniques. I'm worried we neglected the ground game too much."

"I guess I'll have to keep him on his feet then."

"Easier said than done sometimes. Plus, this guy's supposed to be pretty good at stand-up, too."

"You're not giving me too much to look forward to, coach."

Reno blew out a slow breath. "Well, I think you're pretty much as ready as you can be but I still wish you woulda come by earlier like you said you was gonna do."

"Couldn't be helped," Wolf said leaving the rest of his explanation unspoken. Even though he and McNamara had more or less patched up the rivalry between them and Reno, Wolf wasn't about to air Mac's family problems here.

Reno frowned and shook his head.

"Keep in mind that this dude, de Silva's gonna be coming in lean and mean and ready to take your fucking head off."

"Believe me," Wolf said with a smile, "I've been thinking about that. But Mac and I had something to take care of."

Reno seemed to accept this and ran his tongue over his teeth.

"How's the bounty hunting business going these days?" he asked.

"Fair to middlin'," Wolf said recalling Roger D. Smith's unsophisticated choice of words for some odd reason.

Reno's brow furrowed momentarily. "Huh?"

Wolf grinned. "Just something I heard someone say. It's going all right. Could be better but Manny said he might have something for us." He slapped his gloved hands together. "He also said we'd need back-up. Interested?"

Reno's face assumed a wistful expression for a moment then it vanished as he shook his head.

"Nah, they did another MRI on my leg last week to see how it was healing and it looks like they might have to go in and put a steel rod in there as a permanent brace."

The implications of that flashed through Wolf's mind and they weren't good.

Reno must have read Wolf's thoughts.

"Yeah, I know what you're thinking," Reno said. "That'll probably most likely end my chances of making a comeback in mixed martial arts. Plus, I'll be setting off metal detectors right and left as I go through the airports." He barked out a humorless laugh.

Dreams die hard, Wolf thought. He remembered the countless veterans who had sustained far worse injuries from their deployments. It depended on the support network you had but more on the individual's will to overcome, to persevere.

"Maybe not," he said, trying to sound convincing. "There was a boxer back in the day named Greg 'Gator' Bogianowski who lost his lower leg in a motorcycle accident and he came back and fought for the light-heavyweight championship."

Reno snorted. "He win?"

Wolf had to shake his head. "No, but he showed everybody he could do something that nobody thought he could do."

Barbie came running over, all fluffed out hair, bouncing dynamic curves in her turquoise body suit. She called out to Reno that he had a phone call.

"I'm busy," Reno yelled. "Tell 'em I'll call 'em back."

"But it's the sport's network about the fight," she yelled back. Her voice was almost drowned out by the ambient clatter.

"That's different," Reno said. "I'll be right there." He turned and placed a hand on Wolf's shoulder. "This is gonna be big tomorrow. You ain't the main event but you'll be getting network exposure in the pre-lims. Like I said, win and you'll be a contender."

Wolf nodded, once again thinking, but not saying, that it was more about the payday than the status for him. Win, lose, or draw, with the purse from this fight, he'd be able to put Trackdown, Inc. back into the black, and that would go a long way toward repaying his debt to Mac.

Reno turned and started to walk away, then stopped and turned.

"Your girl coming by tomorrow to watch?"

Wolf shook his head. "I told her to stay away, in case I really get my ass kicked."

Reno chuckled. "Now don't go thinking like that. I got a feeling old Steve Wolf's gonna come out of this thing just fine. Even though it's a selected, limited audience in the auditorium, tell her and her girl friends that I'll leave three tickets for them at the gate. And one for Mac and his daughter, too, right?"

"Appreciate it," Wolf said, wondering if Kasey did show up who she'd be rooting for.

Reno glanced at his watch. "Shit, we got to get to that weigh-in tonight by six-thirty." He looked at George. "How we doing weight-wise?"

"He's good," George said. "Right around two-seventeen a little while ago. Since this is non-title cruiser, all he's got to be is less than two-twenty-six."

Reno grunted an approval.

"Okay, do two more rounds on the pads," he said, "and then some easy does it shadow boxing and we'll call it a night. Me and Barbie'll drive you over to the weigh-in and then get some sleep. Rest all day tomorrow."

"Roger that," Wolf said and turned back to face George as he slapped the focus mitts together with a resounding snap.

Rest tomorrow, he thought. But then again, as they say, there's no rest for the wicked.

CHAPTER 5

The McNamara Ranch
Phoenix, Arizona

Wolf found himself sleeping fitfully and occasionally stirring himself awake trying to punch his way out of a bad dream. He stirred awake at his customary zero five hundred hours and realized he was supposed to sleep later, per Reno's orders, since tonight was fight night.

Sleep late and rest the whole day.

And something told him he was going to need all the reserve energy he could muster tonight. From what he's been told, the guy he would be facing, Marcos de Silva, was no push-over. Although this was only his third fight in the United States, he supposedly had a seventeen-and-four record in his native Brazil, with eight wins coming by submission and nine by knockout. He'd also won all of his U.S. fights, two by KO and one by decision.

A Brazilian jiu jitsu fighter, Wolf thought. Reno had said the guy could bang, too, but could he move? Their face-to-face at the weigh-in last night had been uneventful, leaving the posturing hype for the bigger names in the main event to do when their turn came. They'd both been totally professional as they'd stepped on the scale, Wolf coming in at two-sixteen and Silva at two-twenty-six. A ten-pound advantage and he didn't look fat at all.

A jiu jitsu grappler who could bang ... Not a pretty thought.

It has officially started, he decided. The pre-fight jitters ... Nerves ... He was finding it exceptionally difficult to think about anything other than the pending contest that night.

Still, it was only a preliminary bout and wouldn't be attracting that much attention unless either he or his opponent came off looking really spectacular. That meant a knockout or something equally flashy.

The thought of getting separated from his senses tiptoed through his mind's eye and he didn't want to be the one staggering around on the knockout reel or, worse yet, being carried out on a stretcher.

All of this made it impossible to sleep. The luminous dial on his alarm clock now told him it was approaching zero-six-hundred. He found it hard to believe that he'd lain there for more than fifty-five minutes beyond his usual rising time. The day's countdown had started. He had maybe a little over twelve hours left before he'd be taking that long, lonely walk to the octagon.

The longest walk in the world, he reminded himself.

Even the closed curtains, which he normally left open, seemed to be straining under the pressure of the early morning sunlight. Wolf knew this was a stupid supposition but traces of sunlight had worked their way through the slight gaps in the material forming a strip of light on the wooden floor.

It reminded him of the ubiquitous artificial lights that had been his constant companion in Leavenworth just last year. Except for the huge overhead skylight that added to the illumination during the day, most all other light was of the artificial type. What he wouldn't have given back then to have been able to gaze at a window at the morning sunlight as it filtered in and know he was free to go outside and do a morning run.

His thoughts turned from the fight to that of his other, ongoing battle—the one to clear his name and how he was doing on that front.

Not good, he told himself.

Not only had his nebulous primary adversaries managed to remain virtually anonymous, except for a few overheard names, they'd also tried to kill him twice.

At least twice, he reminded himself, thinking about the aborted attempt on his last day in Leavenworth and wondering if they were behind that one, too. All he knew about them was a few names and the seeming object of their interest: the Mexican bandito. He and Mac had mutually decided that until they could figure out the exact reason the statue held so much significance for the bad guys, it was prudent to keep it in a safe place that was accessible to only the two of them. They had originally planned to include Kasey's name on the safety deposit box but subsequently decided against it. Not that they didn't trust her but getting her involved to that degree seemed a bit too dangerous. After all, she'd already lost her fiancé.

But the mystery of the bandito continuously gnawed at him.

Thomas Accondras, the bounty they'd originally been hired to grab down in Mexico, had carried it on his person in a backpack and had tried to convince them to let him go, saying the bandito would make them rich. But he didn't elaborate. It had also been the target of a botched burglary by the South African crew that their old buddy, Jason Zerbe, had brought in. Wolf and Mac had ostensibly been sent down to Mexico to apprehend Accondras at the behest of the Fallotti and Abraham Law Firm out of New York City, which was purportedly representing the family of the child Accondras was accused of molesting.

Cummins and Eagan had been connected to the law firm and an Iraqi named Nasim had also shown up in Mexico. Somehow, there was a tenuous connection to all of this and the court-martial and prison term but the exact particulars had proved as difficult to figure out as an indecipherable conundrum.

Now the Fallotti and Abraham Law Firm was dissolved, most of the principals he'd dealt with were dead, and his old buddy, Cummins, was in the wind. He was the only one who'd appeared in each segment, like a constant in a complex algebraic equation.

Find him, Wolf thought, and he could explain everything, especially the significance of the bandito.

It appeared to be only a cheap, painted, plaster figure from Mexico, so what was all the fuss about?

Maybe it's actually the work of some famous Mexican sculpture, he thought as he swung his legs out of bed and placed his bare feet on the solid floor.

It felt uncommonly cool to his touch but he knew the heat of the day would change that soon enough. Then he was back thinking about the fight that night and debating how to deal with this grappler who could punch. He assumed that the guy might be a counterpuncher, luring an opponent in to throw a punch so the striking arm could be grabbed. That meant that Wolf's best tactic would be to throw a feint and be ready with a counter punch of his own.

In a strange way, all of his adversaries, the Brazilian and the unknown ones, were counterpunchers. They'd lured him into traps too many times.

And maybe it's time I did some luring of my own, he thought.

Before he headed to the shower, he went to his desk and pulled the drawer all the way out. He shoved his hand into the space, palm upward, and felt around for the swath of duct tape. When he found it, he peeled the safety deposit box key from its secreted place and stared at it. The number on the key was 4878.

It was time to get the bandito out of storage.

***

Piccolo Mobile Home Park
Phoenix, Arizona

Cummins awoke feeling spent and sore. Once darkness had descended, the four of them had moved several heavy items from both trailers into the U-Haul. These included Smith's big flatscreen TV, a dresser, a load of suitcases. It had taken them several hours and they didn't finish until close to midnight. It added up to the strong indication that both Smith and Riley would be leaving this place and Cummins wasn't sure where that left him. Besides Keller's rather half-hearted, "Welcome to the Brigade," Cummins had no official ties to Smith and the others. This temporary relationship had served its purpose and allowed him to lie low and figure out his next move. But now that next move included somehow absconding with Riley's kid or at least shadowing the youngster until he could negotiate a trade off with Wolf. That meant sticking close to this bunch of militia fanatics, at least for the short term.

Easier said than done, he thought.

Cummins hadn't objected last night when Keller commandeered the second bedroom where Cummins had been staying. It actually played right into his hands. After packing all of his stuff in his suitcase, along with his toiletries, he'd ensconced himself on the couch where Cherrie spread some sheets and a pillow for him. It had been a fitful and non-restful slumber due not so much to the hard sofa cushions but more to the tangled worries that hung in his mind. Smith originally suggested that Keller sleep in Riley's now unoccupied trailer for the night but Keller was adamant: "Nobody stays there in case them bounty hunters are watching." He wasn't too keen about letting Cherrie come back here and sleep with Smith but the tough hillbilly had drawn the line at letting his lady-love sleep someplace else, much less the motel with Riley and his kid. Keller agreed as long as Cherrie didn't leave the trailer until one of them thoroughly checked the area. Cummins was concerned about being seen as well but not only by

Wolf and McNamara. He had a phone call to make that he didn't want Keller or Smith to hear. So after getting up extra early, putting in his contact lenses, and a baseball cap, he grabbed his burner phone and listened. From the trio of snores he heard as he moved about in the small trailer's living room, he felt confident that all three of them were still asleep. He exited the trailer as quietly as he could.

It was barely past six by his watch but that would make it nine in Manhattan. He mentally debated the wisdom of leaving a message. If the feds had some kind of wiretap going, he'd be cutting his own throat if he said too much. But on the other hand, he had to keep his hat in the ring with Fallotti and VD if he wanted to survive and get his ultimate retirement pay-off. Besides, he was perhaps twenty days or so from being a wanted man himself, once he didn't show up for his court date on the Phoenix PD weapon charge. And who knew if the feds were going to rear their heads again? Regardless, he decided to keep the call as anonymous as he could.

His head bobbled around and he saw no telltale signs of any surveillance activities by Wolf or McNamara. They'd only been interested in Riley and he wasn't there.

There's no way the two of them could even know that I'm here, he thought.

Still, it amazed him how their paths kept intersecting. It almost defied coincidence.

He walked to the front end of Smith's trailer and punched in the number that he knew by heart.

It rang and went to voice mail almost immediately and Cummins was ready.

"You know who this is, so listen carefully," he said, keeping his voice low but trying to imbue a sense of confidence into his tone. "I'm still in the game and I've figured out a way to get you that item you were looking for. But I'm going to need some money and some support. Make that a lot of money. Otherwise, I'll blow the lid off this whole fucking thing. Text me that you've received this message and the next time I call somebody besides a fucking answering machine better answer."

He terminated the call and was feeling pretty damn good about sounding assertive. Setting the conditions and adding that bit of profanity at the end were strokes of genius.

Dealing from a position of strength, he thought, and smiled as he turned. Then the smile vanished as he saw Keller standing by the side of the trailer staring at him.

"Who'd you call?" Keller asked.

His expression was hard and he was clad in a sleeveless T-shirt and jeans. He wore no shoes. Cummins had been right about the plethora of tattoos. The ink scribble covered his upper arms, shoulders, chest, and neck along with the Freedom Brigade emblem on his forearm.

"Call?" Cummins said, trying to buy himself a few extra seconds to figure out an answer.

Even though he hadn't eaten, he felt an unsettling in his stomach.

"Why'd you sneak outta the house to make your call?" Keller took a few steps toward him.

Cummins thought about backing up, even taking off at a run, but he knew the other man would catch him in a few strides. Besides, it would also make him look guilty.

"I didn't want to wake everybody up," Cummins said, trying his best to return Keller's baleful stare with one of his own but knew he was falling far short. Cummins desperately searched for an answer. Should he say he was calling a girlfriend or something?

"How considerate. Now who'd you call?" Keller was within a foot or so of Cummins now and reached out and grabbed the phone.

"Hey, give it back," Cummins said. "Please," he added as an afterthought and then regretted it. The bile did its customary rush up his esophagus and he turned and vomited.

"What the hell?" Keller danced backward.

Cummins recovered enough to straighten up.

"Sorry," he mumbled. "Bad stomach."

Keller blew out a derisive sounding breath as he

checked the phone.

"This is a god damn burner, ain't it?" he said.

Cummins nodded. The sour taste was still in his mouth.

Keller stared at the screen and his forehead wrinkled.

"Whose number is this?" he asked.

Cummins didn't know if the big moron would be able to distinguish the New York City area code but he had to come up with something fast.

"It's a private number," he said.

"That ain't what I fucking asked you, fat boy."

Fat boy? This cretin had no couth.

"All right," Cummins said, coming up with an idea. "It's my ex-boss's private line. I needed to talk to him."

"Talk to him?" Keller's mouth drew back into a sneer. "At six o'clock in the morning?"

Cummins licked his lips. Outwitting this idiot wouldn't be too hard.

"It's nine o'clock on the East Coast."

Keller's face eased a bit and he apparently took this calculation into consideration.

"And what you need to talk to him about?"

"Well," Cummins said. "If you must know..." He was still searching for words when an idea struck him. "I was gonna ask him for some money. He still hasn't paid me the entire sum of my severance agreement and with what you took from me yesterday, I'm in need of some funds."

Putting it all back on his greedy little self, Cummins thought.

Keller dialed the number and listened.

Cummins prayed that no one would answer it this time.

After a few rings, Keller obviously got the voice mail command to leave a message. He terminated the call and tossed the phone back to Cummins.

Fumbling the catch initially, Cummins managed to cradle the phone against his gut.

Thank God I didn't drop it, he thought.

"Don't make no more phone calls till I tell you it's okay," Keller said and headed back for the entrance.

Something's going on, Cummins thought. And I need to find out what it is.

***

The McNamara Ranch
Phoenix, Arizona

After Wolf had finished showering and dressing, he heated up a cup of coffee in his microwave and went again to the window. A solitary figure was proceeding down the access road from the highway at a deliberate jog. Wolf discerned that it was Mac. After grabbing a bottle of water from his refrigerator, he went down the stairs and out to meet him. McNamara's face was covered with sweat. Wolf tossed him the bottle and Mac grinned as he twisted it open.

"I figured you'd be sleeping in this morning," McNamara said after draining half the contents. "You forget you have a fight tonight?"

"Couldn't sleep," Wolf said. "But I skipped the run."

McNamara took another long pull from the plastic bottle.

"And what brings you out this early?" Wolf asked.

"I couldn't sleep neither," McNamara said. "Figured I'd better get in shape for the next time I see that pecker, Riley. In case I have to beat the shit out of him."

Wolf figured Mac could do that whether he was in top shape or not. He was one of the toughest men Wolf had ever known.

"How's Kasey holding up?" Wolf asked.

McNamara took another drink and shook his head.

"As good as can be expected. We spent most of last night trying to find a good attorney look into this custody thing."

"Any prospects?"

"A couple. She's going to follow up with a few of them today. And you and me gotta go see Manny at ten-thirty."

"Manny? Oh yeah, he did say that he's got something for us, didn't he?"

"Yep. Said it was real big and real lucrative. Right up our alley."

Wolf did some mental calculations. As he'd already figured, the money from his MMA fight tonight, win, lose, or draw, would put the company solidly in the black. A big case from Manny would definitely put them on the road to easy street unless some new expenses came along—like a high-priced attorney charging an arm and a leg for renegotiating a child-custody agreement.

But Chad was way too important to both Kasey and Mac to be worried about any expenses. And the boy was important to Wolf as well. Although they shared no blood relationship, Wolf remembered Kasey's castigating line that he was the son her father always wished he'd had. Things had gotten somewhat better between Wolf and her but there was still a ways to go. But little Chad was almost like a relative to him and referred to Wolf as "Uncle Steve."

Wolf wasn't about to let anything happen to the boy but this whole custody thing was a morass with no easy egress. No matter how it turned out, somebody was going to get hurt and most likely it would be Chad.

"You and Kasey are coming tonight, right?" Wolf said.

"Hell, I'll be in the first row," McNamara said. "Don't know about Kase. Have to see how she's feeling."

Wolf almost responded with, *Tell her to come and watch me get my ass kicked and she'll want to be there* but decided not to say anything.

"You know what time's Yolanda getting here?" McNamara asked.

Wolf shook his head.

"Well," McNamara said. "I'm kinda hoping Ms. Dolly and Brenda might be coming along with her. There's nothing like the P-Patrol to help take a man's mind off his other problems."

Wolf said nothing, debating whether he should break the bad news to Mac now about the P-Patrol not coming.

McNamara finished off the bottle, crinkled it up, and tossed it into the recycling garbage container. After dropping the lid, he smacked his hands together in a dusting gesture.

"In the meantime, come on in the house and I'll have Kasey rustle us up some breakfast," he said.

"She's up?"

"Yeah." McNamara's eyes moved to the asphalt surface of the driveway and he sighed. "Poor kid couldn't sleep for worrying about Chad."

"Riley let him call her last night?"

"He did. Chad says he's fine and that daddy's taking him on a trip."

"Well, maybe if she finds the right lawyer, he can slap him with a subpoena when they get back."

"She doesn't want to tip her hand, for fear that Charlie'll pull some kind of vanishing act. We decided it's best to not let on we're planning on anything until the right time." He glanced at his watch. "And let me know what time we got to be at the airport."

"She's not coming," Wolf blurted out. "I called and told Yolanda to cancel."

"What?"

"Yeah," Wolf said. "I told her that I didn't want her to come in case this guy really kicks my ass tonight."

McNamara grinned. "You ain't thinking that's gonna happen, are you?"

"Once you step into that octagon and they close the gate, anything can happen."

"A negative attitude like that's gonna weigh you down some."

"Yeah, but it's the only one I got, so it'll have to do."

McNamara nodded and heaved another sigh. "You know, I'm kinda glad they ain't coming. It's gonna be a limited audience anyway, with all this social distancing bullshit going on and with that asshole, Charlie, on my mind, I'm not in the mood to be showing the P-Patrol around town right now."

"Me either," Wolf said, starting to feel the pre-fight jitters creeping up on him again. And he had a lot to do today before the reckoning. He hoped he'd be able to get it all in.

"Of course," McNamara said over his shoulder.

"That's always subject to change."

He flashed a sly grin.

Wolf forced himself to grin back and thought, Isn't everything?

***

The Von Dien Winter Estate South
Belize

Soraces awoke framed between the two beautiful, brown maidens that had been supplied to him. One was the girl he'd been admiring yesterday. Both of them were caramel-colored honeys and had attended to his every whim, instruction, and desire. As soon as he'd agreed to the assignment, the lawyer had sent an employee to the hotel where Soraces had spent the previous night and picked up his luggage and personal items. Then this guest room suite had been made available, along with a burner phone, a laptop, a bowl of fruit, and the bikini-clad girls who waited on him hand and foot. He'd spent the rest of the day contacting some of his old wet-work guys to see if they were available for this new assignment. Luckily, most of them were: Lucas and Cortez, two of the best on-scene adjusters in the business, and Gunther, whose shadowing and enforcer skills were second to none. He decided on just using Gunther for the time being. By the time Fallotti came in to tell him that the special, temporary position had been created for Soraces at the Phoenix law firm of Bailey and Lugget, it was party time.

"Mr. Von Dien's private jet will be ready to fly you there tomorrow morning," Fallotti had told him.

Everything was falling into place nicely and Soraces knew he was going to take his sweet-ass time with this one. After all those years of being on a Company budget and having to justify every little expense on a DoD report form that was subsequently scrutinized by some pencil-pusher at Langley, it was nice going first class for a change.

Welcome to the private sector, he thought.

Soraces got up to urinate and threw some water on his face. It was relatively early and although he'd pretty much tried every variation with the two girls, he still had a few that he wanted to try again. He was semi-erect as he walked back into the bedroom and pulled back the fine linen sheet. The two girls stirred awake and one rolled onto her side. He grabbed the bondage rope and looped it around her wrists, pulling it taut against the metal framework of the headboard.

"*Por favor. Queremos dormer un poco mas,*" one of them murmured.

Soraces reached over and savagely grabbed her breast, pinching the brown nipple between his thumb and forefinger. She shrieked.

Who did this little bitch think she was, denying him?

"*No dormas nada,*" he smiled lecherously. "*Quiero cingarlas otra vez. En siguida.*"

Just as the girl cried out from the cruel pressure, someone knocked on the door.

Soraces released his hold on the girl and yelled he'd "be right there." Then he leaned close to the girl and whispered, "*Recuerda, perra, siempre tengo lo que quiero.*"

Remember, bitch, I always get what I want.

He strode across the room in the nude, throwing open the door. Fallotti stood there wearing a bathrobe. His hair looked a bit disheveled. His eyes widened slightly as he saw Soraces's state of excitement.

"Sorry to interrupt," he said, smirking slightly. "But we'll be needing you on site in Phoenix a little sooner than we expected. There's been a new development."

"Oh?" Soraces figured it must have been important to get the lawyer out of bed at this relatively early hour.

"Remember that ex-employee I mentioned?" Fallotti said. "Jack Cummins? He's cropped up like a reoccurring case of the clap. He may be causing some problems."

"Is that so?"

The lawyer's mouth drew into a tight line. "Mr. Von Dien has an extreme dislike of loose ends."

Typical, Soraces thought. And also something to keep in mind. I'd better make sure I have my payment in hand before I deliver the goods.

"We'd like you to find him and deal with him."

"Take him out?" Soraces asked. The thought of engineering another assassination was as good of an aphrodisiac as he could ask for.

"Eventually, but not immediately. But he left a message claiming he has a way to get the item and made some demands. We don't know if he's bluffing but we can't afford to take the chance."

"Not a problem," Soraces said using his head to gesture toward the bedroom. "Just give me an hour or so to tie up a few loose ends of my own."

His grin was sardonic.

***

Office of Emmanuel Sutter
Bail Bondsman
Phoenix, Arizona

Wolf and McNamara walked into Manny's office and Mac set the box of donuts down on top of the big desk. It looked fairly orderly for a change and Wolf asked him if he was trying to turn over a new leaf.

The big bail bondsman shot him a wry look.

"Not hardly," he said. "I'm going to be interviewing some girls for a secretarial position and I wanted them to know that I expect things to be kept organized and neat."

"A secretary?" McNamara said. "Where's she going to sit?"

"We got some room over there," Manny said as he tore open the donut box. "Sherman can move his desk over that way a little."

With the mention of his undesirable nickname, Freddie turned to give the finger to his uncle's broad back.

"Hey," Manny said. "I seen that."

Freddie looked startled and quickly rotated his chair around and pretended to be immersed in his paperwork. Wolf noticed that Manny had a small, circular mirror set up on the edge of his desk. Wolf figured it was either to make sure he looked ultra-presentable for the prospective secretaries or it was Manny's way of having eye's in the back of his head to keep tabs on his nephew.

Never a dull moment around here, Wolf thought.

Manny removed a chocolate donut and bit into it, then emitted a grunt of satisfaction as he masticated.

"Hey, Sherman, put us on a pot of coffee, would ya?" Manny said.

Freddie rolled his eyes, stood, and went to the coffee maker.

"Remember you're supposed to be watching your

sugar," Freddie said as he moved into the washroom with the pot and closed the door.

"Yeah, yeah," Manny said, leaning back in his chair and taking another bite. "Sneaky little Judas prick reports everything I fucking eat to his mother, who then relays it to my damn wife."

"Maybe he wouldn't if you didn't ride him all the time," Wolf said.

"Huh?" Manny's mouth gaped exposing some half-chewed pieces of donut. "I treat him like a prince."

"Prince Sherman?"

Manny snorted a laugh and then went into a coughing fit, pounding the palm of his non-donut-holding hand on the desk top. Finally, after a good ten seconds, he leaned over and spat the half-chewed donut onto the waste basket.

"God damn, Wolfman," he said. "You damn near make be bust a gut every time you come in here."

"It's a gift," Wolf said.

"Yeah," Manny said, leaning forward to peruse the remaining selection of donuts. "So what brings you guys in today?"

"You mentioned something about a job for us yesterday?" McNamara said.

"Oh, yeah." Manny bit off another hunk, chewed a few times, and then shoved the rest of the donut into his mouth, pausing momentarily to lick the ends of his fingers. He shoved his enormous body away from the desk and pulled open one of the side drawers.

"You know," he said, sorting through a stack of papers, "with all these damn states loosening up the bail bonds laws, things are getting tighter and tighter. Pretty soon I'll be hiring you guys to start making repossessions on all these damn houses and cars I took as collateral."

"Is that what this big case you mentioned is?" McNamara asked.

Manny was still sorting through some files.

"Nah, this one's a straight-up fugitive case but it could be a little bit tricky. Gangbanger asshole I bonded out for a PCS case skipped out on me to the tune of a hundred and fifty large." He reached over with his right hand and pulled another donut out of the box. This one was tan colored with a coating of white and red decorations on the top. "His poor old mama supposedly put up her house and his sister put up her car as collateral. Now, I either gotta get the punk back in jail or start the proceedings to take the old lady's house and sista's car, neither of which I originally thought were in particularly good shape, bedsides being in the shitty part of town. But that ain't all." He paused to take a huge bite.

"A hundred and fifty large." McNamara emitted a low whistle. "That's a pretty high bond."

"You ain't shitting, it is." Manny shifted his bite of the new donut to his cheek and then yelled out,

"Where's the god damn coffee?"

Wolf heard the toilet flush inside the washroom and Freddie emerged carrying the filled coffee pot. He went to the coffee maker, removed a filter, and began filling it with grounds.

"Turns out—" Manny paused to take another quick bite, "that this wasn't buster brown's first brush with the law. He's got a shit-ton of other arrests under half a dozen or so different names in several states. Lately, he's used just about every bail bondsman in the greater Phoenix area and guess who posted the collateral each time?"

"Mama and sister?" McNamara said.

"Ex-fucking-zactly," Manny said, taking another prodigious bite. "They must've had duplicate titles made up, so even if I did go to court and try to collect on the collateral, I own about as much of that fucking house and the car as I do that old time-share I bought at Disneyworld."

He chewed while he sorted through the file and removed a color picture of a clean cut looking black youth in a graduation cap and gown. "That's his eighth-grade graduation pic." Manny then tossed a color print of the same youth, perhaps ten years older, flashing a gang sign and holding what appeared to be a knock-off AK-47. "This one's more recent."

Wolf compared the two and noticed the youthful innocence and optimism had all but vanished in the second photo. He handed both photos to Mac.

"The shit-brain's real name is Booker Nobles," Manny said. "But he's got a ton of others. At the moment now, he's going by Zeus."

The coffee-maker hissed.

"Zeus?" McNamara said. "He a fan of the classics or something?"

Manny laughed and popped another piece of donut into his mouth. "Yeah, ain't that a good one?"

"Any idea how we can start tracking him down?" McNamara asked.

Manny held up an index finger, which was coated with vanilla frosting and then said, "Not necessary. I got a line on where he's holding up from a guy I know."

"Who's that?" McNamara asked. "And how reliable is he?"

Manny's face scrunched up and for once he concluded his chewing before opening his mouth to reply. "Dickie Deekins. He's golden. Used to work for me. Now he's a reporter."

"A reporter?" McNamara said then looked askance. "For who?"

Manny shrugged. "For himself. He does a podcast. He's an Internet reporter."

"Internet?" McNamara frowned. "I thought you said this guy was reliable?"

"He is." Manny held up his hand and made an O with his thumb and forefinger. "Like I said, good as gold. He sent me some video." Manny broke off a piece of the donut and held it a couple inches from his mouth but didn't stick it in. "And he's waiting to tag up with you guys when you get there. I told him you're coming."

"Pretty sure of yourself that we're going to take this assignment," McNamara said. "Ain't ya?"

Manny shrugged again then hunched over saying, "Let's just say, I'm gonna make you an offer you can't refuse."

"That's the worst *Godfather* imitation I've ever seen," McNamara said.

"Whatever," Manny said. "But take this to the bank, Dickie'll lead you right to Zeus."

"And why's he want to do that? He getting a kickback, or something?"

"Nah," Manny said. "All he wants is the story. He's nursing a hard-on against Zeus."

"For what?"

Manny shrugged. "Don't know. Ask him when you get there."

"I don't understand," McNamara said. "I thought you said this was gonna be tricky or something?"

Manny didn't reply immediately but once more took his time chewing. Wolf thought this looked to be a delaying tactic and wondered what else was involved.

The hammer appeared about ready to drop.

Finally, Manny finished chewing and contemplating. He shifted in his chair and spoke over his shoulder to Freddie.

"That damn coffee ready yet?"

Freddie heaved a sigh, got up, and went to the coffee-maker. Pulling a big mug from the table, he dumped a load of creamer and a pinch of sugar into it before filling the cup with the dark liquid. He handed it to Manny, who took a sip and stuck out his tongue.

"Not enough sugar," he said.

"Too bad," Freddie said as he sat back at his desk. "You're borderline diabetic, remember?"

Manny sneered, pulled open his top desk drawer, and removed three paper packets of sugar and one of an artificial sweetener. He tore open the packets, dumped them into the brew, and grabbed a ball-point pen to use as a stirrer.

"You were about to tell us where this guy's holed up," McNamara reminded him.

"Yeah, yeah." Manny brought the cup to his lips and sipped gently. "You see, this guy's into so many of us businessmen in the area, that we've all got a stake in seeing him brought to justice. So do our insurance companies." He drank some more coffee. "So we all kicked in together and got a little reward going to augment the standard recovery fee."

"Marvelous," McNamara said. "Now quit the run-around. What's the catch?"

Manny ran his tongue over his front teeth and flashed a lips-only smile.

"He's holed up in the FROZ," he said.

"The what?" McNamara said.

"The FROZ," Manny said. "That city called Bendover up near the coast. You probably seen it on the news. The place where they kicked all the cops out, claiming they're a new country, or some other such horseshit. What's it stand for again, Sherman?"

"The Freedom Restricted Occupational Zone," the irritated nephew replied. "And my name's Fred."

Manny smirked at Wolf and McNamara as if the three of them were sharing a private joke.

Wolf thought the nickname joke was wearing a bit thin and he didn't relish the thought of going into a lawless place where the cops were forbidden to enter.

"Bendover... I did see something about that," McNamara said. "But I also heard that the governor's gonna have the state police or the National Guard step in and restore order."

"The governor's a fucking pussy," Manny said. "And that piss-any mayor's claiming it's a peaceful sanctuary or something. It's like a tourist scene during the day but the place goes up for grabs every night. Shootings, rapes, robberies. We're worried that by the time they eventually do step in, old Zeus will have vanished."

"And you'll be out the hundred and fifty grand,"

McNamara said.

Manny took another swing of coffee and Wolf figured this apprehension was particularly serious to him because he hadn't yet touched another donut.

"I don't know," McNamara said. "The Pacific Northwest's a ways from here."

"Only about eighteen or nineteen hours if you're driving."

"Only," McNamara said. "That's a long drive transporting a prisoner back here."

"It's only about two-and-a-half hours if you fly," Manny said.

McNamara frowned. "I left my Superman outfit and cape in the closet."

"You can spell each other and make the trip in under eighteen hours. We'll cover expenses and that reward's substantial."

McNamara and Wolf exchanged glances.

"What do you think, Steve?" McNamara asked.

Wolf shrugged. He figured that Mac was just going through the formalities by asking. He'd already made up his mind.

"Your call," he said.

McNamara turned back to Manny. "We're gonna need back up on this one."

"No doubt," Manny said, a smile starting to form on his lips. "Who you got in mind? Reno?"

McNamara shook his head. "Reno's out. Gonna

have surgery. I'm thinking Ms. Dolly and the gals."

Manny's forehead crinkled. "I don't know. This could be kind of down and dirty. You think they'd be interested?"

"No way to know that without asking them," McNamara said. "Plus, she's got connections in Vegas. Knows somebody that owns a tour bus company. We get one of them things, driving back will be a piece of cake."

Wolf was trying to picture himself behind the wheel of something that large. He'd driven all sorts of vehicles in the army, including having once been trained for a 36-passenger bus and Mac had once owned a motorhome. Driving would be possible but not the piece of cake that Manny had described.

"Look," Manny said. "I don't care if you have to charter a private plane, but just get Mr. Nobles, aka Zeus, back here by next Wednesday and I'll be one happy camper."

"Next Wednesday?" Wolf said. "That's only four days."

"Five, if you count today," Manny said.

"All expenses covered?" McNamara said.

Manny nodded. "Just bring me the receipts so I'll be able to deduct it on my taxes."

McNamara turned toward Wolf and grinned widely.

"Looks like we're going to have to go ahead and

call the P-Patrol after all," he said. "You sure you don't want them to come to the fight tonight?"

"Why not," Wolf said, adding mentally, Why not let everybody watch me get my ass kicked?

***

Piccolo Mobile Home Park
Phoenix, Arizona

It had turned out to be a hectic morning. First, Keller had roused Smith and Cherrie out of bed with the admonishment that it was time to get moving. Then he'd called Riley and told him they'd be coming over to the motel shortly and to get ready. And finally, he tossed the keys to the U-Haul truck to Cummins and told him to drive to the McDonald's to pick up six breakfasts.

"Make one of them a happy meal for the kid," he said as Cummins was going out of the door.

Now I know why he let me keep that extra forty bucks, Cummins thought.

He was about to exit when Smith called out to him.

"Hey, take the Malibu instead," he said. "There's an overhang at the McDonald's and the truck's too high. You don't want to hit it."

They exchanged keys and Cummins left.

This was the first time he'd driven Smith's car

and it handled better than he thought it would. The pick-up went smoothly and when he arrived back at the trailer Keller and Smith were waiting outside, watching his approach like two hawks. Smith looked around, then whistled. Cherrie came prancing down the steps and got into the Chevy's front passenger seat. Smith leaned over, his muscular forearms criss-crossing over the open window of the driver's door.

"You take Cherrie with you," he said. "Follow the U-Haul."

Cummins could smell fresh tobacco smoke on his breath, combined with the reek of an unclean mouth and unwashed armpits. Smith snapped his fingers and pointed at the coffee cups and meals. Cummins handed him two sets and Smith and Keller then went to the truck and got in. They both seemed particularly agitated this morning.

Whatever it was on the agenda, it was starting.

Cherrie grabbed one of the remaining bags and opened it.

"You got all biscuits and bacon and cheese, right?" she asked.

"Yeah," Cummins said. She also reeked of cigarette smoke and body odor, but hers more feminine than Smith's sharp tangy smell. It was obvious that neither one of them had showered this morning. "Where we going?"

"Just follow them," Cherrie said. Bits of biscuit

flew out of her mouth. She popped the slot on the coffee cup and drank some. "You better eat on the way, Jack. Once we get there they ain't gonna give you too much wiggle room."

Cummins debated whether to try and consume anything. The chances were that if things got tense, he wouldn't be able to keep it down, but on the other hand, with his delicate condition, going without breakfast could also give him one of those hypoglycemic headaches.

"Here, sugar," Cherrie said, stuffing the biscuit between her lips and unwrapping one for him. As she shoved it toward his mouth the only thing he could think of was whether or not she'd washed her hands. "Go ahead," she said, her words muffled and distorted by the biscuit still prominent in her mouth. "Eat it."

He reached up and took it, their fingers brushing against each other and he was suddenly curiously aroused by this odiferous hillbilly bitch, not that he held even the slightest notion that he could act on it. Thoughts of an angry Roger D. finding out quashed any thoughts of carnal desire. He didn't even want to think about it.

I've got to figure out an exit strategy, he thought as he bit off a portion of the doughy biscuit, scrambled egg, and half-fried bacon. For me, and the kid, and the bandito.

Suddenly he felt the vibration of his cell phone in

his pants pocket. He took it out and glanced surreptitiously at the screen.

Received your message. Awaiting your call back.

It was from Fallotti. Now all he had to do was find the right time to set up that part of the deal.

***

Garfield and Ollie's Craft's Shop
Scottsdale, Arizona

Wolf watched as Ollie, the distaff half of the jointly-owned husband and wife craft's shop snapped a series of pictures of the bandito with her cell phone. When she'd finished, Garfield, Ollie's husband, gingerly picked up the statue and examined it.

"You say you got it down in Mexico?" he asked.

"Right," Wolf said. "Around Cancun. What can you tell us about it?"

Garfield rotated the statue in his hands, pausing to examine parts of it with a magnifying glass.

"Well," he said. "I'd say it looks like an authentic Mexican piece, all right. Nothing outstanding about it to my eye but then again, I'm no expert. And who'd a *thunk* it that one day a comic book that you bought for twelve cents as a kid would now be worth six grand or more."

"Go figure," McNamara said.

"We can make you a copy for one fifty-six-forty-eight," Ollie said, straightening up from her crouch over the counter. "Add twenty dollars more if you want it painted, but we'll match the paint exactly."

Wolf assessed this and looked at McNamara.

"Ain't that a bit steep?" McNamara asked.

"Well," Ollie said, "we got to make a whole new mold, see. And the paint we gotta match with the computer. Everything's real scientific these days."

"It's gotta be an exact clone," McNamara said. "Can you do that?"

"Even their own mother won't be able to tell them apart," Garfield said with a laugh.

"What kind of time frame are we talking about?" Wolf asked.

The married pair exchanged glances once again.

"Oh, well, we're closed tomorrow," Ollie said. "It's Sunday. Say, a week from today?"

Wolf was about to speak when McNamara said, "Not good enough. We've got an appointment out of town the day after tomorrow or so and I'm not sure when we'll be back."

Garfield scratched his head.

"There's an extra twenty in it for you if you get this all taken care of by Monday morning," McNamara said.

"An extra twenty?" Garfield's face lit up like a Christmas tree decorated with lights of glowing avarice. "Well, I suppose I could get busy on that mold now and then pour it. Then it's gotta set." He looked at Ollie. "And if you can get the paint mixed."

Ollie nodded.

"One other thing," Wolf said. "This bandito has tremendous sentimental value to us. We don't want it damaged."

"Or stolen," McNamara added.

"Stolen?" Garfield grinned. "Not too many people come in to steal our figures but nonetheless, I'll make sure we lock the store securely tonight."

"And I'll put it in our safe when we leave," Ollie said.

"Then it's agreed," McNamara said. "We'll be by at ten o'clock Monday to pick the clone up."

Garfield and Ollie both nodded, smiling with ear-to-ear grins.

Ten o'clock Monday, Wolf thought, fingering the safety deposit box key in his pocket. If I'm still able to walk after tonight, that is.

***

Phoenix International Airport
Phoenix, Arizona

Soraces appreciated the almost flawless landing that the pilot of Von Dien's private Lear Jet made as he touched down on the tarmac. He also appreciated the efficacy of the plan. It was actually a modified version of an acquisition, with a couple of terminations thrown in after the item was acquired. None of the details mattered that much, as long as he kept everything under control. And how could he not with him holding all the cards and setting all the rules?

He sorted through the special envelope that Fallotti had given him before the driver had whisked him away to the airport: a burner phone, blank credit and debit cards that had just been activated, an ample supply of cash, photos of Wolf and McNamara along with printouts of their address, an artist's rendition of what this bandito thing might look like, and the ultimate dealmaker: the flashdrive. The only weak point in the operation was the bandito. He was seeking some statue that neither he nor his employers had ever seen. They were going on the detailed description that Jack Cummins had given them during an interview. They were certain that it existed but not that it absolutely contained that artifact they wanted or even its current whereabouts. The whole thing was based on supposition. It wasn't even known if Wolf knew the significance of what he had. That was the logical assumption, though, and Soraces felt he had to operate under that premise. From what he'd gathered from the reports Jason Zerbe had forwarded before his death about his surveillance and attempts to obtain the bandito statue, both Wolf and his partner more than likely knew by now that the statue was a hot entity.

But did they know why?

That would have to be established. It was like playing poker with a wild card in the deck.

This guy, Cummins, was another wild card. Fallotti had hinted that they suspected that the man was still in Phoenix and trying to insinuate himself back into the game. The lawyer had also said that the original plan had been to dump Cummins due to his unreliability.

He hadn't specified exactly what "dump" meant, but Soraces assumed it was a termination order after Fallotti had said jokingly, "Dead men tell no tales." The big boss, Von Dien, had already expressed his concern about loose ends not being tied up.

Another good point to keep in mind, Soraces thought. I don't want to become one of them.

Years of working for the Agency had taught him how to protect himself through layers of insulation. Once he had control of the artifact, the transfer would be made according to the prescribed procedures that Soraces had used before. Nothing would be left to chance and the item would not be surrendered until the appropriate amount of agreed-upon money had been deposited in Soraces's Cayman Island account.

He slipped the credit and debit card into his wallet and stuffed the envelope into his duffel bag. Customs should be a breeze since he had no extra luggage. Since it was Saturday, a trip to the new law office for his appointment probably wouldn't be until Monday, so today would be a shopping day for new outfits and equipment, plus the continuation of assembling his old team. Back in Belize, he'd left a message for Gunther, who was always the hardest to contact, but the son of a bitch still hadn't responded, despite the suggested urgency. A few of the others had already texted him back that they were interested even though he hadn't specified what the job entailed. Times were hard for wet work teams these days, which meant they'd be eager for a quick and easy payday, especially one that didn't take them to some shithole on the other side of the globe.

As if reading his thoughts, his personal cell phone buzzed and he glanced down at the screen and smiled.

It was Werner Gunther, his favorite wet-works man and best adjuster.

Soraces hit the button and answered the phone with his standard greeting: "Speak now or forever hold your peace."

"I heard through my message service that you were looking for a few good men." It was Gunther's low, gravel-voice, all right. It was practically unmistakable.

"Always," Soraces said. "Interested?"

"Absolutely."

"Good. How quickly can you get to Phoenix?"

***

Algiers's Motel
Phoenix, Arizona

Cummins remained standing in the sleazy little motel room. He was worried about possibly catching bed bugs if he sat on the bed or in the one cushioned chair in the tiny room. Besides, Smith and Cherrie had already plopped down on the rickety bed when they'd all entered the room. Riley was shaving at the sink next to the closet-sized room that housed the toilet and Keller had stationed himself by the solitary window and kept pulling the drawn shade and curtains away to peep out in the parking lot. Riley's kid was playing with some toy truck, pushing it around the musty-smelling carpet.

"What time you gotta check out of this dump?" Keller asked.

Riley scraped some of the shaving cream off the tip of his chin before he answered. He was wearing what appeared to be the same T-shirt from yesterday, with big half-moons of yellowish sweat stains under the arms.

"Check-out's at noon but I paid for two nights already."

Keller was still peering through the open sliver at the window.

"Have the bitch take the kid outta here," he said.

Smith stiffened. "Hey, don't you be calling her that."

Cherrie placed a hand on his arm, shook her head, shrugged. She started to get up.

If Keller had heard, he didn't show it. Instead, he snapped his fingers and said, "Hey, fat boy, give her the keys to the Malibu. I don't want to take the chance on anybody seeing that piece of shit Caravan driving around."

Fat boy? The words again stung Cummins but he knew better than to show a reaction. He glanced at Smith, who didn't look too happy either. Maybe if those two alpha dogs got into it, he'd be able to grab the kid and run.

But where to and for how long?

And there was still Riley to worry about.

Cherrie, too, for that matter, he thought. Better to wait things out.

Besides, something was up. He could sense it. The stagnant air in the room smelled like sour sweat. The tension was palpable.

Cherrie shifted off the bed, leaning over to give Cummins another glimpse of her abundant cleavage. The move almost seemed intentional. Was she coming on to him? Not likely, with her hillbilly significant other sitting next to her.

No, he thought. She's just a prick teaser.

"Come on, sugar," Cherrie said to the kid. "Let's go

get us some ice cream."

"I don't want ice cream," the kid said.

"Chad," Riley yelled from the sink. "Do like she says, dammit."

The reflection of his face in the mirror glared with imminent rage.

The kid grabbed his toy truck and stood.

"Leave the god damn toy here," Riley said.

The kid looked like he was about ready to cry but he set the truck on the floor.

Riley looked at Cherrie. "Get that car seat outta the Caravan for him, would ya?"

"Oh, we'll be all right," she said. "I'll just fasten him in with the seatbelt."

"The hell you will," Keller said. "Get the fucking car seat and use it. I don't want no cop pulling you over for no reason. Drive careful, too."

Cherrie rolled her eyes as she accepted the keys from Cummins.

Smith stared at Keller, who turned from the window.

Cherrie and the kid moved to the door.

After they'd left, Keller once again checked the view through the sliver and stood.

"Okay, Roger D. Let's go get the stuff so we can get ready."

Smith shifted himself off the bed, which creaked like a set of rusty hinges.

Get ready for what?

Cummins watched as Riley wiped the residual shaving cream from his face and neck and studied himself in the mirror.

"How old's your boy?" Cummins asked, trying to sound friendly. Actually, he couldn't care less about the kid or Riley. But the more he knew about this potential bargaining chip, the better.

"Gonna be five come September," Riley said. His tone had that similar-sounding twang as Smith's.

Probably both came out of the same hillbilly mold, Cummins thought.

"Nice looking kid," Cummins said, trying to fill the void.

And what he'd said was true enough, which wasn't any real surprise. Riley actually was what you'd consider handsome, in a hillbilly sort of way. Sort of like a greasy, slicked up version of a young Elvis Presley. From what Cummins had seen of McNamara's daughter, she was attractive and nice looking as well, so the kid had good genes, in the appearance department anyway.

This was all good. After all, he could hardly expect Wolf and McNamara to trade the bandito for an ugly kid.

"Yep." Riley, who was still studying his reflection in the mirror, said, "He is at that."

He leaned closer to his mirror image and brought

both of his hands to his neck, probing with his fingers, apparently trying to pop open a pimple.

The door flew open and Smith and Keller came in carrying the same two old-style army duffel bags that Keller had kept by his bed last night. He slammed the door behind them and paused to set the security lock.

Like that would do much good, Cummins thought. But he found it both amusing and discomforting.

Why did he need to double-lock the door?

A few seconds later he found out.

Keller and Smith pulled out three rifles, two AR-15's and one AK-47, along with several curved, banana-clip magazines. Keller laid the rifles out and then dumped out the rest of the contents from the two bags: four semi-auto handguns and numerous boxes of ammunition. It looked like enough to start a small war.

Keller grinned at Cummins, who wasn't' liking this at all.

This "Freedom Brigade" bullshit was turning into an armed revolution and Cummins wanted no part of it. But from the leering grin on Keller's face, it didn't look like there was going to be much choice on the matter.

Riley picked up the Kalashnikov. It had a metal folding stock and Cummins wondered if it was one of those Chinese knockoffs or an original.

"That one's mine," Keller said. "It's full auto."

Full auto?

Cummins wondered how Keller had gotten that one.

Riley handed him the Kalashnikov and Keller grinned as he pulled back the bolt and checked the chamber.

"Come on over here and help us start loading the magazines, fat boy," he said. "Need us to show you how?"

"No," Cummins said. "I was in the service."

"Good," Keller said. "We want to have everything loaded up and ready by the time Roger D's *lady* gets back with the kid. Then we gotta go out and reconnoiter."

Smith flashed a sullen look as he picked up one of the magazines along with a box of .223 ammunition.

"Okay," Cummins said as he stepped toward the bed. He'd show them that he was no stranger to weapons and magazines. After all, he'd been in the army, too, but some clarification was needed. He wasn't quite sure which way the bullets fit into the magazine. "So are you going to tell me what this is all about?"

"Sure," Keller said, shoving a box of cartridges toward him along with one of the magazines. "We're loading up for bear and tonight we're gonna bag us an armored car."

CHAPTER 6

The Regency Arena
Phoenix, Arizona

Wolf watched as the gauze was wound around his open hand. George seemed to know the exact degree of pressure to assure both comfort and tightness. Occasionally he would pause and instruct Wolf to make a fist. Reno stood off to the side of the table along with an official and a member of the opposing fighter's camp. This was to assure no foreign substance, like plaster of Paris, was sprinkled over the gauze and tape. It was an old-time boxing rule brought about by the abuses of unscrupulous trainers and handlers and had made an occasional reappearance in more modern times. The rule had primarily originated from an unsubstantiated claim that the great heavyweight, Jack Dempsey, had "loaded gloves" when he'd fought

Jess Willard for the championship on July 4th, 1919. Dempsey had annihilated the much bigger Willard in the first round, fracturing his jaw in thirteen places, his cheekbone, several of his ribs, and knocking out a slew of his teeth. Willard staggered around for three more rounds before it was mercifully stopped. Ironic, too, that in those days Dempsey, aka the Manassas Mauler, was allowed to hover over his fallen foe and clobber him as he tried to get back up which was very similar to the loose rules of today's MMA. There'd been a few other examples of loaded gloves in recent years that Wolf recalled and he hoped the observer from Reno's gym, who was monitoring Marcos de Silva's preparation, would be diligent.

I'm going to have my hands full as it is, Wolf thought.

At the weigh-in, de Silva had seemed both aloof and professional. He also looked sleek and very much in shape. Wolf had wondered if the guy's only job was keeping in shape and fighting down in Brazil or if he held down a job as well.

Reno had told him he didn't know but Wolf also wondered if Reno was trying not to undermine Wolf's confidence.

No, de Silva's a professional fighter who trains twenty-four-seven.

Words best left unspoken?

I'll find out soon enough, Wolf thought.

"Make a fist," George said.

Wolf did and George grunted an approval. He clipped the end of the gauze off and picked up a roll of white medical tape, pulling off and cutting eight pieces and clipping them to a specific length of about four inches each.

They were in the red team's dressing room on the first floor. The other group, to which de Silva was assigned, was in the blue team room. Wolf silently hoped that the appellation, red, wasn't a sign of things to come. The case of the nerves hadn't faded yet. It was like waiting to do a big performance and knowing if you didn't perform up to par, you could literally get carried out on a stretcher. The building was a big auditorium that was initially designed to house sporting events of all types. The locker room had a set of lockers where Wolf had hung his clothes, a shower room off to one side, a long metal table, and several chairs along the wall. The place was eerily silent, given that there were other fights on the undercard going on at this time in the central auditorium, with a very limited audience viewing them. Wolf didn't know if that was an advantage or a disadvantage. Usually, the size of the crowd was a distraction only until that opening bell rang. Then everything else, the noise, the cheering, the boos, got blocked out in favor of concentrating on the opponent standing in front of you trying to knock your block off. The ambient noise at times made it virtually impossible to hear any instructions from your corner during the fight. Of course competing in a prison boxing match was a whole different animal: Scores of convicts yelling and screaming and virtually no competent corner-men to advise you one way or another.

This time it would be different. He had both Reno and George in his corner and both of them knew what they were doing. Wolf hoped he would, too.

But, he reminded himself, it's only for the money. Win, lose, or draw.

The indistinct sound of the announcer's amplified voice drifted through the closed door. The preceding fight must have been over with. There was no applause, no cheering. Wolf tried to make out the words but decided it required too much effort.

"What you thinking?" Reno asked.

"About what's gonna happen once I finish that long walk into the octagon," Wolf said.

Reno clapped him on his shoulder.

"You'll be all right. After what I seen you do, it's De Silva that oughta be worried."

Before Wolf could reply the door opened and McNamara came in wearing a wide grin.

He sauntered over to the table, nodded to the others, and then leaned over toward Wolf.

"Looks like you'll be up in a minute or two," McNamara said. "Last fight ended in about sixty seconds."

"Shit," Reno said. "Hurry up with that taping, George. I don't want Steve going in there cold, without warming up."

George grabbed the pieces of tape and began fitting them between Wolf's fingers.

"How you feeling?" McNamara asked. "Ready?"

"As ready as I'll ever be," Wolf said.

"He's ready," Reno said. "Count on it, Mac."

"I am," McNamara said. "Not only have I seen him in action but he's also a Ranger, and they don't quit."

"A Ranger," Wolf said, trying to ease his tension by flashing a smile. "That's almost as good as Green Beret."

"Almost," McNamara said.

"Who's up there in the stands?" Wolf asked.

McNamara took a deep breath and smiled.

"Well, Kase decided not to come," he said. "She's got to finish up a term paper or something for school."

That eased Wolf's mind slightly. He hadn't wanted her to be there anyway, unsure if she would be rooting for him or secretly for his opponent.

"And after I dropped you off, I picked up my gals at the airport. They're all three here and as excited as all get out to see their hero in action."

Wolf smirked. "They've already seen me in action,"

"Not without your shirt off," McNamara said. "Well, I guess one of them has."

Wolf thought about Yolanda, her beautiful dark face, her stunning figure ... He wondered what she'd think if he really took a drubbing tonight, which reminded him once again that he'd specifically told Mac not to bring them here.

"I thought I told you—"

"Aw, hell," McNamara said, interrupting him. "You did. But that was before we got this new gig coming up. We're on a time constraint, remember? This is sorta like a pre-mission briefing."

"What you guys got going?" Reno asked.

McNamara's eyes glanced around the room and then at Reno.

"I'll tell you later."

Reno nodded.

"Just as well," he said. "We got other things to worry about now. Right Steve?"

Wolf didn't reply.

Lots of other things, he thought.

George finished lacing up the gloves and securing them with the band of red-colored tape, signifying the corner designation. Reno told him to get up and do some shadow boxing.

"Worst thing in the world's to walk into that octagon cold," he said. "Break a sweat."

Wolf got up and began dancing around the room, throwing punches and bobbing and weaving. McNamara stood there smiling.

The door burst open and three men came in, two of them on either side, supporting and almost dragging the third man in the middle. His body was slick with perspiration and glistened from a residual layer of wiped off blood. The man's head hung downward and red droplets splashed on the floor from his mouth and nose.

"Clear the table," one of the carriers shouted.

Everyone cleared away and the two men helped the injured fighter onto the metal table. He groaned with each movement.

More men came into the room. Two appeared to be paramedics, from the look of their uniforms, and another was clad in a polo shirt with *Dr. Jay* embroidered on the left breast area. He held a black bag in his left hand.

"What the hell?" Reno said. "What you doing, bringing him here? Shoulda taken him to triage."

"He was in triage," the guy with Dr. Jay on his shirt said. "He declined treatment and then collapsed on the way here."

"We got a stretcher crew coming," one of the paramedics said.

They helped the man stretch out on the table and Wolf saw the guy's breathing was rapid and shallow. His color looked a bit off, too, and the left side of his face was a bloody, swollen mass.

The guy from the opposing camp made a huffing sound and said something Wolf assumed was Portuguese.

Maybe he was commiserating or maybe he was insinuating that Wolf was going to suffer a similar fate.

Reno stepped over, blocking Wolf's view.

"Don't look at him, Steve," he said. "That don't mean nothing unless it happens to you."

Unless it happens to me, Wolf thought momentarily.

"Don't worry about it," McNamara said. "He's seen worse."

And Wolf had, too. A lot worse.

His thoughts went back to the carnage he'd seen overseas on deployments ... GI's with their arms and legs blown off by enemy fire or IED's. Or worse, their bodies riddled and gut-shot. Iraqis and Afghanis, both tangos and civilians, blown apart or curled up in fetal positions nursing a plethora of bullet wounds. The way to not let it affect you was just to not let it affect you, to keep mentally reciting the sacred oath: *Ain't gonna happen to me. Better them than us.*

Two more paramedics came through the door pushing an extended gurney. They glanced around and pushed it next to the supine man on the table.

"Yeah," Wolf said. "I've seen worse."

***

Imperial Armored Car Service
Phoenix, Arizona

Cummins felt the sweat trickling down from his armpits as he watched the armored car pull out of the gate and head down the street in the opposite direction. His hands felt slick inside the latex gloves and for a second he worried that a layer of sweaty water would build up between the rubber and his skin impairing his ability to grip the steering wheel.

"That's gotta be it," Riley said. "The money run."

Cummins nodded and pulled the van out to follow them.

He had a towel over the peeled steering column in the hopes that no one would notice that the van was recently stolen. At least it was tall enough that drivers in regular cars wouldn't be able to look into the interior directly at stop lights and see the draped towel. But then again, he wouldn't be driving this thing that long.

No longer than I have to, he thought.

Riley was gibbering into his cell phone now, talking to either Smith or Keller, who were in the stolen dump truck. It would be Keller most likely. Smith had done the deed on that vehicle, too, as he had on this one. The hillbilly's talents had no end.

Two stolen vehicles, one of them a huge dumper, in less than twenty minutes. It had been phenomenal to watch him work. Less than sixty seconds breaking into and stealing the vehicle each time.

And here I am driving one of them, he thought.

But he was glad that was to be his only part in this venture. Keller had been a slave driver forcing them to go through rehearsal after rehearsal in the hot afternoon sun, imitating the steps they'd take in removing the money bags and placing them in the van. When it became evident that Cummins was not suited to being fleet of foot, Keller assigned him to be the driver. It was simple enough and ironically a role that he was intimately familiar with after his foray at the McNamara Ranch with Zerbe and company. He'd gotten away almost clean from that one and he'd made up a desperation plan for this one as well. If something went wrong, he'd simply take off and worry about the consequences later. It would mean giving up his chance to abduct the kid and make the bandito deal with Wolf, but like he'd planned, it was only to be used in dire circumstances. And from the way these three talked and planned, this operation should go down like clockwork. Cummins got the feeling that it wasn't the first rodeo for any of them. And to make matters worse, the damn kid was nowhere around. Cherrie had him in the Malibu and was supposed to meet them at the assigned rendezvous point.

Still, Cummins thought. I do have a gun.

He felt the metal slide of the Glock biting into the fat of his belly.

It wasn't a far stretch if this thing went totally south and he had to take off, that he could go to the rendezvous point and grab both Cherrie and the kid and take off. He imagined they'd both fit in the trunk of the Chevy. He could reach out to Wolf and make a quick demand: the bandito for the kid, no questions asked. And then he'd be free to make his own subsequent arrangement with Von Dien.

You want it, he imagined himself saying. I got it.

"Yeah, I'm sure," Riley was saying into his phone. "They're going out now with the mother lode to start filling up all them ATMs."

Cummins heard the loud roaring of the big diesel engine as the dump truck fell into view behind them and then soared past.

Riley was listening intently on his phone, then said, "Roger that," and hung up. He dropped the phone into the lower right pocket of his BDU and buttoned it. Then he tapped the magazine of his AR-15 and pulled the mask up over the lower portion of his face. He was wearing the same latex gloves as Cummins. They all were. But Riley had his sleeves partially rolled up and Cummins could see the big bandage he had covering the pus-filled tattoo.

"Better mask up," Riley said.

Cummins grunted and pulled his mask up, too, thankful that he was wearing his contacts and didn't have to worry about the lenses of his glasses fogging up.

"They're gonna slam 'em when they get to McArthur's park like we planned," Riley said. "So get ready. Won't be long now."

Cummins felt the surge of bile rise up and coalesce in his throat momentarily before edging back down.

Oh please, he thought, don't let it happen now.

***

The Regency Arena
Phoenix, Arizona

Wolf felt the butterflies diminishing as he walked down the catwalk alone and stopped for one of the refs to do the body grease check and mouthpiece verification on him. Reno, George, and Reno's cut man, Clancy, joined him as the ref put a thin layer of Vaseline on Wolf's face. After verifying that his corner-men had a second mouthpiece ready in case of damage to the one Wolf was wearing, they did their final, ceremonial hugs and Wolf stepped through the gate and into the cage. He paced around getting the soles of his bare feet used to the somewhat abrasive rub of the mat while waiting for de Silva to complete his own walk and inspection. As the more senior fighter, he had the advantage of coming into the cage second. Usually, it was a standard psychological tactic to make your opponent wait in the ring of the cage as long as possible to let the nerves continue to wear him down, but de Silva hardly took any time with this at all.

He must be as anxious to get to it as I am, Wolf thought.

After de Silva stepped through the gate, the announcer went into his spiel introducing both of them. The guy didn't spare any fanfare as he went about the task, making it sound like he was calling the Kentucky Derby instead of barking into a microphone to an almost empty auditorium. But everything was being recorded and broadcast on a local sports channel so the enthusiasm had to look real. The same could be said about the fights, too. Wolf wondered about the kid he'd seen lying in that semi-conscious state in the locker room.

Ain't gonna happen to me, he thought. *Ain't gonna happen to me.*

Reno was standing there next to him and George was massaging his neck and shoulders.

Across the open expanse, his opponent bounced on his toes. Marco de Silva's body was covered with a network of tattoos and his skin was stretched taut over a network of chiseled muscles. The man looked very fit and then some. His arms and legs were long and loose looking.

A grappler who can bang, Wolf thought.

He glanced up into the stands and although the rest of the auditorium was in semi-darkness due to the bright lights surrounding the fighting area, he was able to make out Ms. Dolly, Brenda, Yolanda, and Mac. Mac sat with one arm around Ms. Dolly and the other around Brenda. Yolanda sat a few feet away from them. He wondered if she was as nervous as he was.

"Seconds out," the ref yelled.

Reno winked at him and said, "Kick his ass."

Everyone else left through the gate leaving only Wolf, de Silva, and the ref.

The fence around the eight-sided ring was jet black and had a black barrier along the top. Sixteen periodic padded posts held the fencing in place.

"Are you ready here?" the ref yelled, glancing at Wolf.

He nodded.

"Are you ready here?" the ref repeated to de Silva.

He nodded as well.

"Then let's get it on!"

Wolf moved to the center of the ring and held up his open palm inviting de Silva to touch-up before they got down to trying to kick each other's asses.

The acknowledging slap felt solid and quick.

***

McArthur's Park
Phoenix, Arizona

They were approaching the far end of the park now, the same route that Riley said they'd go. He said he'd driven it over a hundred times at the planning session and his prognostication had now come to fruition.

Habitual behavior is the faithful ally of the ambush, Cummins remembered hearing from his military days. Not that he'd ever been on either side of an ambush.

He heard the accelerating diesel whine of the dump truck and looked through the windshield at the unfolding scene, the accident to be.

Seconds later, he heard the crunch of metal striking metal as the front bumper of the bigger vehicle, the dump trunk, smashed into the side of the armored car right by the driver's door. Sparks flew from the impact and the grinding of the big truck's gears squealed with a high-pitched radiance. The cab of the armored car crinkled like an accordion as the dump truck pushed it off the street and over the empty parking spaces and over the sidewalk.

Cummins pulled up next to the crash site and Riley was already leaping out of the door, his rifle held against his shoulder at the ready, a ring of keys jingling in his left hand. He rushed over to the undamaged right side of the armored truck's cab. The driver was not visible and Cummins assumed he'd been knocked over by the impact. Keller was there now tearing open the door, his Kalashnikov held with his right hand in firing position.

"Open the fucking back door," Keller yelled, the mask slightly muffling his words.

"Do it, Thompson," Riley shouted. "Do it, or he'll shoot ya."

A few seconds later Keller's rifle exploded with a staccato burst and he stepped back yelling, "You do it now, idiot, and use your damn key. That's what you stole it for, ain't it?"

Cummins strained his eyes to try and see what had just happened.

Did Keller execute the driver?

Riley looked stunned for a moment and then reached inside the cab of the truck. He did something, which Cummins assumed was the flipping of the security switch to disengage the rear doors and then ran around to the back. Smith was already standing by the rear of the armored truck, training his weapon on the door. All the windows were bulletproof and there were three gun ports on the back and side portions. If the guard inside had recovered from the stress of the crash, there could be more shooting.

Cummins shifted into reverse and backed the van up and swung it around so the side door, which Riley had left open, was now adjacent to the rear of the truck. The intention was to afford them an easy transfer of the money bags from the armored truck into the van. Riley grasped the door handle and twisted it.

It was apparently still locked.

Cummins saw him swear and then bring the ring of keys up to the lock. He inserted one.

Keller was next to him now, pointing the Kalashnikov at the door.

Riley twisted the handle again and this time the door popped open. Smith edged the end of his rifle into the open door and yelled something. Seconds later a guard stumbled forward out of the rear section, his hands raised. Smith pulled the man all the way out, stripped the pistol from his belt holster, and pushed the guard all the way to the street and away from the opening. Riley slung his rifle over his shoulder and hopped up into the truck. Keller motioned for Smith to shoulder his rifle as well as one of the heavily laden canvas bags was tossed out of the rear section of the armored truck.

Smith grabbed it and heaved it into the van. It landed with a clunk.

Riley tossed another bag and Smith caught it and flung it into the van as well.

The impact made a jarring thud and Cummins felt a flood of bile rush up and settle in his mouth. He clenched his jaws, trying like hell not to lose control.

The two of them, Riley and Smith, moved like two automatons in tandem: toss, catch, throw, toss, catch, throw ...

Cummins watched the process continue for the

better part of a minute as the stack of canvas bags continued to grow behind him.

"That's it," Riley yelled, popping his head out of the rear door.

"Go," Keller shouted and motioned for both him and Smith to enter the van. They both did, the foul sweat pouring off both of them. Smith slammed the door shut.

They waited for Keller who was still standing over the prone guard. Keller stooped and retrieved the guard's pistol, looked at it, then shoved it on the side of his pistol-belt.

Smith ripped off his mask and yelled, "Let's go, dammit!"

Keller glanced at him through the windshield, then rotated his head back toward the ground.

The sound of another staccato burst tore through the air and a spray of ejected shells poured through the Kalashnikov's ejection port.

It was too much for Cummins. He pulled off his mask, pushed open the door, leaned out, and vomited. By the time he'd pulled himself back fully behind the wheel, Keller was in the front passenger seat with his rifle resting between his legs. A trail of acrid smoke rose from the barrel.

"If you're done, fat boy," he said, holding his mask away from his face. "I suggest we get the fuck out of here."

***

The Regency Arena
Phoenix, Arizona

Wolf plopped down on the stool as George placed an icepack against the back of Wolf's neck. The instant chill revived him somewhat but his breaths still came in gasps. Round one had gone pretty much as expected with both fighters tentative at first, throwing jabs and kicks. As the round progressed, Wolf began to connect with a few punches and then was taken down after de Silva grabbed him. They struggled together on their knees at first. Wolf vaguely remembered Reno yelling for Wolf to "Get back up, dammit."

I can't let him keep me on the ground, Wolf remembered thinking, and tried to maintain his hold on his opponent's body. Wolf had his arms around de Silva's chest and had one leg in a scissor-lock. The Brazilian felt slippery and the pungency of his scent seemed to overwhelm everything else. They flopped together like ungainly lovers until de Silva managed to attain a mounted position and began raining punches down on Wolf. He managed to block a number of them with his arms, vaguely cognizant of Reno's shouting. His words were indecipherable as they mixed with the heavy sounds of his own breathing and the shouts in Portuguese from de

Silva's corner on the opposite side of the cage.

Each blow seemed like a hammer coming down, and not just any hammer, a sledge hammer. When de Silva leaned back a little too far to take in a deeper breath, Wolf somehow managed to flip onto his side and then onto his front. This proved a dangerous move in that de Silva immediately went for a naked-rear-choke. Luckily, Wolf was able to grab hold of the other man's arms and avoid the encirclement of his neck. And just as he thought de Silva had finally managed to slip his forearm into the proper place, the air-horn sounded signaling the end of the first round.

Saved by the bell, Wolf thought as he got to his feet. His arms and legs felt like lead.

It had only been five minutes but Wolf felt like it had been five hours. He struggled to get his breathing under control now as Reno's voice suddenly became understandable.

"You listening?" Reno placed a hand on Wolf's shoulder. "You gotta pick it up this round. He won the last one. He gets this next one, it's over, understand?"

Wolf understood all right. One round down, two to go. He had to do better, stay on his feet, find the range.

"Seconds out," the ref called.

Had it already been a full minute?

Wolf stood and George grabbed the stool and he and Reno headed out of the cage. De Silva's corner-men followed.

The air-horn sounded again.

Time for Round Two.

***

Underneath the I-94 Overpass
Phoenix, Arizona

They were under a cement overpass with the traffic whizzing by on the freeway about forty feet above them. Cummins had driven the van to the place where Cherrie had been waiting with the U-Haul. The kid was in the car seat in the cab. While Cummins had been driving, Riley, Smith, and Keller had used the keys Riley had stolen from his former employer to unlock and open the metal clasp-locks securing the bags. The material was so tough, Riley had explained, that they couldn't be cut with a regular knife. They'd emptied each bag into open cardboard moving boxes and secured them with packing tape. Riley pointed out the GPS monitors that each bag contained.

"Want me to smash 'em?" Smith asked.

"Just toss 'em," Keller said. "And hurry up and get us on the freeway, fat boy."

Keller's continuing use of that pejorative angered Cummins but he kept his mouth shut. This guy Keller was a fucking psycho. The capricious way he'd killed those two guards, without the slightest compunction, clearly exemplified sociopathic tendencies. Cummins could put nothing to chance with this guy.

Got to keep my mouth shut and bide my time, he thought. Wait for the right moment to bail.

And he still needed to grab the kid, too. Although it would be dangerous, it was his only way out, his only trump card, his only chance of getting the bandito.

"Get the boxes transferred while I douse this sucker," Keller said. He jumped out of the van with the duffel bag containing the rifles and ran to the rear of the parked U-Haul truck. He twisted the securing hatch and raised the door. The bed was filled with various pieces of furniture that they'd taken from Smith and Riley's trailers.

Keller tossed the bag containing the rifles into the back.

Riley and Smith carried two boxes each and ran to the open rear of the U-Haul. Cummins grabbed a couple of boxes and joined in. Keller retrieved a red, plastic, three-gallon can of gasoline from the truck and splashed some of the contents around inside the van. Riley and Smith returned for the remaining boxes. Cummins was out of breath and panting by the rear of the U-Haul.

"That's all of them," Smith said as he shoved the two boxes he'd been carrying into the bed of the U-Haul.

He hopped up into the rear, as did Riley, and Smith

extended his open hand down toward Cummins.

"You done good, Jack," the hillbilly king said.

Cummins grasped the man's hand, jammed his right foot onto the rectangular metal guard attached to the rear frame, and managed to climb up into the bed of the truck. It was more like Smith had lifted him up but Cummins was still a bit winded and rolled back onto his haunches. Keller set the red plastic can on the floor of the van and removed a book of matches from his pocket. He broke one off, struck it against the striking board, and then lit the entire pack. Stepping back, he threw the blazing match pack inside the van and seconds later it ignited with an exploding, vacuous boom.

Keller ran over to the U-Haul and ascended to the bed with a nimble vault. He motioned for Smith and Riley to get back and then reached up and grabbed the nylon rope to close the big door. As it started downward, he said, "I'm gonna ride up front."

"Hey," Riley said. "How about letting me do that. I want to be with my kid."

"Check on him later when we switch cars," Keller said and slammed the door all the way down.

The three of them were suddenly plunged into total darkness.

***

The Regency Arena
Phoenix, Arizona

Last round, thought Wolf as the air-horn blared once again.

He felt that he'd won Round Two and Reno had agreed.

"This one will decide it," he said into Wolf's ear as the command for seconds to vacate had been given. "Dig deep, Steve."

Wolf's arms felt so heavy that it required an effort to hold them up. His breathing had almost returned to normal between rounds and he silently thanked all those mornings of early roadwork. Hopefully, he'd find that special reservoir of energy to marshal another commanding performance this time.

Dig deep.

The word rang in his ears.

His opponent looked to be doing the same thing. He hadn't come all this way to lose and probably had more riding on it than Wolf did.

Only in it for the money? He asked himself as they met in the center of the cage and touched gloves as a sign of mutual respect.

Wolf threw a quick jab and caught de Silva on the cheek. He lurched forward trying to throw a straight right over Wolf's jab but was a tad slow and Wolf pivoted and delivered a straight right of his own.

De Silva went down and Wolf hesitated a moment too long before making another move and didn't follow him down to the mat. Instead, he stepped back and waited for his opponent to rise.

"What the hell are you doing?" Reno's voice yelled from the sidelines. "Go after him. Mount him. Ground and pound."

The thought of delivering punches to a semi-conscious man in a sporting event was anathema to Wolf, a holdover from his boxing days: You didn't hit a man when he was down.

"Christ," Reno yelled again. "You got him."

But from the way de Silva quickly rolled to his feet, Wolf wasn't so sure. He'd been stunned, sure, but he was also like a python on the mat. He could have been playing possum to lure Wolf down to the mat where the Brazilian definitely had the advantage. That added to Wolf's decision to stay on his feet.

Or try to, at least.

De Silva sprang to his feet and charged. He and Wolf collided and went crashing into the black fencing, their arms locked around each other's bodies. They danced together, twisting and turning, their bodies undulating, locked in a mocking imitation of lover's embrace.

More twisting and then they both tipped over. Wolf fell with his back against the fence. De Silva drew his arm back and delivered two solid punches to Wolf's face. He was so adrenalized he barely felt the impact. He struck out with a punch of his own, a looping left, delivered from his semi-supine position.

It was an arm-punch, with little power due to no thrust from his legs, but it caught de Silva squarely on the mouth.

An eruption of blood spewed forth, spraying Wolf with the crimson mist. His opponent's head jerked back slightly and Wolf slid forward, got his arms and legs planted, and straightened up. De Silva smashed an overhand right to Wolf's temple and the black lights suddenly swarmed in front of his eyes, then vanished. He retaliated with a solid body blow that backed de Silva up a few steps. Wolf backpedaled to the center and waited as de Silva whirled and lumbered toward him.

Wolf shot out a quick combination that stunned de Silva. He did a little stutter-step but when Wolf moved in to deliver another punch, his opponent lurched forward and encircled his waist, lifting him off the mat.

The mat slammed against Wolf's back as he hit the floor, the wind expelling from his lungs. He tried to inhale but his chest ached. Fighting through the pain, he took shallow, rapid breaths as de Silva undulated against him trying to pin him down, his arms still encircling Wolf's waist.

A warm torrent of de Silva's blood poured forth

over Wolf's abdomen, mixing with the sweat. Wolf felt almost unable to move but somehow managed to deliver a crisp punch to de Silva's left temple. The punch had little effect.

An arm punch, Wolf thought, still trying to work his legs to escape being mounted.

De Silva's body edged upward, his bloody mouth spewing forth a steady crimson flow.

Wolf got his right foot under de Silva's left hip. The Brazilian scissor-locked Wolf's left leg.

More struggling, more pain, more warm blood flowing over his heaving abdomen and pouring onto the mat.

Wolf delivered another punch.

De Silva did as well.

After an interminable thirty seconds of pain, sweat, and blood, the air-horn sounded once more, signaling the end of Round Three. It was over.

I finished on my ass instead of my feet, Wolf thought.

But he was certain that he'd won.

***

I-10 South of Phoenix
Arizona

Cummins could feel the big U-Haul truck slowing to

a bumpy halt as he, Riley, and Smith bounced around in the darkness of the truck bed. It was insufferably hot and no one had thought to bring water. To make things worse, the two of them lit up cigarettes and the tobacco fumes filled the air.

"Reminds me of the Sandbox, don't it?" Smith said.

Riley grunted. The red glow of the cigarette partially illuminated his face. He was clearly worried about his kid.

Cummins was, too. His original hope that the robbery would go bad, allowing him to escape and leaving him open to drive to the rendezvous point and meet Cherrie and the kid hadn't materialized. It was a hastily conceived option anyway. The snatch would have to be done with a bit of finesse, perhaps after building some trust between him and the boy and Riley.

Mind if I take your son for ice cream?

That could work. One thing was for sure, however, things had to be handled just right. After the way Keller had dispatched those two guards, and Smith and Riley going along with it, meant that any such move on his part would be fraught with danger ... Extreme danger.

Did he have the stones to carry it off?

Good question, he thought.

Then again, they were on the move now, to where he wasn't exactly sure. But once they got there, an alternate plan would have him contacting Wolf and merely giving him the location of the kid in exchange for the bandito. That would take him out of the equation. Let Wolf and McNamara deal with the fanatical psychos while he sold the bandito to Fallotti and VD for a healthy retirement price.

The rear door rose upward letting in a cool breeze and ambient lighting from some sort of parking lot. Cummins struggled to get to his feet. Smith and Riley were already jumping down. Riley disappeared around the side of the truck as Smith and Cherrie embraced.

Cummins saw they were at a rest stop on the Interstate. A long building with glass walls was about twenty-five yards away.

"Go on inside and use the facilities if you have to," Keller said. "And anybody wants anything from them vending machines, get it now, cause we're heading south shortly."

Riley was carrying the car seat with his kid inside, the boy's leg dangling from the seat. He appeared to be sound asleep.

"You give him something?" Riley asked Keller.

Keller shrugged.

"Relax," Cherrie said. "I give him half of one of my sleeping pills."

"What?" Riley's mouth curled up in anger.

"It was more like a quarter of one," Cherrie added.

"Don't never do nothing like that again," Riley shouted.

"Hey," Smith said. "Easy."

"Fuck easy," Riley said.

The two men glared at each other, Riley looking white hot with rage and Smith as cool as dry ice.

Then Riley blinked and walked to Keller.

"Gimme my keys," he said.

Keller stood there for several seconds not moving, then reached into his pants pocket and removed a set of keys.

Riley shifted the car seat with his son and grabbed the keys.

The movement stirred the boy awake.

"Where we going, daddy?" the kid asked.

"To a place where we can get a new start," Riley said as he walked toward the building.

Keller tossed a set of keys to Smith, who caught them.

Cummins assumed they were going to the Malibu, which was parked on the other side of the building next to the Caravan in the Cars Only section. The king and queen of the hillbilly royalty sauntered their way toward the building, arms around each other and looking joined at the hip.

"That leaves you riding with me, fat boy," Keller said. "I might even let you drive."

Cummins nodded, reviewing his options, which

were few and far between. He had little choice to go along with the ride. But he felt he was still entitled to a few answers.

"Where we going?" he asked.

Keller lifted an eyebrow and then winked.

"You heard the man," he said. "To a place where we can get a new start."

CHAPTER 7

Former Fort Lemand
Southern Arizona

They'd driven for a couple of hours into the settling darkness bound for their new destination. Cummins hadn't had the slightest idea of what that was or even where they were. He only knew that Keller, who was beside him in the U-Haul truck, kept saying just to follow the other two vehicles. The stop for gas and to use the washroom facilities was coordinated by cell phone. It had been a tedious and boring trip, with Keller continually checking the truck's side-view mirror and spouting off some nonsense about the coming social revolution and how the Brigade would find him ready. A few times he mentioned something about the "Colonel," but didn't go into details. After a while, he quit talking and just told Cummins to keep driving and follow Smith's Malibu.

"He knows the way," Keller said. "And we shouldn't oughta have to stop for gas again."

Cummins wondered about a personal relief stop but didn't ask.

He knew they were more or less heading south but they'd exited the freeway and began a circuitous trek on some side roads. When they finally turned onto a paved road that seemed to cut between two small hills, Cummins thought he saw several pinpoints of reddish light up ahead in the distance which quickly disappeared. Peripherally, he caught sight of some movement to his right and realized Keller had dozed off.

The big man stretched and yawned.

"Nothing like a good combat nap," he said.

"Where the hell are we?" Cummins asked.

"Close," Keller replied. He turned toward him. "Past the point of no return."

Cummins didn't ask what that meant. He was afraid to ask. Once again, he found himself in a tricky and perilous situation but he still had the Glock 43 that Keller had given him before the robbery. The big goon had made no attempt to get it back.

Trust … What a wonderful thing. But how long would it last?

Apparently, his participation in the robbery had been sufficient enough to engender a place in "the

Brigade." His plan was to go along with the program, figure out a way to get the kid out of there and contact Wolf about a trade.

Keller took out his cell phone and made a call. It seemed to go through without a problem, which meant Cummins's own cell, the burner phone to contact Fallotti, probably had reception out this way, too.

More good news, he thought.

He'd need to somehow find Wolf's cell phone number so the trade could be set up when the time was right. But it was going to take some planning.

"Let us pull ahead," Keller said into his phone. "Tell Riley to pull behind you."

Cummins heard a muffled reply and Keller pressed a button to dial again. This time his voice had a ring of command authority when he spoke.

"This is Captain Keller," he said. "Myself and two other vehicles are approaching the main gate. I'm in the U-Haul."

A muffled response came, sounding militarily crisp and totally obedient.

Captain Keller?

Cummins thought Keller had all the earmarks of a lowly enlisted man. Now, he'd made himself into an officer. Or at least, somebody had.

Up ahead, Cummins saw the Malibu pull over to the right, followed by the Caravan. He glanced at Keller, who told him to drive around them. His headlights washed over both vehicles and then he saw the red lights flash again in the distance. It was just a brief illuminated dot, gone in a second, but something was out there. He could sense it. Shapes were getting more distinct in the distance. He flicked on his high beams hoping to get a better fix.

"Shut them damn things down," Keller said. "Low beams only. And roll down your window all the way."

Cummins complied and suddenly a long cyclone fence became visible. The top of it was adorned with a roll of concertina wire. It ran along both sides of the roadway. Then straight ahead he saw the fence lines fold perpendicularly together forming a large gate with a cement guard post building in the center. A red light flashed inside the guard shack and a man ambled out holding what looked like an AR-15. He wore a set of blackish BDUs and had a thick nylon pistol belt with a leather holster hooked on the right side. His black baseball cap was centered low on his forehead. He walked to the left front of the vehicle, standing off to the side so as not to be illuminated by the headlights, holding the rifle at port-arms.

"Halt. Who is there?" he shouted.

"A friend of the Brigade," Keller shouted.

The guard stiffened, then said, "Identify yourself."

"Captain Louis Keller." He then rattled off a series of numbers that had the same ring as an Army serial number. "Returning from mission."

The guard snapped his rifle into a salute position, held it for several seconds, and then ran back toward the gate. He flipped up a big metallic latch and walked the gate back.

"Well, go on in, fat boy," Keller said. "We're home."

Cummins hit the gas ever so slightly and crept forward, feeling the big truck's gears grinding in slow motion.

Ahead, he could see an array of buildings, some two- and three-story brick, others rows of half-moon structures. He could hear the thrumming sounds of a couple of motors—generators, most likely. Several vehicles, cars and pickup trucks, were parked in lots off to the left, and piles of debris—bricks, broken lumber, and various boxes sat in quiet repose along another street. The lights of the truck illuminated an uprooted metallic sign leaning against one of the brick buildings, its two long, horizontal metal poles showing remnants of broken concrete and clusters of dried earth on the lower portions. Three metallic arches were affixed between the two poles that had once been implanted in the ground but were now uprooted and apparently discarded. He could discern peeling paint and black lettering on the arching signs: a white background upon which were some once bold black letters:

YOU ARE NOW ENTERING
FORT LEMAND

U.S. ARMY BASE.

Fort Lemand? Cummins had never heard of it. The writing on the strips of metal looked time-worn and ancient.

The place must have been closed down decades ago.

But from the looks of it, a new army had taken it over.

"Straight ahead to the orderly building," Keller said. "We got to report in."

"What the hell is this place?" Cummins asked as he lights swept over another guard post, this one housing two more men in uniform along with what appeared to be an M-60 machine gun.

An M-60, Cummins thought. My God. Where the hell did they get that kind of ordinance?

Again, out of the corner of his eye, he caught Keller smiling.

"Welcome to Base Freedom," he said.

***

The McNamara Ranch
Phoenix, Arizona

The jarring vibration stirred Wolf out of his slumber. Initially, it was just a vague disturbance to a nonsensical dream but his old combat acuity snapped into place awakening him, and he saw the cell phone on the bedside table. As he reached for it Yolanda stirred awake as well and murmured something unintelligible.

"It's my phone," he said, noticing the time.

Who the hell would be calling him at seven-thirty-five on a Sunday morning after his big fight?

It was an unknown cell phone number.

He contemplated the possibilities, figuring that it was probably either something really bad or really good.

"Steve?" Kasey's voice asked, sounding a bit tentative. "I didn't wake you up, did I?"

Resisting the temptation to reply with a smart-ass comeback, he told her no.

"What's up?" he then asked.

"Um, how'd it go last night?" Her voice was sounding extra tentative, which given the often-contentious nature of their relationship, didn't surprise him. He was still trying to fathom why she'd called him when she quickly added. "Did you win?"

"No," he said. "It was a draw."

Memories of the cage announcement came flooding back to him like the rerunning of a bad commercial: the announcer saying there was a split decision, his voice highlighting the scores, the final judge's being even, making the match a draw. Reno had been more disappointed than Wolf had been.

At least I didn't lose, he remembered thinking, and

I was only in it for the paycheck, anyway.

From the expression on de Silva's face, it was hard to tell his opinion. They'd done the customary fighter's embrace after the ref had pulled them both to their feet after the air-horn had blasted. Mutual respect had been achieved and Wolf recalled having nothing but respect for the tough Brazilian, who had had more on the line than he did.

"Shit," Reno said, as they made their way back to the dressing room. "You won that one, hands down. Those damn judges must have had their heads so far up their fucking asses they needed to cut holes in their stomachs to see out of."

Wolf reached up and clapped him on the shoulder. "Sorry I let you down, coach."

Reno was silent for the rest of the walk and virtually all Wolf was thinking about at that point was getting under a shower to wash de Silva's blood off of his body.

"I thought you won, too, boo," Yolanda said as they continued toward the locker room.

"Yeah, well, win, lose, or draw," Wolf said. "I still got the same amount of money."

She'd been a little bit miffed when they wouldn't let her into the locker room, but McNamara, Ms. Dolly, and Brenda quickly joined her in the hallway.

Wolf had wanted to leave right after showering and changing clothes. He felt like he'd been run over by a ten-ton truck. Mac, Ms. Dolly, and Brenda had elected to stay for the rest of the fights, with Wolf's blessings, and he and Yolanda had taken Rideshare.com back to his apartment at the ranch even though Reno had offered to have Barbie drive them. It hadn't been real late and the lights had been on in the house, but he didn't know if Kasey had seen them arrive.

"If you and your friend want to come over to the house," Kasey said. "I'm fixing some eggs and bacon."

I guess she had seen us, all right, he thought.

He didn't know whether to feel self-conscious or not. Kasey wasn't exactly on the best terms with the P-Patrol.

"I appreciate the offer," he said. "But I'm kind of sore. I think I'll sleep in little bit more."

"Oh, I'm sorry," she said. "I did wake you, didn't I?"

"Not a problem, Kasey. But did you have something other than inviting us to breakfast on your mind?"

Yolanda, who was wide awake at this point, effected an expression of total shock and surprise and mouthed, Wicked Witch of the East?

That was the informal nickname Ms. Dolly had given to Kasey after their last, less than cordial meeting.

"Yes." Her voice was still tentative, unsure. "I was just wondering if you knew where dad was. He didn't come home last night."

Wolf surmised that Mac had spent the night in

good company in Ms. Dolly and Brenda's hotel room, but he didn't say that, nor did he say that her father was a big boy. Instead, he asked if she wanted him to call around.

"I'm sure he's okay," she said. "But when I woke up this morning and saw he wasn't here..."

The rest of her sentence trailed off. Wolf reflected on how much she'd changed in the last month. She'd gone from totally resenting him and blaming him for everything wrong in the world, to now coming to him like a worried little sister.

"Well," he said. "It's still kind of early. And I'm sure he would've called you if anything was wrong."

"Yeah, I know," she said. "But it's just that ... Well, Chad didn't call me last night and nobody answered when I tried his cell. I'm kind of worried."

She'd gone through a lot lately: the death of her fiancé and the financial problems with the business, and now this escalating new custody dispute. It was a heavy load for her to carry and Wolf didn't want to make it any heavier.

"Let me see if I can get a hold of your dad," Wolf said, feeling almost like he was helping to conceal a transgression or something. "I'll get back to you."

"Okay, thanks," she said and hung up.

He tried to sit up a little more and felt the instantaneous bolt of pain along his abdominal wall. His arms and shoulders ached, too but it was a good pain.

It meant that he'd taken most of his opponent's blows on the arms and body instead of the head. But seconds later Yolanda's finger traced along his cheek and he felt a sting there also, reminding him that he hadn't blocked all of them.

"Does it hurt much?" she asked.

"Only when I laugh."

"What did the Wicked Witch of the East want?"

Wolf chuckled and that hurt his stomach again.

"She's worried about her father," he said. "And don't make me laugh."

She ran her hand over his bare chest and shoulders.

"You're gonna have some bruises here, boo."

"Tell me something I don't know," he said, punching in McNamara's cell phone number.

It went straight to voice mail.

Wolf tried the number again, with the same result. He looked at Yolanda.

"Don't suppose I could persuade you to call Ms. Dolly to see if Mac's with her,?"

"Maybe," she said, pressing her naked body against him. "For a price."

Wolf felt the sexual stirring in his groin and more than anything wanted to toss the cell phone onto the floor and get some morning delight.

"What's the price?" he asked playfully.

"I'm still thinking about it but you're gonna like it."

She disengaged her body from his and slipped from

under the sheet. The movements rocked the mattress a bit and Wolf once again felt the effects of having been in a three-round fight where the rounds were five minutes long.

Seventeen minutes of hell, he thought, with a one-minute break in between minutes five and eleven.

Yolanda came back and sat on the bed, dialing. After a few rings, she smiled and said, "Hey, Ms. Dolly. How you doing?"

Wolf could hear a loud voice replete with a Texas twang. Apparently, Ms. Dolly didn't like being woken up either. After about thirty seconds of conversation, Yolanda said, "Hold on," and handed the phone to Wolf.

"Honey," Ms. Dolly said. "Why in the hell are you having that girl wake me up this early on a Sunday morning?"

"I thought you might want to join us at Church," Wolf said.

"What?" After a few moments of silence, Wolf heard her throaty laugh. "Sugar, you'd better have a better reason than that or I'm gonna tan your backside next time I see you."

"That'll give me something to look forward to," Wolf said. "But really, I need to talk to Mac. Is he there?"

"He sure is, snoring away. Or at least he was until all the commotion started. Here."

McNamara's gruff voice came on the line. "What

the hell you want?"

"Kasey's worried about you," Wolf said.

"Huh?" Wolf heard him sigh. "What the hell's the matter with that girl. I thought her mama raised her better than that."

"She's got a lot on her mind," Wolf said, wondering how much to tell him.

Break it to him gently, he thought. But break it.

"She's worried about you," Wolf said. "And she's also concerned about Chad. Apparently, he didn't call her like he was supposed to and there's no answer on that cell phone she gave him."

McNamara groaned in disgust. "That no good piece of shit, Riley. I'm gonna have to kick his ass all the way up to his mouth the next time I see him."

"Better get up and do your roadwork then," Wolf said, trying to inject a bit of levity. "Or did you get enough of a workout in last night?"

That elicited a chuckle from McNamara.

"Someday, when you're older," he said. "I'll tell you about last night."

Wolf felt Yolanda's body pressing against his again. Her hands began roaming over his bruised and battered body. Each pause, each squeeze, each caress, brought an exquisite mixture of pain and pleasure and his breathing quickened.

"You want me to call her and say you'll get a hold of her later?" Wolf asked.

He silently hoped that he wouldn't have to explain Mac's whereabouts.

"No, hell," McNamara said. "I better do it. Anyway, I want Kase to start researching that FROZ place and that dude we're after. I got it all set up for us to fly up to that Bendover place tomorrow. All five of us. I'll give you today to rest and recuperate since you fought one hell of a fight last night but then it's back to business. We gotta get ready and pack, too."

"Sounds good," Wolf said as Yolanda's hands continued their exploration.

He was about to say something more when she sat up and reached over to pluck her phone from his hand.

"He'll call you back later, big boo daddy," she said. "Right now we got some business of our own to attend to." With that, she terminated the call. Dropping the phone, she smiled down at him from her dominant position.

It was a deliciously wicked smile.

"You asked about that price before," she said. "I'm ready to collect."

***

Summerlin Hotel
Just outside of Phoenix, Arizona

Soraces waited for Gunther to join him at the restaurant table. He'd told the maitre d' that someone would be joining him and requested a table in the far side of the restaurant, away from the other tables. He'd slipped the man a twenty as he made this request. It was a lot of fun spending someone else's money with carefree abandon. He laid another twenty on the table as the waitress was pouring his coffee from the carafe and he took delight in watching her dark eyes widen. She was young, pretty, and Hispanic—just the type he liked and she had eyes for the money, too.

Great fun, manipulating others, he thought. Especially the venal and the malleable.

He hoped that this guy Wolf would prove just as easy to manipulate.

But then again, he told himself. It's all in how you bait the hook.

He did another assessment of the waitress's breasts. Even through the cloth prison, he could tell they were substantial—again, just the way he liked them.

Perhaps he should get her number for later but that could wait. There was no sense rushing things. He was still setting up the pieces on the metaphorical chess board.

His food had just arrived and he was doing his customary pre-consumption meal ritual: cutting the toast into equally spaced quarters. He preferred to instill order into all things, including his meals as well as his plans of operation. It was the way things were built and allowed careful consideration of every facet.

So far the setup was proceeding as planned. After arriving yesterday, Soraces had checked into the luxury hotel and then gone over to get acquainted at the Bailey and Lugget Law Firm. Even though it had been a Saturday, one of the senior partners had met him there to welcome him. Obviously, his new employers, Fallotti and Von Dien, had a lot of clout. Not as much as Uncle Sam but the pay was better. Much better and he didn't have to justify his actions in a report to some pencil-necked bureaucrat. And the array of tools he had to work with in this little excursion was sheer artistry.

Gunther entered the restaurant and came walking over to the table. He was a huge black man with a shaved head and this morning he was dressed in a tan polo shirt and brown Dockers.

A study in monochrome, Soraces thought and motioned for the waitress to bring a new cup and saucer.

The big man slid into a seat across from him and smiled appreciatively as the waitress poured the coffee and asked him if he needed a menu.

"I'll have what he's having," Gunther said and reached for the sugar packets.

When the waitress had left, he leaned forward and asked, "What's the status?"

"Everything's on track," Soraces said. He set the

knife down and speared one of the squared-off pieces of toast with his fork.

"Meaning?"

"I'm all set at the law firm." Soraces had ordered his eggs sunny side up and now dipped the toast into one of the yolks. "I'll call him tomorrow and leave a message to set up an appointment this week."

Gunther tore two packets open and dumped the contents into the dark liquid.

"I thought you said that this one was time sensitive?" Gunther brought the cup to his lips and sipped.

"Is that sweet enough for you?" Soraces said, placing the toast into his mouth.

"Hot, sweet, and black. Just like me."

Soraces's mouth formed a lips-only smile as he masticated. When he'd finished chewing, he set the fork down, wiped the edges of his mouth with the linen napkin, and then drank from his own coffee cup.

"It is time-sensitive," he said. "But only to a degree. I expressed urgency on my initial call to you because one of our employers was hovering about listening. It was all about the image."

"Doesn't sound like you've changed much since you officially left the Agency."

Soraces picked up the fork and speared another fragment of toast. "As far as the call, I want it to be during regular business hours. One thing we don't want is to appear either over-anxious or the least bit suspicious."

Gunther savored more of the coffee. "Wouldn't it be quicker to just abduct the guy and force him to give up whatever the hell it is our employer's looking for?"

Again, Soraces didn't answer until he'd finished chewing.

"That's been tried twice already," he said. "Both times this fellow's proved very formidable. Ex-Ranger, and his partner's ex-Special Forces."

Gunther's bald head gleamed under the florescent lights as it moved up and down with a slight nod.

"So we're up against a couple of tough pros," he said.

"Exactly. And remember, this isn't Kabul or Baghdad or Mogadishu. Our employer also wants this matter kept on a low-key basis. We're to use finesse if at all possible."

Gunther shrugged. "Well, I ain't complaining. Like you say, this place is a hell of a lot better than some Third World shithole."

"Precisely." Soraces raised an eyebrow. "Additionally, we don't know where our quarry's stashed the item."

Gunter set the cup down and seemed about to speak when the waitress appeared again, smiling brightly, and set the hot plate down on the table in front of him.

"Do you need anything else?" she asked, her eyes drifting down to the spot where he'd laid the twenty.

"We'll let you know," Soraces said.

As she left Gunther was already smearing a layer of strawberry jelly over his toast. After quickly glancing around, he leaned forward again and said in a subdued tone, "What is this item we're looking for again?"

Soraces dipped another of the cut squares into the now depleted yolk.

"A bandito," he said. "A plaster statue of a Mexican bandito."

Gunther shoveled some of the food into his mouth.

"You're kidding, right?"

Soraces shook his head.

"You bringing in anybody else on this?" Gunther asked.

"I reached out to a couple others." Soraces wiped his mouth again with the napkin. "I have them on stand-by in case we need them."

"So what do you want me to do in the meantime?" Gunther said.

"Just sit tight for the time being." Soraces speared the last bit of egg white and then used the final square of toast to blot the final remnants of the yolk. The plate looked almost immaculate now, almost totally devoid of bread crumbs. "Just be ready to shadow the guy and take him out if and when I tell you."

***

Former Fort Lemand
Southern Arizona

Cummins was stirred awake by Keller's boot kicking the edge of the metallic bunk in the room. Morning sunlight shone through the window and Cummins managed to sit up.

"What time is it?" he asked.

"Time to get up, fat boy," Keller said. "We let you sleep past revelry because we got in a little late." He tossed a plastic bucket down on the tiled floor. "The latrine's down the hall at the other end but Sergeant Smith and his lady love are using it now, so if you have to go, use the bucket and dump it when the latrine's clear."

Keller turned to go but stopped at the open door and pointed down to Cummins's suitcase under the bed. "Oh, I suggest if you have a change of clothes in that bag there, you make use of them. You all are gonna see the colonel after mess. That's in fifteen minutes. They're holding it for you."

After mess, Cummins thought. What the hell kind of rag-tag outfit had he gotten sucked into?

Last night, after they'd parked all three vehicles, Keller had escorted Cummins and the others to one of the buildings adjacent to the Quonset huts. Unlike the standard army billets he'd seen pictures of at such places as Fort Polk, these had been sectioned off into individual rooms inside the structure. Each room had a window, which was without a screen and standing open, which was a good thing considering the desert environment. A couple of large fans had been set in the hallway and rotated with clamorous monotony but Cummins had been so exhausted he almost welcomed the unceasing noise as he tried to sleep.

He got up and closed the door after Keller had gone, making sure not to slam it. The last thing he wanted was to provoke the big stooge.

Captain Keller ...

Yeah, Cummins thought. Definitely officer material.

He quickly urinated into the plastic bucket and set it aside. After placing his suitcase on the bed, he opened it and assembled a presentable pair of dark slacks and a loose-fitting short-sleeve shirt. After finding his dopp bag he removed the special eye drops and dumped a few drops into each eye to lubricate the extended-wear contacts. His cheeks felt rough with beard growth but that would have to wait until he found a decent water supply. Then he stripped out of his old garments and rolled them into his laundry bag, keeping on the same pair of underwear. Although both he and his underclothes were getting more than just a little ripe, there was no sense changing those until after he'd had a chance to shower.

If the showers even worked around here. Last night when they were given access to a washroom they were admonished to flush the toilet by using the bucket of standing water beside the bowl.

"Don't use it all up for one flush," Keller had told them.

Smith had explained that the water was drawn from a well and they had to conserve it. Thus, buckets of standing water were placed next to every toilet.

Cummins had wondered whose job it was to keep them filled

That most likely meant that if there was any running water around here, it was at a premium.

He'd slept in his clothes, which suited him just fine. His main concern was that someone might see the money belt, which he still had secreted around his ample waist. The Glock had been under his pillow all night. He looped his leather belt through the belt loops and cinched it, then reached under the pillow for the Glock, securing it inside his pants. He wished he had a pancake holster. He thought again about the M-60 he'd seen as they'd driven in and the sentries with the AR-15s. And Keller had his big Desert Eagle in a glossy black leather holster this morning. The man's fatigues looked crisp and pressed and he'd been wearing the old-fashioned black leather boots, Cummins had no doubt they were spit-shined.

But enough of that, he thought as he stooped down to grab the plastic bucket and wait his turn at the latrine. He grabbed his shaving kit just in case there was some water available that the hillbilly king and queen hadn't used up in one flush.

***

The McNamara Ranch
Phoenix, Arizona

Wolf and Yolanda had just finished showering and cleaning up, with Yolanda complaining about having to wear the same clothes from yesterday.

"I told you we shoulda stopped by the hotel last night," she said. "At least I could've grabbed my overnight stuff."

"Just be glad I had a spare toothbrush," Wolf said as his cell phone rang. He picked it up and saw that it was Mac.

"You two up?" McNamara asked.

"Yep. And raring to go. What's the plan?"

"Come on over to the house. Kasey's fixing us all breakfast."

He hung up.

"She ain't gonna try to poison me, is she?" Yolanda asked with a sly grin.

"She's had it kind of rough lately," Wolf said and proceeded to tell her about Shemp's unfortunate death and the ongoing custody problem involving Chad.

Yolanda was silent as they crossed the expanse of asphalt to the ranch house.

Inside Wolf saw Mac, Ms. Dolly, and Brenda all seated around the big dining room table. McNamara had had it quickly installed to change the appearance of the room after the recent, brutal scene. To his surprise, Wolf saw Kasey laughing as she was making the rounds with a pair of well-stocked plates. Ms. Dolly was laughing too, like they'd just shared a really funny joke.

McNamara pointed to the two chairs on his right and Wolf and Yolanda sat down.

"I hope you like your eggs scrambled," Kasey said to her. "With so many for breakfast it was easier to fix them that way."

Wolf was again surprised to see the smile on Kasey's face after the less than hospitable welcome she'd shown the P-Patrol the last time.

"That'd be fine," Yolanda said. "You need some help serving?"

Kasey declined, in demure fashion, and began preparing two more plates.

Yolanda's joke about the poison came floating back to him.

When had that been? All of five minutes ago?

It was as if he'd stepped into an alternate reality, like on that old TV show, *The Twilight Zone*. Things were a little bit off kilter, and everybody, all of whom hated each other, was getting along.

But I'm not complaining, he thought, and realized again how much Kasey had changed in recent days.

"We got to figure our plan for grabbing this guy," McNamara said. "We're going to have to infiltrate this FROZ place."

Wolf nodded as Kasey set two plates replete with eggs, bacon, and toast in front of him and Yolanda. The smell was tantalizing.

"Kasey's been researching the situation for us," McNamara said. His plate was practically empty now as were Ms. Dolly's and Brenda's. He picked up his coffee cup and asked Kasey what she'd found out.

Kasey set her big laptop on the counter next to the stove and turned it so they could all see the screen. Then she made a few clicks with the wireless mouse and the screen illuminated with the frozen image of a slender man with jet black hair and a goatee standing in front of a city street blockaded by several cement barricades. Kasey clicked the mouse again and the image came to life.

"We're here in Bendover at the scene of FROZ," the bearded man said, stepping back and allowing the cameraman to pan over the three-foot-high barriers. They were covered with a variety of crudely painted bits of graffiti. The barrier in the center had FROZ spray-painted in ungainly large capital letters that looked like they were scribbled by a recalcitrant grammar school student.

"FROZ," the reporter continued, "is an acronym for the Freedom Restricted Occupational Zone. It began ten days ago when a large group of protesters took to the downtown business section of Bendover and declared it theirs, banning police from entering this six-block square area and declaring themselves a separate and sovereign entity."

Crowds of people milled about on the other side of the barriers and numerous port-a-potties lined the street. The cameraman apparently moved in closer to the barriers and zoomed in on a group of young people sitting in a circle singing an undecipherable tune.

"The leader of FROZ," the reporter said, "Or at least one of them, has declared that they have no intention of leaving or altering their stance until all of their demands have been met. Just what those demands are has yet to be formally established but they are said to include abolishing the police department, amnesty for all those in prisons, and free food and medical care for everyone, including the large homeless population, which has doubled in size since the occupation started. The main leader, Zeus, as he calls himself, has purportedly met with both the mayor and city council members to discuss the situation but no agreement has been reached at this time."

The grainy footage of a black man with a huge network of dreadlocks streaming from his head and dressed in a flowing dark overcoat filled the screen. He appeared to be addressing a substantial crowd of onlookers. The image shifted back to the reporter who said that the mayor's office could not be reached for comment at this time but also added that the mayor was in negotiations with all of the leaders of FROZ and hoped to have a solution worked out shortly.

Kasey froze the screen on the laptop.

"That's allegedly your man," she said. "Zeus, aka Booker Nobles. He's twenty-six years old, with seventeen arrests ranging from shoplifting to armed robbery and attempted murder. He's served no prison time and he's currently wanted under five different aliases in three states."

"Show us a close-up of him," McNamara said.

She clicked the mouse again and a full facial mug shot appeared of Nobles without the dreadlocks.

Wolf hadn't liked the way Kasey had said "allegedly."

"We're sure that this guy's the same one we're after?" Wolf asked. "Manny mentioned something about a reporter who located him."

"That's him on the video," Kasey said. "Dickie Deekins."

Yolanda laughed and tried to disguise it as a cough.

"Yeah," Ms. Dolly said. "I know, girl. How we supposed to place any credulity in a guy with a name like that?"

"Why's he diming him out?" Brenda asked.

"He's got his reasons," Kasey said. "Watch."

She held up the mouse and gave it another click. The mug shot vanished and another grainy video started playing on the screen. This one was obviously taken at night and showed a bunch of graffiti-laden boarded-up windows, piles of garbage littering the street, and two vehicles with their windows broken and tires removed. What appeared to be a homeless man wallowed on the street, defecating and puking.

"This is Dickie Deekins coming to you from inside FROZ," the man's voice on the video said in a hushed whisper. He wasn't visible and the camera kept panning around, going back to focus on the homeless man. "We've come into the FROZ zone tonight to get a glimpse of what's actually going on. They're restricting entry at the main entrance so we had to—"

The screen went suddenly blank and after several seconds the image resumed but it was obvious that the camera now lay on its side recording an ongoing scene in front of it. The same black-bearded man who'd done the other segment was being held by two men, while a third man was in front delivering slaps and punches.

"Hey, don't," Dickie Deekins yelled. "Please. I'm on your side."

"That why you be sneaking around in my hood, motherfucker?" a deep, baritone voice said. "What I tell you about sneaking 'round in here without permission?"

"No, please," Deekins said. "I wasn't—"

His words were truncated by a sharp body-blow. The puncher followed up with several more, then stepped back and delivered a kick to Deekins's groin.

"Ouch," Ms. Dolly said. "That looks like it hurt."

"It does," McNamara said. "Been there, done that."

Ms. Dolly flashed him a wry grin.

Kasey froze the image.

"As you can see," she said. "Deekins harbors some animosity regarding Mr. Nobles, aka Zeus."

"That's putting it mildly," Wolf said. "That was some beat-down."

"What I'm concerned about," Kasey said, "is another report I've found about shootings going on in the Zone. It's rumored that Nobles has his own contingent of armed security with him at all times."

"Which is why we're flying up with our own little arsenal," McNamara said. "Hell, me and Steve have been dealing with a lot worse adversaries than those punks."

"And, honey," Ms. Dolly said. "Me and the gals ain't gonna let nothing happen to your daddy. Take that to the bank."

"You're strictly on the perimeter on this one," McNamara said. "Steve and me will be the ones going inside."

"Hey," Yolanda said. "Me and Brenda are probably

the only ones out of the five of us that can infiltrate this place without being noticed."

"*No creo que pueden ir en todas partes sin mucho notados,*" Wolf said.

Brenda and Ms. Dolly both laughed.

"If it's one thing I can't stand," McNamara said, "it's not being in on one of your smart-ass comments. You want to repeat that for the rest of us?"

"He said they can't go anywhere without being noticed," Kasey said with a smile. "And I'm inclined to agree, as pretty as they both are."

Brenda and Ms. Dolly exchanged glances with Wolf, who was equally surprised. They'd both made somewhat derogatory comments in Spanish about Kasey in the past, due to her less than friendly attitude, and now realized she might have understood what had been said.

But now it looked as if all was forgiven.

"We can discuss all that on the plane tomorrow," McNamara said. "We'll need to do some recon once we get there." He stood up. "Come on, clear these dishes and let's get ready."

I guess that means we're shipping out, thought Wolf. As he stood, McNamara leaned close.

"Don't forget tomorrow morning we got to pick up the clone," he said.

Wolf wondered if both of them would fit in the same box.

***

Former Fort Lemand
Southern Arizona

Cummins waited in the hallway of the biggest of the brick buildings. This one had half a dozen fans rotating at full speed and they actually created a half-decent breeze. He held his hand next to the crack in the closed double doors and could feel a minute stream of air conditioning. This was the room into which Keller had ushered Smith and Riley. Cherrie was down the hallway sitting with the kid. For a brief moment, Cummins fantasized about pulling out his Glock, taking both her and the kid as hostages, and commandeering one of the cars to beat feet out of this nightmare. But the way these mercenary morons were armed, he doubted he would get very far.

No, he thought. I'm going to have to do some reconnoitering first.

There had to be a back way out and once he found it, then he'd grab the kid and make his escape. And then he'd do the trade off with Wolf.

Luckily, no one had taken his cell phone or his Glock. Once he'd finished this meeting with the Colonel here, another phone call would be in order, but it would have to be when he was safe and secure. That bastard, Keller, was like Big

Brother—always watching.

The doors opened and the three men came out. Riley and Smith were beaming as they marched in step with military precision. They nodded a greeting to Cummins and proceeded down the hallway toward Cherrie and the kid.

"Your turn, fat boy," Keller said. "But first, give me that gun you got stuck in your belt."

"What?"

"You heard me." Keller's expression was flat and hard. "Nobody sees the Colonel with a weapon, unless they got special clearance."

He patted the handle of the Desert Eagle.

Not wanting the big goon to extract the Glock himself, lest he notice the money belt, Cummins pulled the weapon from his beltline and handed it to Keller, butt first.

"You'll get it back when we're sure you've been properly cleared," Keller said. "Square your shirt away."

Properly cleared? What the hell did that mean?

In the meantime, Cummins thought, while he did his best to make himself more presentable, I'll be walking around with a bunch of armed fanatics.

Keller's nostrils flared a bit as he gave him a final once-over, then he opened the door and whispered, "Stand at attention when we get up there."

The room was exceptionally large and had several rows of chairs set up facing the front. Numerous portable air-conditioners were stationed around the room and hummed steadily. Cummins appreciated the cool air. Directly in front of them, on a podium about forty yards away, a big man with a blockish build stood with his back to them, his hands clasped behind his back. He was wearing the same black BDUs that Keller, Smith, and Riley had on. As Cummins drew closer he saw the man had three concentric rings of whitish sweat stains under each arm and, despite the reasonably effective air-conditioning, he was working on a fourth. It almost looked decorative. His hair was dark and clipped militarily short. An enormous red banner affixed to the wall directly behind him. In the center of the banner was a white circle outlined in black, and in the center of the circle was a huge black swastika.

Cummins was mildly shocked.

Were these guys Nazis?

He studied it closer as they marched toward the front.

No, it wasn't a swastika per se. It had been altered somewhat. One of the arms on the pattern had an arrow at its end. And there was something else about it that looked different but Cummins wasn't sure what it was.

A lectern was off to the side of the podium and a long table was on the floor in front of it. The boxes that housed the stolen money reposed upon the table.

He and Keller marched up to the long table and Keller gave the command to halt.

Cummins did and remained at attention. The large man turned and Cummins saw that he had the silver insignias of a full-bird colonel on the collar of his blouse. His name tag, also in silver, read BEST. His face was block-like, too, with deep creases extending from both of his nostrils to frame his mouth. The man's eyes were pale blue and piercing.

"Captain Keller reporting, sir," Keller said, whipping his hand up in a full military salute.

Cummins didn't know whether to do the same and then figured he'd better.

This movement elicited a slight twitch of the large man's eyebrows, then his lips curled into a faint smile momentarily. He returned the salute and said, "Stand at ease."

Cummins started to relax but Keller immediately slipped into a parade rest position.

Assuming that pose was a bit difficult, but Cummins did his best. He was feeling nervous that his gut was protruding as much as it was and hope to God that the colonel didn't notice his protruding neoprene back brace, which concealed the money belt.

"Captain Keller has told me a bit about you," Best said. "You have military experience, do you not?"

"Yes, sir," Cummins said. "Second lieutenant, army. Military intelligence. Did a tour in Iraq, sir."

This was stretching his truncated, politically arranged three-month deployment a bit but Cummins didn't figure this outsider would have any way to check it out. Besides, he hoped to be out of here sooner rather than in the movement for the long haul.

Best's head bobbled up and down minutely.

"Very good," he said. "Captain Keller also tells me you've made a substantial monetary commitment to the Brigade as well as assisting in this fundraising operation."

Fundraising operation? That was an interesting euphemism for armed robbery and murder. But why mince words?

"That is correct, sir."

Best studied him for several seconds without saying anything and then began speaking.

"In the bygone days of our once-great country, patriots had to rally against the forces of tyranny. They did this by forming a militia, an army of minutemen, who would work their fields but be ready to grab their weapons and fight at a moment's notice." He paused and got a serene look on his face. "We are now at a crossroads once again, when patriots like Captain Keller and myself must take the helm and lead the way through a tempest of anarchy and recrimination that threatens to topple our precious republic."

Best turned and held his hand up toward the immense banner.

"I saw you studying our insignia as you came in, Lieutenant Cummins. Tell me, what do you think of it?"

Not sure how to answer, Cummins said, "Impressive, sir."

This brought a smile to Best's lips. "I know what you're probably thinking." He paused again, letting the silence settle over the three of them for a moment, then said, "Nazis. Am I correct?"

Once again, Cummins was unsure of what to say but was beginning to get the feeling that if he gave the wrong response the consequences could be fatal. He felt the resurgence of the bile beginning to creep up his throat.

Oh, no, he thought. To lose control here and now would probably get him shot. Still, what was the alternative?

"Speechless?" Best said, his lips twisting into a grin and he laughed.

Cummins was now feeling a growing pressure in his bladder as well.

This madman's either going to kiss me or kill me, he thought.

"No," Best continued. "Not Nazis. Do you think that I would besmirch our rich history of fighting for freedom by incorporating a symbol of our former enemies?"

Cummins was sure his knees were trembling but

hoped the table was blocking them for the Colonel's view.

Best started walking around on the podium, his hands clasped behind his back.

"Actually, the symbol of the swastika is very old, predating Hitler by many decades," he said. "It was originally an Indian symbol and it has been a symbol of mysticism through the ages. Ours bears no resemblance to the Third Reich. The Nazi swastika has arms that run in a clockwise pattern, which is a mirror image of ours."

Cummins glanced upward and saw the distinction. The arms of the cross were pointing counterclockwise and the end of the horizontal middle one was in the shape of an arrow. Best stopped and gazed up at the banner. Out of the corner of his eye, Cummins saw Keller looking up at it, too.

Christ, Cummins thought. A pair of fanatical lunatics.

He felt as if he were going to lose control of both his bladder and his stomach simultaneously.

"So the question remains," Best said, still gazing at the banner. "When the bell of liberty rings, will you step up and answer its call?"

"I will, sir," Cummins managed to say, cognizant of the fact that the sweat was now beginning to pour down his face and neck.

Best whirled to gaze down at him, his eyes widening.

"Good," he said. "The Brigade needs patriots, good soldiers, for make no mistake, the forces of darkness are nipping at our heels. We have to remain vigilant. And ready."

The pressure was almost unbearable but something told Cummins that if he did lose control now, and puked all over the table, he'd end up being disciplined by a bullet.

"You will report back here tonight at nineteen-hundred hours," Best said. "We will administer the oath to you and the other two civilians. As a prospective militia member, however, I expect you to present yourself in a proper military manner. Remove that unseemly patch of facial hair, and dress yourself in proper military attire. I will consider restoring your officer's rank once you've been evaluated and have completed our training cycle."

The idiot was starting to ramble and Cummins felt like he might pass out.

"Any questions?" Best said.

"Begging your pardon, sir," Cummins said. "But I have a medical condition that sometimes arises at inopportune moments and this is one of them. May I be excused momentarily?"

Best didn't answer immediately but seemed faintly amused. "Captain Keller, escort soon to be reinstated Lieutenant Cummins to the latrine."

Thank god, Cummins thought.

They snapped to, did a left-face and Keller walked him to a door on the far wall below the big banner. Cummins was relieved to see the sign marked *MEN*. He rushed in and threw up in the sink. When he finished he straightened up, wiped his lips with the back of his hand, and twisted the faucet.

No water came out.

He heard a chuckling behind him and turned to see Keller watching. He had a wicked grin on his face.

"What did you say it was that causes you to blow chunks like that all the time?"

"Dyspepsia," Cummins said, already regretting that he hadn't tried to make it to the toilet bowl instead.

"There's a bucket of water inside the stall," Keller said. "Make sure you clean it real good and don't leave no stink. Colonel Best sometimes uses this latrine."

He stepped out and the door softly closed behind him.

Colonel Best, Cummins thought as he staggered to the urinal and relieved himself. Afterward, he retrieved the bucket from the stall, making sure to not let any of the water slosh over the side. The vomit was all spit and bile and easily dispersed down the drain. He poured a little bit in the urinal for good measure. As for the odor, he took out his lighter and lit a bit of rolled up toilet paper to consume any residual smell. When he finished, he wanted to rinse his mouth out to get rid of the sour taste but realized his only choice would be to use the water in the bucket. Using the back of his hand, he once again wiped off his lips and then replaced the bucket by the toilet.

This obviously wasn't going to be a pleasant stay. He had to figure out an escape route and a chance to grab the kid if that would even be possible at this point.

When he exited the latrine, Keller was nowhere to be seen. He stepped closer to the door leading to the big auditorium found it locked. He could hear voices speaking on the other side.

Best and Keller, but the exact nature of the conversation was indistinguishable. Cummins walked down the long hallway, relishing the opportunity and excuse to look around a little and came to another door. This one was unlocked and led to a perpendicular hallway that seemed to lead back to the main one in front. He glanced around and saw no sign of Keller. After checking the knob to make sure the door wouldn't lock behind him, Cummins went into the new hallway and strode down to the end, which had still another closed door. This one was unlocked as well and he pushed it slightly to allow a crack of visibility.

Smith, Riley, and Cherrie were engaged in some kind of argument. Riley held his kid, who looked to be in a stupor, against his shoulder.

"Why didn't you tell me you done that last night?"

Riley said. "You had no right not to."

"I told you," Cherrie said. "It was a fucking accident, for Christ's sake."

"Charlie," Smith started to say.

"You shut the hell up, Rog," Riley said. "She's wrong and that's all there is to it."

"Will you just relax," Smith said, raising his hands in a placating gesture. "She didn't mean nothing by it."

"And fucking Keller told me to anyway," Cherrie added.

"Yeah," Riley said. "Just like he told you to dump that other phone, huh? The one my ex gave him."

"I don't know what happened to it," she said.

"I'm only gonna tell you this once," Riley said, shifting the kid's body so that he could hold him with just his left arm while shaking the extended right index finger in front of Cherrie's face. "Don't you never give Chad no more of that sleeping medicine shit. Never. Understand?"

Smith grabbed Riley's extended finger and did something that put the other man in a crouching position with a look of pain on his face. He struggled to maintain his footing.

"And you understand," Smith said in a calm but firm tone. "Don't you never talk to her like that again or I'll kick your ass so bad it'll be all the way up around your fucking ears." He held the grip a few seconds more, then asked, "Got it?"

Just as Riley was about to reply Cummins heard some scuffling behind him and turned to see Keller.

"What the fuck do you think you're doing?" Keller asked.

Cummins felt a wave of panic but had his answer ready.

"The hallway door was locked," he said. "I heard you and the Colonel in conversation so I was trying to go around to the other door."

Keller's eyes narrowed slightly as he regarded Cummins, then he said, "Come on with me. We ain't got nothing at the quartermaster's that'll fit you, fat boy, so we gotta go into town to army surplus to see if we can find you some proper BDUs."

Into town? At least that sounded promising. Perhaps he would be able to figure out an escape plan sooner than he thought. Maybe he'd even be able to contact Fallotti and Wolf.

It was time to start playing both ends against the middle.

CHAPTER 8

The FROZ
Bendover, Oregon

As they took the first pass by the Freedom Restricted Occupational Zone, Wolf observed the same crudely painted cement barriers in the street that he'd seen on Kasey's presentation. A pair of 50-gallon oil drums, with a long two-by-four suspended between them, was stationed next to the substantial cement barriers. The make-shift gate looked flimsy by comparison and would definitely not be substantial enough to prevent a vehicle from barreling though and proceeding down the avenue. But two men clad in black, apparently some sort of gate guards, stood next to the oil drums and both were armed with AR-15s. They had scarves pulled over the lower portion of their faces, each making their visages look like a smiling skeleton.

Beyond them, groups of people walked calmly in the early late afternoon sunshine. Wolf's body still felt bruised and sore from the fight and he reflected that he wished he had a few more days to recover before venturing into what could be a hornet's nest.

"We're passing by the front," McNamara said into his blue tooth. He'd purposely gotten a nice Lexus RX350 from the car rental place at the airport. The P-Patrol had opted for a big Ford van with a sliding door on the side that Ms. Dolly said was tailor-made for an urban abduction.

"And we're coming up on your six," Ms. Dolly said.

McNamara laughed and kept driving. The plan, after taking their chartered plane from Phoenix to here, renting the cars, and checking into a hotel on the outskirts of the city, was to get an idea of the dimensions of the FROZ. So far, Wolf was less than impressed.

"Think those guys know the first thing about maintaining perimeter security?" he asked.

McNamara snorted. "Shit, I probably forgot more than they ever learned." He guided the Lexus down a side street and continued the slow roll.

They still had to tag up with Dickie Deekins, as Manny had suggested, but so far, everything was going according to plan. However, Wolf couldn't shake a feeling of uneasiness. It had started before they'd even gotten on the plane. Picking up the cloned bandito had gone smoothly but Garfield's pronouncement had puzzled Wolf.

"Here they are," the old man said. "Betcha can't tell which is which, right?"

Wolf assessed the two identical banditos and had to agree. He told Garfield he'd earned the promised bonus.

"Not quite yet I haven't," Garfield said. "Ever hear of Archimedes?"

The name rang a faint bell with Wolf but he couldn't quite recall why.

"Eureka," McNamara said. "That was him, right?"

Garfield smiled and nodded, obviously impressed. "I see you paid attention in physics class."

"Hell," McNamara said. "I slept through most of it and spent the rest of the time stealing glances at the pretty girl who sat next to me."

"How about you two scholars enlightening me?" Wolf said.

"Archimedes was a Greek mathematician," Garfield said. "The king ordered him to check to see if the crown they had was pure gold, as it was supposed to be, or a mixture of gold and silver."

"This was back in the day," McNamara added.

"I'll bet," Wolf said.

"Well, the thing was," Garfield continued, "the king forbade him to damage the crown, but how else was he going to tell? He knew if he displeased the king and didn't deliver the answer, it would mean death, the same if he damaged the crown."

"Talk about being between the king and the hard place," McNamara said.

"You two ought to start working on a stand-up routine," Wolf said. "What's the point?"

"Well," Garfield said. "Let me finish the story. I used to be a teacher, after all."

Wolf rolled his eyes. "You know, we have a plane to catch."

"Okay." Garfield took a deep breath and continued. "Archimedes was in a quandary, not knowing what to do, so he decided to take a bath. Well, when he got into the tub, he noticed that the water rose once he lowered himself into the water. He then realized he'd figured out a way to tell the if the composition of the crown was pure by placing it in a tub of water and seeing if it displaced the same amount of water as the exact amount of gold that was supposed to be in it. It's called the theory of displacement."

"And he was so happy," McNamara said, "that he jumped up and ran through the streets naked yelling, 'Eureka, I've found it.'"

"Was he arrested?" Wolf asked.

"Not at all," Garfield said. "The Greeks used to run their marathons in the nude."

"Sounds like a great way of showing off their shortcomings," Wolf said.

Both McNamara and Garfield laughed.

Garfield picked up the closest statue and handed it to Wolf, who accepted it. After a moment, the old man took the statue back, set it down, and handed Wolf the second one.

"Notice anything?"

"Yeah," Wolf said. "They weigh a little different. So what?"

Garfield shook his head. "Precisely. I noticed the difference, yet I was careful to use the exact same type of plaster for the duplicate. It's called stone and is known for its sturdiness. It has a yellowish color."

Wolf nodded, wondering where this was going.

"It was my Archimedes moment," Garfield said. "The two statues should weigh exactly the same but they don't. This one is slightly heavier."

"Which one is that?" Wolf asked.

"The copy. I was curious as to why, so I ran the original over to the medical center. My son works there as an x-ray technician. He snuck it into the room and did a quick shot for me." Garfield pulled open a drawer and removed a 10 x 14 envelope. After undoing the metallic clasps, he flipped up the paper flap and slid out a translucently dark photo. Holding it up to the light, he pointed. "There's something buried inside of this statue. The plaster is very thick, so the image is not distinct, but there's definitely something there. It looks to be about the size of half a grapefruit."

Wolf studied the picture.

Was this what everybody was after?

The bandito was a Trojan Horse of sorts. Or rather a riddle wrapped in an enigma.

"I didn't want to break it open to see what it was," Garfield said. "Because you were so explicit that I not damage the statue. But I couldn't help feeling a bit like Archimedes."

"Eureka," Wolf said.

***

The Pittsfield Building
Phoenix, Arizona

At the Bailey and Lugget Law Firm, Soraces settled into the office cubicle of one of the junior partners who was in court. Scrolling through the numbers on his phone, he found the one he needed for Trackdown, Inc. and dialed. A woman answered with a crisp, business-like greeting. From what he'd gathered from the report that the PI, Jason Zerbe, had filed before his untimely demise, it was most likely Kasey Riley, the daughter of Wolf's bounty hunting partner.

"Yes," Soraces said, putting on his most cordial and professional tone. "I'm trying to get hold of Mr. Steven Wolf please."

The woman hesitated and asked, "Who's calling please?"

"My name is Richard Soraces and I work for the Bailey and Lugget Law Firm." He spelled out his last name.

"And what's this in reference to?"

Soraces assumed the air of a busy attorney and answered with a standard sounding spiel. "I have a legal matter that I wish to speak to him about. Is he available?"

"I'm afraid he's not in the office at the moment."

The office?

From what he'd read in the report, Trackdown, Inc. operated out of McNamara's ranch house.

Who was she trying to kid?

She was being as evasive as he was but he was prepared for this. It was imperative that he make sure his ruse held up under scrutiny.

"Well," he said. "I can leave my number and if you could have him call me at his convenience I would appreciate it." He rattled off the law firm's number and figured it would be better not to give out the cell phone just yet. It was a burner and if they had the capabilities, they might be able to trace it, which might arouse suspicion.

No, for now, I'm a simple lawyer working for a ho-hum law firm, negotiating a tricky deal for an anonymous but generous client.

"Okay," she said. "I'll give him the message when he comes in. And what did you say this is in reference to again?"

"I didn't say," he said, trying to come off sounding both amused and insouciant. "I'm afraid I'll have to discuss that with Mr. Wolf."

After terminating the call, he walked out into the main office and stopped at the receptionist's desk. Soraces explained that he was going out for the day but he was expecting a call back from a prospective client and if it should come through, roll it over to his voice mail and notify him on his cell.

"Yes, sir, Mr. Soraces," she said.

Now all he had to do was wait for a call back. So far this was going about how he expected.

But that could always change.

***

Flying Tigers Army/Navy Surplus
Desolation City, Arizona

Cummins was delighted when Keller had said to follow him in the U-Haul truck, which had to be returned to the renting place in Desolation City. According to Keller, the town was about ten miles west of Base Freedom. He got into a black pickup truck and pulled ahead of him. They went through a back checkpoint adjacent to the big brick building that housed the auditorium. Another guard pulled back the long cyclone fence gate and waved them through.

Alone at last, Cummins thought.

It was the perfect opportunity to make that quick phone call to Fallotti but when he took out the phone his signal reception was spotty. Additionally, he didn't want Keller to spot him in the rearview mirror on the phone. The eavesdropping in the auditorium had been a close call. He didn't want to give Keller another reason to be suspicious. He kept monitoring the signal bars as they traveled down the asphalt road toward the highway. Earlier Cummins had spotted something else of interest: row after row of dilapidated wooden and brick buildings. As he looked closer, he saw a maze of crumbling walls and caving roofs amongst some more sturdy structures that had seemed to have withstood the ravages of desert winds and time. It was what appeared to be an old abandoned ghost town about half a mile or so from the west side of the base. At one time, when the base was in operation, it must have housed the typical attractions of such places—shops, restaurants, bars, barber shops, tattoo parlors, and who knew what else. Now it was just a ramshackle collection of old, crumbling buildings.

But not a bad place to hide a kidnapped kid, while waiting for an exchange to be made.

The kid's in the old hotel in the ghost town, he imagined himself saying to Wolf over the phone as soon as he had possession of the bandito and was on his way. The notification would naturally be made hours after and once he was well on his way out of the area.

Which brought up another question: stay in Arizona or maybe flee the area altogether. With the funds he had in the money belt, he could afford to do some limited traveling. It would just be a matter of finding a way to deliver the bandito to Von Dien after receiving a hefty payoff. It had to be a place where he could have the money transferred and then withdrawn. Mexico was out of the question… Perhaps Canada if he could get across the damn border.

But first, he had to get things set up, and that started with the phone call to Fallotti.

The bars on his phone suddenly appeared indicating once again that he had enough signal power. He quickly hit the button and waited.

The phone rang once, twice, three times, four, and then someone picked it up.

"Jack." Fallotti's voice sounded warm and friendly. "I'm glad you finally called back. Where are you?"

"Never mind where I am," Cummins said, marshalling all his strength and trying his best to imbue confidence into his tone. "Tell Von Dien that I'm close to getting his precious artifact for him and I expect to be compensated. Well compensated."

Fallotti said nothing for a few seconds, then, 'Great. Glad to hear this. Let us send you some help."

"How'd that worked out the last few times? I don't need any help, just money."

"That can be arranged." The prick was sounding genuinely accommodating. "Just tell me where you are and we'll send—"

"Bullshit!"

Cummins felt a thrill at using the word to cut off his old boss. For the first time in their relationship, he felt he had the upper hand.

"Now, Jack, let's not be—"

"Shut up." He felt the thrill double. This was like a power trip. But he also knew it was all or nothing. "Do you think I don't know what you had planned for me the last time? With Zerbe?"

Cummins waited as Fallotti made a stuttering sound like a doctor had told him to stick his tongue out and say, "Ah..."

Feeling he had the advantage and not wanting to lose it, Cummins continued.

"This is the way it's going to be," he said. "*I'm* calling the shots. You're going to do exactly as I instruct, or you and fat boy will never see the fucking other half of the Lion Attacking the Nubian again. Understand?"

"You're being... rather unreasonable, aren't you?"

Cummins knew he had him. The use of Keller's persistent pejorative to now designate Von Dien was icing on the cake. He'd laid all the ground work except the specific amount.

"I want six million wired to the account," he said. "When I give you the number."

"Six million."

"Yeah," Cummins said, realizing it was still to his advantage not to appear weak or conciliatory. "That does seem a little bit thin especially when you consider the fact that you two were intending to cut me off without a cent last time."

"What?" Fallotti made his confusion sound halfway believable. "You know that's not the case."

Typical lawyer, always obfuscating the facts.

"True," said Cummins. "You were more than likely planning to pay me off with a copper-jacketed hollow-point."

"Aw, Jack, you're talking crazy now. You know we always take care of our people."

"Just like you take care of those loose ends, huh?"

He looked ahead and saw they'd entered the main section of the small town and the brake lights of Keller's pickup flashed on. It was time to go.

"I'll call you when I've got things set in place for the trade," he said and hung up.

He felt totally satisfied that he'd accomplished what he needed to accomplish for now. The stage was now set.

Part of it was, anyway.

***

The FROZ
Bendover, Oregon

Wolf had been so caught up in his reverie about the bandito that he was only vaguely conscious that McNamara had asked him a question.

"Say again?" he said, falling back into his army terminology.

"I said, where the hell's your damn head at?" McNamara's voice was raised and irritated. "We got us a damn mission to chart out and I don't see you doing any diagramming."

"Sorry," Wolf said. "I can't help wondering about the bandito, wondering what's inside of it ... Wondering how it all fits together."

McNamara sighed. "Which is exactly why you shoulda let me bust the damn thing apart back at Garfield's place. At least then we might've known something."

Or not, Wolf thought.

"You know what they said about Humpty Dumpty," he said.

McNamara snorted a laugh.

He'd picked up a wooden hammer and chisel at the shop but Wolf had stopped him. He didn't want to take the chance on doing some inadvertent damage to whatever it might contain. So for now, it remained a mystery.

"A mystery wrapped in an enigma inside of a conundrum," he said. "Isn't that what Winston Churchill said about Russia?"

"Something like that," McNamara said. "But right now the only enigma I'm worried about is how to get in and out of this damn FROZ place."

Actually, Wolf had been paying limited attention as they circled the six-block sealed off area and he'd noticed something.

"They've got the main roads blocked off," he said. "And guards posted, checking IDs. But it's obvious that's intended for keeping the police and vehicular traffic out. The rest of the perimeter looks pretty porous. They've probably got roving patrols but limited communications and equipment."

"Not to mention a fundamental lack of knowledge and tactics," McNamara added, shaking his head. "You kind of expect to see this shit in Mogadishu but this is hitting a little too close to home."

Wolf agreed. The sight of the boarded-up stores, piles of garbage, and smoldering fires everywhere was a depressing sight. Even Baghdad during the occupation hadn't looked quite this bad.

"Why do you suppose the politicians are letting these assholes get away with it?" McNamara asked.

"I'm sure they have their reasons," Wolf said. "And none of them are good. But eventually, they'll have to step in."

"And we've got to be in and out before that happens." McNamara was about to say more when his cell phone rang. He pressed the button and answered it.

"Hey, sugar," Ms. Dolly's voice said over the dashboard speakers. "You ever seen anything like this shit?"

McNamara laughed. "We were just talking about that."

"Well, what do you say we go meet this Dickie Deekins guy and figure out our plan?" she said. "What do you figure? Tonight's reconnoitering and tomorrow the big game?"

That would mean we'd have to fly back, Wolf thought.

"Let's see if we can grab him tonight," McNamara said. "We gotta get him back for his Wednesday court date."

"Tonight would be better for us, too," Ms. Dolly said. "We got a corporate meeting on Wednesday I'd really like to be back for and I gotta get ready."

"Honey," McNamara said. "You were *born* ready."

Wolf heard Ms. Dolly's throaty laugh. They agreed to meet back at the hotel and McNamara terminated the call.

"After we meet this reporter fella," he said. "Let's you and me have the gals drop us off in the south perimeter so we can get a look inside this shithole."

Wolf agreed, thinking that it would be better if the vehicles were seen as little as possible.

McNamara's phone rang again and he answered it.

"Dad," Kasey said. "How was the flight?"

"Smooth as a satin pillow, honey," he said. "How's things back at the Ranch?"

"Oh, all right," she said.

From the sound of her voice, Wolf figured it was anything but.

Apparently, so did Mac.

"What's wrong?" he asked.

"I still haven't heard from Chad," she said. "Or Charlie, either, for that matter. I tried calling that cell phone but there's no answer."

"You got Charlie's number, right?" McNamara asked.

"I do but he's not picking up either. It goes directly to voice mail and he never calls back."

"When we get back we'll take another ride over to that damn trailer of his," McNamara said. "We'll track his sorry ass down."

"Another thing," she said. "He said he was going to the Grand Canyon before but I'm not sure about that. I've called most all the hotels in the area down there and they're not registered at any of them. No credit card activity, either, from what I could find."

It was obvious she was putting her tracking skills into play. Wolf wondered if she'd been trying to track

Riley's cell phone as well.

"We'll find him," McNamara said. "And Chad, too. And this'll be the last the little guy sees of that son of a bitch."

"Oh, dad, stop. He's Chad's father for Christ's sake."

From the sound of it, she was on the verge of tears. Wolf knew better than to say anything. Mac did, too.

After a few moments of awkward dead noise, she came back on the line.

"Oh, is Steve around?" she asked.

"He's right next to me," McNamara said. "You're on speaker."

Her breath came in a hiss. "I wish you would have told me that before." Wolf could hear her taking in a deep breath, composing herself, before she continued.

"Hi, Steve. Some lawyer called for you earlier," she said, speaking rapidly now. Her voice seemed more under control. "Soraces is his name. Wanted to talk to you but wouldn't tell me any specifics about what he wanted."

This sounded disconcerting to Wolf. Lawyers reaching out usually meant one thing: trouble.

"He say where he works?"

"Bailey and Lugget Law Firm. They're local. I checked them out and he is employed there."

That narrowed the possibilities a bit but Wolf still had no idea what this was about.

Wolf scribbled down the number as she read it off,

along with the spelling of his name.

"Thanks, Kasey," he said. "And try not to worry too much. We'll find Chad and make sure he's safe."

She murmured a "Thanks" that was accompanied by what sounded like a burst of tears as she terminated the call.

Wolf and McNamara exchanged glances and Mac shook his head.

"I'm gonna take particular pleasure in kicking that fucker, Riley's, ass," he said. "Sounds like we'd best try to pick up this asshole, Zeus, as fast as we can."

Wolf nodded in agreement but his thoughts were now centered on Kasey.

The last thing in the world he'd wanted to do was say something to make her cry.

"Sor-ac-es," McNamara repeated slowly, drawing out the word. "That sound Greek to you?"

"It's all Greek to me," Wolf said.

***

1871 Fornaux Street
Bendover, Oregon

In person, Dickie Deekins didn't look much like the suave podcast journalist Manny had described or even the one they'd seen on the video clips. His face was now swollen on both sides to grotesque proportions and the area under each eye contained a drooping black loop. His upper lip was distorted on the left side as well. He lay back on the cushions of the sofa in the cluttered living room of the old house. His mother stood at the edge of the room, which was adjacent to the kitchen watching over the conversation. Wolf, McNamara, and the P-Patrol stood in a semicircle around him and it was clear that he was enjoying the audience.

"Zeus and his boys prowl mostly at night," Deekins said. "That's when they jumped us. We were trying to film some of the stuff that's been going on in the Zone."

"We saw that video," McNamara said. "Looked like they worked you over pretty good."

"There was nothing good about it," Mrs. Deekins said. "Those beasts hurt my baby and the damn police won't do nothing about it."

"A damn shame, ma'am," McNamara said.

"Ma, please," Deekins said. "Leave us alone, will ya?"

The older lady made a huffing sound and went into the other room.

Deekins rolled his eyes and appeared to instantly regret the movement, punctuating it with a groan.

"Right now you got three different factions vying for leadership domination in the FROZ," he said. "One is a mishmash of white radicals and blacks called the Mez, as in mezzed up. They're mostly into yelling and screaming on the street corner about social justice. Then there's another group of Hispanics called the *Vaqueros*. They mostly keep a low profile but are strong-arming what businesses that are still open for protection money."

"Protection from who?" McNamara asked.

"It's whom," Deekins said. "And that's just it. They pay because they're afraid and the *Vaqueros* don't do shit to protect them. Zeus and his boys just walk around and take whatever they want, including taking turns with any nice-looking girls they see."

"*Vaqueros*," Brenda said with disgust. "*Ladrones. Pendejoes cingados todos.*"

Wolf couldn't agree more and the more he heard, the less he was liking this.

"Who all's armed in the Zone?" he asked.

"Shit, every fucking body," Deekins said.

"Dickie," Mrs. Deekins said from the other room. "Watch you language, sweetie. There are young ladies present."

"Yeah, yeah, ma."

Yolanda and Brenda exchanged grins and Ms. Dolly said, "Don't worry, it wasn't nothing we hadn't heard before."

"What kind of weapons they have?" Wolf asked.

Deekins shrugged. "I don't know too much about guns. I got some videos that might show something."

Wolf nodded and Deekins swung his legs off the

sofa. His white socks had numerous holes in them and smelled like they hadn't been washed in days.

"Where does Zeus hold up?" McNamara asked.

"He stays in this apartment building that's right across from the city hall," Deekins said as he looked through a bunch of flashdrives. "That's how this whole mess got started. They had this big protest at the city hall, marched in, and took over. The city council all got evacuated and the next thing you know the mayor ordered the police to leave the police station rather than stand their ground. The next thing you know, they'd barricaded the streets and wouldn't let anybody in or out without permission."

"Bend over, Bendover," McNamara said.

"Sounds all too familiar," Wolf said.

"Don't it," McNamara said. "Welcome to Somalia West."

"*Cuando llega la revolución*," Brenda said. "*Lo devora todo.*"

"When the revolution comes," Ms. Dolly translated. "It devours everything."

Wolf couldn't agree more. Deekins had plugged a flashdrive into his laptop and clicked on a file. A video filled the screen but it was hard to distinguish much due to the grainy nature of the picture. It did show a group of black men wearing hoodies. One held an AR-15. Another a shotgun. Two more flashed what looked to be blue steel semi-autos of some kind. Wolf couldn't tell the makes.

"Can you draw us a map of this Zone area?" McNamara asked. "Pointing out where the city hall and the police department are."

"I can do better than that," Deekins said. "I can go to Google Earth."

His fingers swept over the keyboard.

"Zeus has proclaimed himself the leader of the FROZ," Deekins said. "Him and his guys, about fifteen of them, take these nightly patrols around, starting at around eight-thirty or nine."

"Patrols?" McNamara asked, looking at the screen, which was now showing an overhead, long-distance shot of Bendover, but obviously in better, bygone days. "What does he do on them?"

Deekins enlarged the image showing a close-up of the apartment building. It looked like a four or five-story structure with numerous balconies.

"Whatever the fuck he pleases," Deekins said.

"Dickie," his mother yelled from the kitchen area. "Language."

Deekins rocked his head back and forth and then winched.

"That's when they beat me up," he said. "Me and Henry were following them, trying to document some of the shi— errr, stuff they do, and they seen us. Beat us really bad. Henry's still in the hospital. We were lucky they only beat us and didn't shoot us."

Wolf and McNamara looked at each other. They'd brought two handguns, extra magazines, a Taser, handcuffs, leg irons, a sap, and a roll of duct tape. The P-Patrol had three more handguns between them but they were going against at least one AR-15 and a shotgun.

They were already way outgunned.

CHAPTER 9

Fort Lemand
Southern Arizona

Cummins shoveled some of the gruel-like stew into his mouth and tried not to concentrate on the salty taste. The mess hall was immense but like many of the other buildings in the compound, uncomfortably hot and gritty. He'd counted perhaps twenty-five other soldiers at Base Freedom, excluding himself and Colonel Best. Only a handful of them were armed but he had no doubt there were more weapons available in the arm's room. His Glock 43 was one of them. Besides those on guard duty and the one stationed by the M-60, only Keller and Best were armed. He'd heard the sound of rifle fire earlier and peered out his window but saw nothing. The gunfire seemed far off and Smith later told him that they'd had range practice earlier. Smith seemed a bit disgruntled and Cummins wondered if it was due to the spat he'd overheard between Smith and Riley. But now all five of them, Smith, Riley, Chad, Cherrie, and himself, sat together for evening chow a few tables away from most of the others. A couple of the younger guys stole glances at Cherrie from time to time but Smith's returning glare made them look away quickly. She appeared miserable.

The kid didn't seem to like it much either and kept complaining. Riley had to tell him to be quiet numerous times and finally threatened to swat him. As far as Cummins could tell, Chad was the only child and Cherrie was the only female on the compound. Neither Smith nor Riley seemed too happy that Best was making both her and the little kid attend the swearing-in ceremony tonight. In fact, they had less than twenty minutes now. At least Cummins had found a clean bucket of water in the latrine and managed to shave off his newly grown goatee. The room Keller had told him to bunk in was hardly luxurious and he doubted that Smith's accommodations were much better.

I wonder if he's sorry he brought the flat screen, he thought, recalling loading the item into the U-Haul truck.

Smith seemed to read his thoughts.

"This sure ain't nothing like I thought it would be,"

he muttered as he scooped more of the lousy chow from his plate. "Nothing like they promised."

"Sure ain't," Cherrie said. "And I don't like the way that Keller guy keeps looking at me, neither."

"He touches you," Smith said. "I'll kill him."

You'd better be ready to use your bare hands, Cummins added mentally. Because I've never seen him without that big Desert Eagle and they took away your handgun just like they did mine.

"And we made over a hundred grand hitting that armored truck," Smith continued in a low voice. "And so far we ain't seen none of it. We was supposed to get bonuses."

"Bonuses," Riley accompanied by a disparaging laugh. "And Keller said I gotta go on training maneuvers all day tomorrow. I asked him, who's gonna take care of my kid? Know what he said back?" Riley scraped some more of the gruel with his spoon, looked at it, then shoved the plate away. "The prick said it was my problem for bringing him. Can you imagine? I got a good mind to vacate this place."

"If it gets much worse," Smith said. "We'll go with you. I didn't sign up to be another fucking grunt crawling in the sand."

"I can take care of him again," Cherrie said. Her voice sounded weary.

Riley turned to stare at her, his lips curled back from his teeth in a semi-snarl. "Okay, but like I said, don't be giving him no more of that medicine."

"If need be, I can give you a hand, too," Cummins said. "All they have me doing is some bookkeeping right now." He forced a laugh. "Guess they don't trust me with a weapon yet."

Everyone fell into an uneasy silence for a few moments, then Riley said, "Appreciate that, Jack."

And I'll appreciate the opportunity to be alone with the kid for a bit, he thought. Get the little shit use to good old Uncle Jack.

Maybe this was going to be easier than he thought. Disgruntled personnel, hints at a way out ... Maybe it was time to call Wolf and start setting up that trade.

***

Near the FROZ
Bendover, Oregon

Dickie Deekins had proved more resourceful than Wolf had anticipated and loaned them a pretty sophisticated miniature body cam and recording mic. All they had to do was promise to email him back any videos of the apprehension of Zeus. Ms. Dolly readily agreed to do that. She'd brought along her radios, with the lavaliere mics as well. The only question that remained as they got assembled in the rear parking behind a closed, boarded-up drug store was how to proceed.

Wolf and McNamara donned raggedy-looking sweat shirts with hoods, and Mac made sure his covered the Glock 19 he had in a pancake holster on his belt. He placed a black baseball cap on and pulled the hood portion over it. Wolf's sweat shirt was a couple sizes too large to cover the Taser and the Glock 21 that McNamara had insisted he carry on this one.

"An ex-con carrying a gun," Wolf said with a grin. "You know what'll happen to me if we get caught?"

McNamara snorted. "I guess we'd best not get caught then. Besides, you know what'll happen if we get caught up in a fire fight with these sorry-ass jokers with you only armed with a Taser. Better to have a gun, than not."

"Y'all come up with a plan yet?" Ms. Dolly asked. It had pretty much been agreed that she would be on the perimeter in the van, waiting to pick them up.

"Listen," Yolanda said. "Me and Brenda are the only two of us that can go inside this FROZ place without being conspicuous. Let us go in, play up to this dude and get him alone."

"And then what?" Wolf said. He didn't like the thought of exposing them to the danger but after all, it was what they did.

"We taze his sorry ass and handcuff him," she said. "You guys can be standing by to carry him out."

"Too risky," McNamara said. "We have no air support, no reinforcements … We can't afford to get into a fire fight with a numerically superior and better armed force."

"Oooh," Brenda said. "You know I love it when you talk military stuff like that, big guy."

Mac grinned. "Glad you liked it but it don't change the facts. We can't even call nine-one-one if the shooting starts."

"In other words," Wolf said, "we need this to be a stealth op. In and out without being noticed."

"Exactly," McNamara said.

"Which is why me and Brenda need to get him alone in his little room," Yolanda said.

"This ain't exactly our first rodeo," Ms. Dolly said. "Trust us and let us do what we do best."

"And that's looking bad-ass and kicking butt," Brenda said with a deliciously wicked smile.

Wolf and McNamara looked at each other.

"You think he'll take the bait?" Wolf said.

She batted her eyes and puffed out her chest. "Wouldn't you?"

He smiled.

Actually, the idea was making more sense to him now. If they could tag up with Zeus and if they could somehow separate him from his protection detail, on the pretext of wanting to get intimate, it could give Mac and him a chance to sneak in and subdue their quarry. But, there were a lot of "ifs" and a lot of intangibles.

"It's getting dark now and from what we heard, this asshole's like a vampire," McNamara said. "Let's go reconnoiter a bit."

"And if we see him?" Yolanda asked.

"Then we watch and figure out a way to take him down." McNamara turned to Ms. Dolly. "You ready to drop us off darling?"

Her hand caresses his jaw. "Just tell me where, sugar."

"Where" for Wolf and McNamara turned out to be on a side street a block or so away from the abandoned police precinct. Yolanda and Brenda said they were sure they'd be allowed inside the front gate. They'd all communicate by radio or text until they rendezvoused inside. The code word, "bailout," meant that something was amiss and they were all to make their way out of the Zone as quickly as possible. "Evergreen" was the distress word that meant immediate help was needed.

Ms. Dolly slowed the van and pulled down a side street while Yolanda and Brenda got out. Both were wearing tight-fitting blue jeans and brightly colored tank tops. Yolanda's was bright orange, Brenda's was red. Both of them had ear mics for their radios and fanny-packs for their weapons. They were both wearing gym shoes for good foot speed. As they wiggly-walked together, laughing and touching and looking at their smart phones like any two young ladies out for a good time in the FROZ, Wolf felt overcome with concern.

"Don't let nothing happen to my girls," Ms. Dolly said, shifting into gear to spin around to the next drop off point.

"I'll scrub this whole thing before I let something like that happen," McNamara said.

Just then his cell phone rang and he pulled it out and frowned.

"Yeah, Kase," he said. "What's up?"

Wolf reminded himself to turn his own phone on vibrate and slipped it back into the backpack that had their other equipment. McNamara continued to listen and murmur into his phone.

"The son of a bitch has got an ass-whipping coming," McNamara finally said. "As soon as we get back me and Steve'll go check that damn trailer park again. In the meantime, you keep checking as best you can."

From the sound of it, Wolf surmised that she still hadn't heard from Chad.

"Yeah, he's here. Why?"

McNamara raised an eyebrow and handed the phone to Wolf. "She wants to talk to you."

Wolf took it figuring it was going to be another admonishment from Kasey about making sure her father didn't take too many risks or get hurt.

He answered and waited.

"Steve, another guy called here and was trying to get

ahold of you," she said. "He used a blocked number."

"Okay." Wolf tried to assess this new information. "He give his name?"

"Well, yes and no. He said, 'Tell him his old army buddy, Jack, called.' Said he'd be calling back."

Army buddy? Jack?

Could it be Jack Cummins?

Just what I need at this point juncture, Wolf thought. Another distraction.

After thanking her, he handed the phone back to Mac and ruminated on this new development but after a few seconds, he pushed it out of his mind.

Concentrate on the mission at hand, he told himself. Deal with this other stuff later.

"Here y'all go," Ms. Dolly said, stopping the van on a dimly lighted residential street.

McNamara leaned forward and kissed her and Wolf regretted that he hadn't kissed Yolanda before she'd departed.

Another time, he thought as he pulled back the sliding door and jumped out. Another place.

They walked to an intersecting street and then came to an open field about forty yards long that led up to a twelve-foot cyclone fence topped with concertina wire. Beyond it was the abandoned police building but in between a motley collection of make-shift tents redolent with the pungent odor of unwashed bodies and human waste.

McNamara sniffed the air with exaggeration.

"Guess we know where the homeless are hanging out," he said. "Better watch where you step."

Wolf regretted not bringing any heavy-duty wire cutters, but as they got closer to the fence he saw that someone had already done the job for them. A large section had been cut and pulled back allowing easy access. Both he and McNamara slipped through quickly.

"Check that out," McNamara said, indicating the shattered glass rear doors of the police building. "Might as well take a look-see."

Wolf nodded and held up his hand. After glancing around to assure their privacy, he keyed his mic and said, "Sit-rep."

"We're on Main Street heading your way," Yolanda said. "How about you?"

"At the PD," he said.

"Anybody there?" she asked. "I thought it was empty?"

"Abandoned but hopefully not totally empty," he said, wishing they'd spent more time going over radio protocol. Gabbing about trivia wasn't the best tactic for a mission.

"If you two love birds are finished," McNamara broke in, "let's clear the net."

"Roger that, boo daddy," Yolanda said. "I think I see something interesting anyway. Don't call me. I'll call you. Or maybe I'll text."

Wolf and Mac exchanged grins as they zigzagged through the sea of tents toward the building and finally went up the cement steps leading into the station. Spray painted graffiti was everywhere, most of it profanity directed against the police. The shattered doors led inside a glass foyer of sorts where a solid metal door lay on the floor after evidently being torn off its hinges. The long brick hallway was dark, except for moonlight streaming through an overhead skylight. More crudely scrawled messages, all of them profane, decorated the walls. The floor was littered with more broken glass, ceremonial plaques, and trampled pictures of groups of uniformed police.

"Watch it," McNamara said, pointing to a pile of human feces on the floor ahead. Several more piles formed scatological trail markers up to an empty door frame leading to the outside.

"Sorta feels like we stepped off into a new version of *The Lord of the Flies*," Wolf said.

"Plenty of them around," McNamara said, then stopped. "Aw, hell."

A filthy, trampled American flag lay crumpled in a corner.

Wolf stooped down and grabbed the flag and shook it vigorously.

"Let's fold it until we can dispose of it properly," McNamara said.

They went off into an adjacent corridor, removed their tight-fitting leather gloves, and held the flag out between them. Wolf had the end with all the stripes, so after folding it length-wise two times, he began to make the triangular folds with rote skill, recalling the many times he'd done it before, including over the caskets of fallen comrades. He was sure that Mac had lost way more of them than he had. McNamara tucked the flag's edge into the triangular field of blue with white stars and nodded. Wolf slipped the back pack off and placed the folded flag inside.

A rat scurried across the room and disappeared into a crack in the wall. The room had numerous windows, all with holes of varying sizes. More papers and other items were strewn about. A broken telephone had been ripped from the wall and two large sections of smashed black plastic, seeming to be radio recharging stations, were in a corner. McNamara nudged Wolf over to another dangling door. This one was listing lugubriously, still being attached by one hinge. The sign on the front read *EQUIPMENT*. Wolf pulled the door open the rest of the way and saw a jumble of detritus on the floor of what had been a large walk-in closet. He pulled out his mini-mag flashlight and shone it around, stopping on a box that contained two reels of nylon rope.

"Lookie what we got here," McNamara said, stooping down and removing the reels. Wolf held the beam over the box as Mac reviewed the contents.

"Seems like two rolls of three hundred feet each," he said. "Got some D-rings in here, too."

The sound of laughter crackled in his ear from his radio, and a feminine voice saying, "Hey, hey, hey, boo. You must be *the man* 'round this place."

Wolf realized it was Yolanda sending him a message. McNamara caught it as well.

"So you gonna take us up to your place and show us the most elegant bachelor pad in the FROZ?"

It was definitely her voice.

"Maybe smoke us a little weed, honeybunny?"

That was Brenda. One of them was keying her mic to let them know they'd located the target and were headed back this way.

"Maybe do a little dancing, make a little love," Yolanda said and then both girls chimed in together to sing, "And get down real good tonight."

"You got it, sweet things," a deep, masculine voice said. "And I got the baddest shit in town, too, and I ain't just talking about what's in my pants."

More giggles and laughter.

"Lemme text my other boo," Yolanda said. "Tell him it's off for tonight."

Wolf quickly removed his cell phone from the backpack and watched the screen. Presently, a text appeared.

Hey, boo. I'm busy tonight.

It was obvious that the plan to tag up and do some recon had been accelerated, whether by design or serendipity. What was clear was that it was time to improvise. Wolf stepped to the window and gazed out.

K, Wolf texted back. *Keep in touch*.

"Didn't Deekins say that Zeus's apartment was in the building across the street?" he said.

"Yep." McNamara joined him at the window. "Top floor."

"The girls are headed there now," Wolf said.

McNamara studied the building across the way.

"You thinking what I'm thinking?" Wolf asked, pointing to the open balcony facing this way.

"Let's do it," McNamara said and grabbed the two rolls of nylon rope.

***

Fort Lemand
Southern Arizona

Cummins lay on his bunk staring at the ceiling. Keller had declared "Lights out" an hour or so earlier but slumber wouldn't come. His mind raced trying to figure out his next move. Then he heard the faint knock on his door and recognized Smith's whispering voice.

"Jack, open up."

Cummins swung his legs out from under the sheet and made sure he'd tucked neoprene money belt under his pillow before padding to the door and unlocking it. He'd felt compelled to take his extended wear contact lenses out earlier to put them in the cleaning solution, so the room's interior was a soft, myopic blur. So was Smith's face as he slipped through the opening.

"What's going on?" Cummins asked. "Where's Cherrie?"

"She's in our room," Smith said. "Me and her been talking. Charlie, too. We ain't liking it here much, especially since they promised they was gonna give us something good for hitting that armored car. Turns out the fucker didn't give us shit."

Cummins remembered Keller promising the three of them a substantial bonus for doing the deed. He nodded.

"One of the other guys we served with in Iraq overheard Keller and the Colonel talking about maybe making Cherrie and Charlie's kid move out," Smith said. "Get a room in Desolation City and stay there while we train."

That might make an abduction easier, Cummins thought. But, then again, all he had to do would be to tip Wolf where the kid was ... After he had the bandito, of course.

"You listening to me?" Smith asked. The irritation

was easily perceivable in this tone.

"Yeah," Cummins said. "Just thinking, is all. He give you any reason?"

"Shit, he's talking about taking us all out into the desert to conduct some desert warfare drills. I had enough of that shit in the Sandbox, didn't you?"

Cummins really hadn't done any of that but he nodded in agreement—playing kindred soldiers was the name of the game right now. "Why are they so hot on doing all this training?"

"Best's going off the deep end. Says the government's gonna be coming for us. For him, actually. He's talking crazy, like it's the end of the world's just around the corner."

Armageddon rising, Cummins thought.

"He's fucking nuts," Smith said. "Like I told you, me and Charlie's been talking. We been thinking that getting out of here might be a real good idea right now."

Cummins wasn't totally sure where this was going but he figured he'd better play along.

"I'm with you on that."

The corners of Smith's mouth curled into a smile and he clapped Cummins on the shoulder.

"That's what I wanted to hear," Smith said. "We got to figure a way to get into the safe where they got all the money locked up. We take our fair share, what we were promised, that's all, and then take off. Me, Cherrie, Charlie and his kid, and you, if you want to come."

Take their fair share?

Or maybe a little extra, Cummins thought. A bit more cash never hurt.

"Well," Smith said. "Whaddaya think?"

"But how would we gonna do this? The guards at the gate would never let us leave. They took my gun, and they took yours and Riley's too, didn't they?"

Smith nodded. "They did, but if we do it right, we shouldn't oughta need no guns."

Cummins looked skeptical. "How's that?"

Smith glanced around, even though they were alone, then leaned close, his voice a low conspiratorial whisper.

"There's a secret way outta here."

***

The FROZ
Bendover, Oregon

As Wolf and McNamara walked across the abandoned parking lot in front of the police station, they saw numerous homeless people crouching and scurrying about. One was standing off to the side urinating. Another stopped a staggering walk, pulled down his pants and defecated. Wolf and Mac gave both of them a wide berth and almost collided with a seated figure who emitted a growling sound. Wolf looked down and saw the man manipulating a syringe that he had jammed into a vein at the crux of his elbow. The hollow syringe filled with blood, then drained slightly, then filled up again. His mouth gaped with each breath and he made a gasping moan.

The soles of their shoes made a crunching sound as they walked, crushing the mosaic of discarded syringes on the asphalt. In the middle of the street, a group of three youths pushed a homeless man to the ground and started pulling stuff out of the shopping cart he'd been pushing. The man protested as he got to his knees but one of them kicked him in the side and he fell over moaning. The youths laughed.

"What were you saying about *Lord of the Flies?*" McNamara said.

"Those bastards." Wolf started to head toward them but McNamara grabbed his arm.

"Hey," Mac said. "We're here on a mission and we got the gals depending on us. We ain't got time to play the Lone Ranger."

Wolf knew he was right and kept walking.

A waspish young black man who'd delivered the kick to the homeless man broke off from the group and approached them with a grin, holding a folded packet in his open palm.

"Hey, dudes," he said. "Looking for some good shit?"

They both ignored him but he followed.

"I got some," the young man said. "If you got the bread."

They said nothing, continuing their trek.

"Hey, man, I know you two?" the slender man asked, following them.

"*Lo siento,*" Wolf said. "*No hablo inglés.*"

"Huh?" The young man frowned and spat. "Hey, the *Vaqueros* knows they ain't supposed to be coming 'round here, Pancho and Cisco. You'd best get your beaner asses on the other side of Main Street 'fore Zeus sees y'all or he'll kick your asses all the way back to Mexico." After a few seconds assessment, he added with escalating bravado, "Motherfuckers."

Wolf and McNamara exchanged glances and Wolf figured it wouldn't be prudent to leave this loudmouth alerting people to their location. He turned and gestured to the young man, saying, "Come, come. We buy from you."

"Now you talking," the young man said with a smile.

They stepped over to the corner of the apartment building and Wolf clenched his fist, ready to ram it into the young drug pusher's gut but McNamara beat him to it. The pusher folded in half and collapsed onto the ground gasping.

"Oooh," McNamara said. "That felt good."

McNamara straddled the pusher and after twisting his hands behind his back and securing them, along with his feet using heavy-duty plastic zip-ties, McNamara wound a section of duct tape around the guy's mouth a few times. He squirmed a few times and McNamara placed the sole of his shoe on the young man's face holding him still.

"Better not leave him out in the open like this," he said. "Liable to attract too much attention."

"This is our stop anyway," Wolf said. His radio crackled and he heard what he took to be Yolanda's voice saying, "Is this *your* place?"

"Sure nuff, baby," a male voice replied. He was still speaking with an affected, exaggerated deepness.

Wolf's phone vibrated with an incoming text.

We here.

K, he texted back. *Us 2.*

Wolf moved to the edge of the building and did a quick peek. Yolanda and Brenda stood with five black guys, two of whom carried rifles.

The AR-15 and the Kalashnikov, he thought. The others are probably armed, too.

The guy in the middle had the same set of dreadlocks as in the picture Manny had shown them. It had to be Zeus, aka Booker Nobles. The group piled in the front door and he overheard Yolanda saying, "Wait a minute, why don't you leave your entourage outside, baby."

"Where the king goes," Zeus said, "the entourage

follows."

They piled in the front door and Wolf ran back to give the update to McNamara.

"Guess we'd better shake a leg then," he said. He stooped down and grabbed the trussed-up drug dealer and hoisted him up like a sack of potatoes. After adjusting the man's bulk a bit and trying to control the squirming figure, he lowered the man feet-first to the ground. He then straightened up and delivered another solid bolo punch to the pusher's abdomen. Twin plumes of air expelled out the man's nostrils, accompanied by thin ribbons of snot.

"That's better," McNamara said and replaced the man on his shoulder.

They walked to the rear of the building and found another black guy leaning against the wall next to a solid metal door. The guy was sucking hard on what smelled like a marijuana cigarette and a shotgun was leaning against the wall next to him. His eyes widened as they came around the corner and he bounced off the wall.

"What's the story?" he said.

Wolf snapped off the cartridge and brought the Taser up, pressing it against him for a drive-stun. The device crackled and the guard stiffened and dropped. McNamara let his burden fall to the ground and knelt beside the quivering guard. After handing the shotgun to Wolf, Mac repeated the binding ritual on this second subject. He then patted the man down and came up with another gun, a Taurus 9 mm, and a set of keys.

Straightening up, he moved to the metal door and started trying to keys in the lock. After a few times, it opened. McNamara eased the door open, peered inside, then looked back to Wolf.

"I think these two might be more comfortable inside in that corner," McNamara said. "Don't you?"

"Absolutely," Wolf said and grabbed one by the feet and the other by the collar.

After secreting both captives in the corner under the staircase, Wolf and McNamara made their way up to the fifth floor. The staircase ended but there was a ladder built into the wall that led to a trapdoor, which Wolf figured went to the roof. He went to the door opening onto the fifth-floor hallway and eased it open a crack. Perhaps thirty feet away, two of them, the ones with the rifles, stood outside the middle door passing a hand-rolled cigar back and forth. The sweet odor of burning marijuana was noticeable even from a distance. That meant the other three, including Zeus, were inside the apartment.

So much for the girls getting the target alone.

This wasn't going according to the plan but that was the norm. Every plan looked good on paper until it was executed. Then Murphy's Law—whatever can go wrong, will go wrong, usually came into play.

And it'll go wrong at the worst possible moment,

he thought.

He eased the door back closed and relayed the information to McNamara, who frowned.

"I'd say our best shot is coming in from the balcony," he said.

Wolf agreed. Taking out both of the hallway guards would be easy enough but most likely noisy. That would alert the ones inside, who were probably just as high and prone to shooting first and asking questions later.

"Let's open this patio door and let some night air in here," a feminine voice murmured on his radio.

It was Yolanda again, signaling them that they were opening the patio doors. Maybe she figured it would designate which apartment they were in. She and Brenda had no idea that Mac and he were in the building already. Wolf wanted to text her but figured he'd better not. What if Zeus or one of his henchmen saw it?

Wolf and McNamara went to the ladder and Wolf scaled it quickly, then halted as he got to the top. Two wires dangled from the handle securing the trapdoor.

It might be a burglar alarm, he thought, and if it is, there could be an audible alarm attached.

He debated what to do and McNamara said, "Pull the god damn thing. Fortune favors the bold."

Wolf put his hand on the lever but stopped. He reached into his pocket and withdrew his knife. Flipping the blade open, he severed both wires.

No alarm sounded and he worked the lever. The trap door opened and exposed a view of the velvety sky. He crawled through the opening and immediately began searching for a place where they could tie off their ropes. The roof was flat and was covered with a layer of small, oval-shaped bits of gravel. It also had a massive air-conditioning unit in the center. McNamara looped two bow-line nooses around the base of the structure and then brought both lines to the edge of the roof. Wolf was busy cutting two three-foot sections of line for him and Mac to tie into Swiss seats. They had the lines spread and the knots tied in about ninety seconds and McNamara handed Wolf a D-ring. After clipping them in place, they both went to the edge of the roof, straddled the crenulated barrier on the edge, and dropped the rest of their lines over the side.

Wolf heard them both hit the ground below. He hooked the rope through the D-ring.

They'd heard nothing on the radio since the last transmission a few minutes ago.

"Time's a wasting," McNamara said and straightened his legs and leaned back. Wolf assumed the same position and then shoved himself off the wall. They descended in tandem, halting their flow in front of the banister of the fifth-floor balcony. Wolf hooked his boot over the banister and saw that Mac was doing the same but his made a thumping sound. Swinging his other leg over the barrier, Wolf landed on the solid cement platform and shoved open the sliding door.

Good girl, he thought, for leaving it open.

The three men inside looked up in surprise. They, too, had been leisurely inhaling on fat, hand-rolled cigars that smelled of cannabis. One of them held an open bottle of whiskey. Wolf centered the laser dot on the chest of the closest one and squeezed the trigger of the Taser. A burst of miniature confetti burst forth with a snap as the prongs shot outward, snagging the guy's shoulder and chest. As the guy went down, Wolf brought his foot up in a kicking motion striking the second man under the chin. He dropped like he'd been pole-axed. Wolf pivoted, doing a hook kick, and caught the third one in the temple. McNamara was inside now using the zip-ties and duct tape. Wolf kept his finger depressed on the Taser until Mac had secured the last of the three. There was no one else in the room. A door on the left side was closed and soft music and a rhythmic moaning were audible. He moved toward the door but McNamara grabbed his arm.

"We gotta take out those other two guards first," he whispered. "The gals'll have to fend for themselves right now. You don't leave a rear echelon force available to attack your flank."

The sound of a female's loud moan, followed by

a gasp of what sounded like delight, made Wolf's blood boil.

Were they having sex in there?

Was forcing them?

He didn't want to think about that but knew Mac was right. They moved to the door and Wolf inserted another cartridge onto the Taser. The confetti would provide minute and traceable serial numbers of the weapon but Wolf wasn't too worried. So far they hadn't had to shoot anybody and it was dubious that any of Zeus's henchmen would call the police or be sophisticated enough to do a CSI sweep of the apartment later. Wolf positioned himself to the left of the door as McNamara gripped the doorknob. After seeing Wolf's nod, Mac ripped the door open and Wolf burst through. He pointed the Taser at the guy standing to the left, the aiming crimson laser light centering on his mid chest. Wolf squeezed the trigger and the prongs once again shot outward. The man stiffened and teetered over backward. The second man made a grab for his rifle but Wolf slammed a sidekick into the man's gut. He grunted as he slammed against the wall. When he straightened up, McNamara smacked him right behind the ear with a leather sap. Wolf kept the trigger depressed, keeping the second man writhing on the floor until they were both dragged inside along with the two long guns. The moaning had intensified behind the closed door and Wolf was verging on anger and concern for the two women, especially Yolanda.

Was she all right?

After securing and gagging both hallway guards, Wolf got up and strode to the door, taking out his gun. He gripped the knob and twisted, but it didn't open.

Locked, he thought, then took a backward step and delivered a solid, full-footed kick just below the doorknob. Raising his gun to the combat-ready position, he peered cautiously around the door jamb and saw Yolanda and Brenda fully clothed and sitting on a settee at the end of the bed. Their feet rested on the supine figure of Zeus, who lay in a tangled mess on the floor. His arms were obviously cuffed behind his back and a swath of duct tape secured a rag that was partially protruding from his mouth. A pornographic movie played on a large, flatscreen television next to the bed, the volume on high, emitting a series of ecstatic moans and groans from the female actress.

Yolanda looked up at him and winked.

"Sure took you long enough," she said.

CHAPTER 10

Ghost Town Near Fort Lemand
Southern Arizona

Cummins backed Riley's Caravan between the standing walls of two buildings that looked sound enough not to collapse. Smith pulled the Malibu up in front and gave him a thumbs-up as he got out of the Chevy. They made quick work of covering the white Dodge with some camouflaged netting that they'd taken from the supply room and anchored it with some discarded bricks from a nearby fallen wall.

When they'd finished Cummins felt out of breath but at least he didn't have to throw up.

Smith paused and took out a pack of cigarettes, offering one to Cummins, who declined.

"That oughta do it, all right," Smith said as he held the flame from his lighter against the tip of the cigarette.

"You think Keller will buy the story?" Cummins asked.

Smith shrugged as he exhaled some smoke through his nose.

"I expect he might get suspicious eventually," he said. "But for now, I think everything'll be okay."

They'd gotten special permission to take Riley's car into town to get a purported radiator leak fixed. It was a total fabrication but Keller seemed to buy it because Riley was supposed to be getting his kid's stuff ready for transfer into Desolation City. Cherrie was assisting him. Smith casually mentioned that he and Cummins could drop it off while he booked a room at the hotel for Cherrie and Chad to stay in for the next few days.

Keller had agreed but Cummins was worried that the big goon was a bit suspicious. Maybe he was smarter than he looked. And there were a lot of intangibles.

"You're still planning on going tonight?" Cummins asked.

Smith nodded. "We ain't got no other choice. The training's supposed to start tomorrow. We're supposed to be taking Cherrie and Chad into town tonight to stay at the hotel."

"What are we going to do about the safe?"

Smith drew deeply on the cigarette and let the

smoke drift out of his mouth with his next words. "Only Keller and the Colonel supposed to know the combination. Guess I'm going to have to make one or the other of them give it to us."

Having seen Smith in action in the lock-up, Cummins knew the man's physical prowess but Keller was physically bigger and looked just as tough. Plus, he was armed with that massive Desert Eagle. It might be easier to force Best to comply but that would be equally risky and he had a sidearm as well.

But if Smith and Keller and Riley all cancelled each other out, it would leave a free path to grab the kid and the hillbilly queen and sneak away through this secret tunnel Smith had mentioned.

"So are you going to clue me in on the secret passageway?" Cummins said.

"Sure," Smith said. "Come on."

They walked about forty feet down the street to one of the few buildings that remained intact. It was a solid-looking, three-story brick structure and actually had a solid wooden door that was still operational.

Or, as Cummins saw as they drew closer, what seemed to be operational. When they got there, Smith took one more drag on the cigarette and tossed it down. He grabbed the edges of the door and lifted it up and out. It had merely been wedged into place in the door frame. He stepped through the opening and motioned for Cummins to follow him through the first floor. A large staircase was off to the left and the midmorning sun filtered in through the sections of barren windows and sent beams of sunlight dappling over a floor that had been swept relatively clean. Some piles of broken bricks and smashed wooden timbers were piled off to one side but the room was in better shape than Cummins would have imagined.

Smith pointed to another door, this one metal and obviously in working order, that was on the back wall.

"On the other side of that wall's another room," Smith said. "Looks like a loading dock. Secured by a big overhead door."

They came to another pile of what appeared to be stacks of rippled fiberglass panels. Smith stopped and squatted down.

"Grab that other end there," he said. "It ain't heavy."

A couple of small lizards scurried off the fiberglass as Cummins reached down to lift it. After putting the stack aside, Cummins saw a hinged, stainless steel door fitted into a triangular cement base. A keyed handle, shiny as a new nickel, was centered halfway down the left side.

"You got to unlock it from the other side," Smith said, grinning. "There's a ladder that goes down to a flat area next to the ramp that's connected to the tunnel. There's another set of doors so you can't see the ramp unless you know it's there. The tunnel's about thirty feet down and it's big enough to drive a fucking pickup truck through. Goes all the way back to the bunker."

"The bunker?"

"Yep." Smith pulled out another cigarette and lit it up, blowing out a wispy haze of smoke as he continued. "Back in the day, when the fort was operational, they built this underground bunker. It was for the command staff in case of a nuclear emergency. There was an engineering company stationed here and they were told to do all the construction work. A couple of them got this idea to extend the tunnel all the way over to here, so they could sneak shit in and out of the fort undetected." Smith's lips curled back over his teeth in a smirk. "You know, black market stuff to sell, as well as bringing booze and whores in and out." He waved his arms at the empty building. "That's what this place was before, back in the day. A whorehouse."

Cummins looked around, trying to imagine the place in its heyday.

"And the tunnel's still there?" he asked.

Smith nodded. "It's built like a brick shithouse."

"It's got to be a long hike all that ways," Cummins said, moving to the window and looking out toward the very distant fort.

"It's a ways, all right, even to the bunker," Smith said. "But our lazy-ass colonel's got some golf carts that he keeps down there. Shouldn't take us that long at all."

And it would be a lot easier to transport Cherrie and the kid in a damn golf cart than pulling them both along on foot.

"Where's the entrance to this bunker?" Cummins asked.

Smith took one last drag on the cigarette and tossed it through the door as a larger lizard scaled the empty doorjamb.

"You know that big auditorium building where you took the oath?" he said.

Cummins nodded.

"It's in the basement," Smith said, with a crafty smile. "Right next to the fucking vault. There's a sliding metal door underneath the stairs. I'll show ya when we get back."

Cummins smiled and nodded.

Things were starting to take shape. All he had to do now was time it so that he could get hold of Wolf and have him bring that damn bandito here.

***

The Pittsfield Building
Phoenix, Arizona

The drive through the night from Bendover had taken them a little less than fifteen hours, which they'd done in shifts so no one got overly tired. They'd stopped for food one time, for gas twice, and once again along the freeway to allow Zeus, aka Booker Nobles, to empty his bladder while standing by the side of the road. Wolf temporarily removed the handcuffs but left the leg irons on. Nobles had complained that he couldn't urinate while Wolf and McNamara were watching.

"That's something you better get used to, where you're going," McNamara said. "Now get to it or we'll zip you up in one of them body-bags and let you piss all over yourself."

"You can't do that," Nobles said. "It's against the law."

"Listen, asshole," McNamara said. "Right now, I am the law. Now either complete your business or I'll tie your fucking body in a knot and say you got shot trying to escape."

Something in Mac's tone convinced Nobles to be cooperative. He was able to successfully urinate and was meek and mild for the rest of the trip.

After arriving back in Phoenix in the early afternoon, they'd called Manny who met them at Central Detention to assist in getting the bond revocation recorded when they dropped off the prisoner. Ms. Dolly announced that the P-Patrol had a couple pressing engagements back in Vegas and Wolf and McNamara agreed to drop them off at the airport and send them their portion of the recovery fee and reward bonus later. All of them were feeling exhausted.

"I know y'all are good for it, sugar," Ms. Dolly said.

Wolf had more that he wanted to say to Yolanda, like asking her to stay and spend a few days with him but before he could ask, he got the first phone call. It was from that lawyer named Soraces asking that Wolf stop by the law offices of Bailey and Lugget on "a matter of mutual concern and great importance."

Wolf agreed, more out of curiosity than anything else, and McNamara agreed to drop him off and then stop back to pick him up after he'd dropped the girls off. His goodbye kiss to Yolanda has been little more than perfunctory due to the audience watching but they made the most of it.

Best be careful, McNamara had subsequently texted him after he'd dropped him off in front of the Pittsfield Building. *Or you'll end up getting serious with that gal.*

She's way out of my league, Wolf texted back, set his phone on vibrate, and went inside the building to check the legend. His thoughts once again turned to his bleak financial situation and the lack of anything tangible in his life. It was foolish to think he could go on sponging off Mac's largess forever. He owed the man way too much as it was, and being an ex-con with DD from the military left him with few options. At this point, there was little he could offer a high-maintenance girl like Yolanda.

Bailey and Lugget were in suite 402. Wolf pressed

the button for the elevator and when the doors open he got in.

Here goes nothing, he thought.

The pretty receptionist at the law firm gave Wolf the once-over as she pressed a button on her phone and whispered into it that "Mr. Wolf" was here. She hung up and stood, giving him ample time to appreciate her svelte figure in the tight-fitting business attire. Wolf had to admit that everything about the office area looked first class. After ushering him down a hallway which had frosted glass doors and fine mahogany frames, she paused, knocked, and opened one of them. She stepped in and to the side, allowing Wolf to enter.

Richard Soraces looked to be in his late forties as he rose from behind a large desk, his back to an expansive window affording a pleasant view of downtown Phoenix. His blond hair was long and swept back, showing a bit of curl and some artistic and expert coiffing. The charcoal gray suit hung somewhat loosely on his frame, indicating that he had a rather slender build but his grip was firm and strong as they shook hands. He flashed a flawless smile that was either the result of expert orthodontics or dazzling veneers.

"Ah, the elusive Mr. Wolf," he said. "We meet at last."

He held his hand out toward the chair positioned in front of the desk.

As Wolf took a seat, the receptionist asked if they

needed anything.

"Coffee?" Soraces asked.

Wolf, who was actually feeling like he could use some, shook his head.

Soraces dismissed the receptionist and leaned forward, his elbows on the top of the glass covering of the desk. Stacks of paper were all arranged in symmetrical stacks, each seemingly placed at exact separations. Wolf saw a double-framed photograph off to the left side and since his chair was positioned in the center, he caught a glimpse of the photo. It was an apparent family photo, showing a man, a woman, two children, and a dog. The man in the photo didn't resemble Soraces.

"You're a hard man to get ahold of," Soraces said. "I appreciate you coming in."

"I move around a lot," Wolf said, still trying to size the man up.

"Sort of the embodiment of the peripatetic bounty hunter, eh?" Soraces said and flashed the smile again. When he saw that Wolf didn't react, it faded and his tongue flicked over his lips. "I know you're a busy man, and so am I, so if you don't mind, I'll cut right to the chase."

"I don't mind," Wolf said.

"First, let me say that I'm not from this area." The smile reappeared. "I saw you looking at the picture on the desk. Actually, I'm employed by another law firm back East. I'm here on a special assignment, under the largess of Bailey and Lugget."

"So you work for Fallotti and Abraham?" Wolf asked, tossing out one the mystery names that he knew. He was keen to see the other man's reaction but it was flat and unexpressive.

"No," Soraces said. "I'm based in Maryland but I have done occasional work for Mr. Fallotti in the past. I believe his firm was recently dissolved."

Wolf nodded. The guy was sharp and observant. Wolf waited for him to continue.

"I have been retained by a client, who wishes to remain anonymous," Soraces said. "To approach you about a matter of certain delicacy."

"Anonymous?" Wolf said. "Why's that?"

"He has his reasons, which will become clear shortly. It has to do with a certain piece of property that he wishes to acquire. He's willing to pay a substantial amount for its acquisition."

It had to be the bandito and the anonymous client had to be that Von Dien character. Maybe this would provide some answers.

"What property?" Wolf asked. "I think he has me mixed up with someone else. I don't have very much."

Soraces lifted an eyebrow. "Perhaps the word property was not the best choice of words. It's actually an item you acquired during your trip to Mexico."

"The bandito."

"Ah, it's refreshing to deal with a man who doesn't mince words."

This run-around was starting to wear thin. Wolf was tired and he wanted answers but it was obvious this guy wouldn't be giving out any unless he was prodded.

"It's a pretty sought-after item," Wolf said, deciding to take the initiative. "But I'm sure you already know that."

"Indeed. And since you seem to be a man of action, shall we discuss price?"

"Not quite yet," Wolf said. "Why does your client want this bandito?"

Soraces waited the customary few beats before answering. "He didn't say."

"Any ideas?"

Again, the customary two- or three-second pause before answering: "I'm not in the business of speculating. My only role is to try to facilitate an agreement and acquisition. Now, am I correct in assuming you have this item in your possession?"

Wolf took his time answering and decided to be just as evasive. "A lot of people seem to think so."

Soraces sighed. "We seem to be backtracking into the avenues of evasiveness. My client is aware that you've come under severe hardship over the past few weeks. He wants you to know that although he regrets what has happened, he had no knowledge of or participation in any of it. It was the result of unscrupulous individuals seeking to take advantage of both you and him."

Unscrupulous individuals?

Give me a break, Wolf thought.

"And," Soraces continued, "he's willing to pay you substantial damages, no questions asked, for the inconvenience you've suffered."

"I'd hardly call two attempts on my life an inconvenience."

Soraces raised his eyebrows once again. "Nor would he. And while he does not in any way want to suggest culpability brought on by these rogue elements, he is open to paying substantial reparations, in addition to a finder's reward."

This was getting interesting. Wolf was pretty sure he could keep fencing with his guy all day and not get more than a whole lot more double-talk but he wanted to see just how far "the client" was willing to go.

"I'm listening," he said.

"I'm authorized to do a reparations fund transfer to your bank account today, as a show of good faith."

"A reparations fund transfer?" Wolf felt slightly amused at the verbiage.

"Shall we say, fifty thousand dollars?" Soraces canted his head slightly and Wolf knew the lawyer was trying to gauge his reaction. Wolf did his best not to show him one.

"Fifty thousand dollars for two attempts on my life?"

"Yes, that does seem a bit paltry, doesn't it?" Soraces smiled again. "Why don't we raise it to say ... a hundred thousand?"

Wolf had to consciously stop himself from showing any reaction whatsoever. This was either a real lucrative, no questions asked deal or one hell of a setup.

Soraces picked up a cellphone from the desktop and waggled it.

"If I may have your preferred bank account number I'll have the money there in an hour. Again, this is a show of good faith. We can discuss adding the finder's fee later."

Wolf was tempted. After all he'd been through, giving up some stupid plaster statue for that amount of money seemed like a no brainer but there was more to it than that. Someone had tried to kill him twice and he still had no total understanding of why. Plus, there was the little matter of what was inside the bandito. He wanted answers more than money and an assurance that he would stop being a target. But he was bush-leaguer compared to these guys ... a welterweight in the ring with the heavyweight champ. They knew who he was, and seemingly everything about him, and he was still punching at shadows. Treading cautiously was the best course now, especially as tired as he was.

"Let me think about it," he said.

The space between Soraces's eyebrows formed into twin creases.

"We have more to offer, Mr. Wolf." He waggled the cell phone again. "And I'm not just talking about money." He pressed a few buttons on the smart phone, then rotated the screen toward Wolf. "We're also offering something worth much, much more."

A frozen video hung on the screen. Soraces punched another button and it sprang to life as an obese man sat at a table obviously engaged in a conversation with an unseen party. The obese man was Jack Cummins.

"Sure, we set him up over there," Cummins said. "But that was Eagan's doing, not mine. Him and Nasim were the ones that killed those ragheads."

The image disappeared.

Wolf was stunned.

A confession by the man he was seeking ... This was all tied not only to the debacle in Mexico but to four years ago in Iraq as well. A confession that could be the proof that could provide exculpatory evidence and maybe get him a new trial, get his conviction tossed out. It was a chance to clear his name.

He felt a surge of anxiety as his heart sped up. This was it—the Holy Grail, but there had to be a catch.

You've seen the bait, he thought, but don't swallow

the hook just yet.

Soraces sat there with a triumphant grin on his face. He'd obviously played what he thought was going to be the trump card.

"Well, Mr. Wolf? I'm told that this was only a taste. Believe me, I've been authorized to tell you that the entire video would get you completely exonerated. I'd be available to prepare an appeal to your conviction, introduce this new, exculpatory evidence." He canted his head to the side and shrugged in a nonchalant manner. "A new trial would be a given. Most likely we'd be looking at an outright dismissal. Imagine, clearing your name, a reinstatement of all rank and benefits, not to mention a lucrative wrongful conviction suit which I'd also gladly handle for you." Soraces brandished the phone as if he were holding a bar of gold.

"Well," he said. "What do you say?"

It was like a dream come true but Wolf was still a bit mistrustful. Why the sudden overture to play let's make a deal after two failed attempts on his life? Was it true that the client, whom Wolf figured had to be that Von Dien character, wanted to pay him off? Or would the ultimate payoff come in the form of a jacketed hollow point?

This whole scenario was skewed. Wolf knew he wasn't dealing from a position of strength and didn't like it. Hell, it wasn't even a level playing field. He had the bandito, but his adversaries had all the money and power at their disposal. It left him feeling powerless and more than just a little angry.

Wolf was about to speak when his cell phone chirped with a text. He pressed a button and saw it was from Mac.

TROUBLE. YOU AVAILABLE? 9 1 1

The 9 1 1 after the message was their personal signal for something really serious and requiring immediate attention. Wolf pocketed the phone and stood up.

"You've given me a lot to think about," he said, turning toward the door. "I'll get back to you."

Soraces looked confused. It was clear that he hadn't expected this reaction.

"But," he said. "Our proposal…"

"I'll have to get back to you, Mr. Soraces," Wolf said. "Something's come up."

Soraces nodded, compressing his lips. His nostrils flared a bit and he asked for Wolf's bank account information.

"At least let my client follow through with that show of good faith on my client's part to show our commitment," he said. "May I have a bank routing and account number?"

Wolf considered the offer and thought, why not? There was next to nothing in it anyway. He took his bank card out of his wallet and read off the routing and savings numbers. It was amusing to watch Soraces scramble to find a piece of paper and a pen before scribbling them down.

"Look for the deposits by this afternoon," Soraces said. "Reparation showing our remorse over your pain and suffering and as a show of our good faith."

Wolf nodded and extended his hand. As they shook, Wolf's cell chimed again.

YOU THERE? 9 1 1

On the way, he thought, and wondered what this was all about.

***

Fort Lemand,
Southern Arizona

Both Smith and Cummins immediately knew something was wrong when they were denied access by the state police to get on the main highway from the access road from the ghost town. Rather than stop and get an explanation from the trooper, Smith wheeled the Malibu into a U turn and sped back toward the ghost town.

"What the hell's that all about?" Cummins asked.

"Who knows," Smith said. "But I ain't about to stick around and find out. We can get in the back gate."

But as they approached the macadamized road

leading to the rear entrance of the fort, they saw a column of military-style vehicles and dark sedans moving toward them from the opposite direction.

"What the fuck?" Smith said and stomped on the accelerator. They arrived at the back gate and skidded to a stop. The gate guard made no move to exit the gate shack and open it for them. In fact, he peeped up from the window and pointed an AR-15 in their direction.

"Shit," Smith said. "Everybody gone nuts or something?"

He swung the door open and got out with slow deliberation, keeping his hands elevated.

"Hey," he shouted. "It's us. Smittie and Cummins. Open the fucking gate, would ya?"

The gate guard picked up a telephone and began speaking into it.

Cummins couldn't control himself any longer and pushed the car door open. He leaned forward and vomited copiously. Everything he'd had for breakfast, the toast, the powdered eggs, the coffee, came roiling up from his stomach and out through his mouth. When he'd finished, he wiped his mouth with his fingers, and then wiped those on the seat of the Malibu, hoping that Smith wouldn't notice. Cummins was glad to see Smith had stepped closer to the gate shack and was now engaged in a conversation with the guard. He'd lowered his hands and came back to the front of the Malibu.

"Come on," he said. "He's under strict orders not to open the gate. We gotta leave my car here for now."

Cummins managed to extricate himself from the vehicle and step around the puddle of vomit. He slammed the door and joined Smith by the fence.

"What's going on?" he asked.

"Don't know," Smith said. "Could be another one of the colonel's bullshit alerts or something. He gets a hair up his ass every once in a while but I don't like the looks of them other vehicles we seen, neither."

The gate guard walked over and stuck a key into the heavy-duty security lock. It was one of those massive locks that was about the size of a pint-sized water bottle with a hasp that dropped inside leaving little area on the hasp that could be cut. The guard looked young, maybe eighteen or nineteen, and totally wide-eyed and petrified. It was plain to see he was scared.

Cummins wondered again what the hell was going on.

"You're both to report to the auditorium at once," the gate guard said. "By order of Colonel Best."

Oh, my God, Cummins thought.

Had their little escape plan been discovered?

***

The McNamara Ranch
Phoenix, Arizona

McNamara was waiting, double-parked in front of the office building when Wolf pushed through the doors and Mac took off as soon as Wolf slid inside. The expression on his face was one of tension and concern.

"Trouble?" Wolf asked. The adrenaline was kicking in and he felt the fatigue vanish.

McNamara nodded. "Kase called." He darted around several vehicles, then made a sweeping right turn in front of a line of cars stopped at a red light.

"What'd she say?" Wolf asked, buckling himself in.

McNamara passed two vehicles and zoomed down the roadway.

"Only that she needed us home right away," McNamara said. "And that the FBI was there."

"The FBI?"

Wolf tried to assess this new information.

What was this all about?

He knew they were investigating the recent shooting at the Ranch and also Franker and Turner still had their ongoing investigation of the murders of the American citizens in Mexico. But he'd gotten the impression that Franker was going to let the clock run out of that one because Wolf had warned him of the pending danger prior to the South African mercenary shooting incident. Maybe he'd read the FBI man wrong.

Time will tell, he thought. If we make it there, that is.

"I hope to hell they ain't serving a search warrant or something," McNamara said as his eyes darted back and forth between the mirrors and the road ahead. "They're liable to find my weapons stash."

Wolf hoped not too but he really had little to hide at the ranch.

"Like you always say," Wolf said. "Let's not worry about something until we know exactly what we have to worry about."

McNamara was breaking all speed records for city driving and had apparently thrown the Rules of the Road book into the toilet.

They arrived in record time, scarcely fifteen minutes after Wolf had exited the building. He thought about making a joke about Mac doing the flying the next time they had to go somewhere out of state but Wolf kept his mouth shut. They'd hardly spoken at all on the ride back and he figured that was the way McNamara wanted it.

As they got out of the Escalade they saw a solitary navy-blue Crown Vic parked next to Kasey's car.

No SWAT Bearcat, Wolf thought. And only one sedan. Last time they had three cars.

He took it as a positive sign.

McNamara grabbed Wolf's arm and said, "Remember, we don't say shit to them without a lawyer. That guy Soraces seem like a possibility?"

"He's sharp," Wolf said, "but definitely not on our side."

They practically ran to the front door and McNamara thrust his key in the lock, only to find the door open. He burst through and there was Kasey, a box of tissues on her lap, with two FBI agents in blue suits, one standing, one sitting, next to her.

"What's going on here?" McNamara said, striding over to them.

Kasey jumped up, the tissue box tumbling to the floor, as she ran to her father's embrace.

Wolf could see that her face was red and pinched looking. She'd been crying.

"Oh, dad," she said. "They're here about Charlie. He's into something awful. And he's got Chad."

The seated agent stood and produced his badge case with his gold shield and ID card.

"Mr. McNamara," the agent said. "I'm Special Agent Decker. This is my partner, Agent Vincent. We work in Special Operations, the bank robbery detail."

Bank robbery, Wolf thought. What the hell's going on?

Both of them looked to be mid-thirties with slender builds and short-cropped hair. Decker appeared to be the senior of the two.

"What do you guys want?" McNamara said. "And

what the hell did you say that upset my daughter?"

Before the agents could respond, Kasey unburied her head from her father's massive shoulder and said, "No, dad, no. They've been very nice. It's Charlie. They think he's involved in that armored truck robbery the other day."

Wolf had heard a brief mention of that on the news but the details had been vague. It was only noted because the two armored car guards had been murdered.

"You might have seen it on the news," Decker said. "It happened Saturday night..." "What's this about my no-good ex-son-n-law being involved?" McNamara asked. Kasey had reburied her face in his shoulder and he softly patted her shoulders.

The two agents looked at each other, then Decker resumed talking.

"I'm afraid we've found some evidence linking him to the crime, sir. Would you happen to know his whereabouts?"

"Don't call me 'sir.' I work for a living," McNamara said.

Wolf figured he was using the old army NCO refrain to buy a few seconds of time.

"What kind of evidence?" he asked.

Agent Decker shook his head. "I'm not at liberty to discuss the particulars but I'm afraid it's pretty compelling. That's why it's imperative that we locate Mr. Riley as soon as possible."

"You check that piece of shit trailer park?" McNamara asked.

Decker nodded. "Apparently, he's moved out of there. Your daughter said that he has their son and was purportedly going to the Grand Canyon?"

"I already told you, he was lying," Kasey said, easing away from her father. "I don't think he went there at all. I checked with all the hotels in the area and he wasn't at any of them."

Mac held her hand and she resumed her seat on the sofa.

"I gave them his phone number, too," she said. "And the number of Chad's phone."

Decker gave a slight acknowledging nod to her and continued to address McNamara. "Any idea where he might have gone? Whom he might be with?"

McNamara shook his head slowly. "All I can think of now is that he has my grandson with him."

"So your daughter's told us," Decker said. "We'll see that the local authorities place an Amber Alert for the child's safe return."

"We went looking for him at the trailer park the other day," Wolf said, figuring neither Mac nor Kasey was thinking clearly enough to give information to the FBI. "There was a guy in the adjacent trailer that seemed to know him. Name's Roger D. Smith. Drives a black Malibu."

The two agents made eye contact again. Decker

nodded but made no effort to write the information down.

Either the guy's got a photographic memory, Wolf thought, or they already know that.

Decker shifted his shoulders a bit and Wolf got the impression that this interview had run its course. The FBI man took a card out of his breast shirt pocket and handed it to McNamara.

"Sir," he said. "I know how stressful this must be but are you sure you don't have any idea of your son-in-law's whereabouts."

"He's my ex-son-in-law," Mac said, his voice a low growl. "And if I did have, do you think I'd be standing here?"

Decker's head tilted to the side. "Mr. McNamara, believe me, the best thing to do, if you do receive any information as to his whereabouts, is to contact the Bureau." He handed the card to Mac, who made no effort to touch it.

"The son of a bitch is out on bond," McNamara said. "And now he's robbing and killing people, and he's got my grandson with him."

Decker compressed his lips and nodded. "I understand how disconcerting this is. That's why—"

"You guys must know more than you're telling," McNamara said. "Tell me what you know and I'll track him down myself."

"That wouldn't be a good idea, sir," Decker said.

"Don't you listen?" McNamara said. "He's got my grandson."

"And the Bureau will do everything it can to make sure the boy is recovered safely," Decker said.

"If we call him," Wolf said, "can you triangulate off the phones?"

Decker raised an eyebrow.

"We're already doing something of the sort," he said. "It would be better if you'd refrain from trying to take any action yourselves at this point. If you do hear from him, urge him to turn himself in and contact us." He offered the card to McNamara, who now accepted it.

"You said you'd do one of them Amber Alert things?" Mac said.

"We'll look into having that done immediately, sir," Decker said. He and his partner repeated the admonishments they'd already given and headed for the door.

Decker seems like a consummate professional, Wolf thought.

Once they'd left, Kasey burst into tears.

"Oh, my God, dad," she said. "He's got Chad. What are we going to do?"

Mac shook his head and said nothing.

For the second time that day, Wolf felt powerless and angry and he liked it even less this time. There was way more at stake.

About ten minutes later, the phone on Kasey's desk rang and she jumped up and ran to answer it, saying, "Maybe that's him."

At the desk, she stopped and glanced down at the Caller ID screen. She looked up at Wolf.

"It's blocked," she said.

Wolf strode over to the desk and picked up the phone, answering with the standard, "Trackdown, Incorporated."

For a few seconds, there was nothing but silence, then, "That you, Wolf?"

It was Cummins. Wolf was sure of it.

What a time for this to happen.

"Yes," Wolf said. "Who's this?"

"I think you know the answer to that, soldier," Cummins said. "Don't you?"

"Look, Cummins," Wolf said. "Give me a number where I can reach you and I'll call you back. Something's come up here and—"

"And I bet I know what it is. He's about two-and-a-half feet tall, with blond hair and blue eyes, and answers to the name of Chad. Right?"

Wolf felt like somebody had struck him in the gut with a baseball bat. His reply came out in a hoarse whisper.

"What are you talking about?"

"Simple," Cummins said. "I'll trade you the kid for the bandito statue."

"What?"

"Cut the shit," Cummins said. "And listen real good. Give me a cell phone number where I can reach you and only you. No feds, no cops, nothing. Be ready for me to call you back with the details of the deal. And bring me the bandito from Mexico."

Wolf repeated his personal cell phone number.

After a moment, Cummins came back on the line. "Okay, like I said, wait for my call. No cops, otherwise, you'll never see the kid again, Understand?"

"You touch him, motherfucker, and I'll kill you," Wolf said.

Peripherally, he saw Mac and Kasey look up.

"Like I said, spare me the threats," Cummins said. "I don't want the kid to get hurt any more than you do but it's all contingent on me getting what I need, no questions asked."

"What do you need?" Wolf said but he already knew what Cummins meant.

"Yeah. The bandito. Just be ready to deliver it to me, safe and sound, if you ever want to see the kid again."

He hung up and Wolf kept staring at the phone.

"Steve?" Kasey said. "Who was it? Did he say something about Chad?"

Wolf turned to her, the feeling that somehow, someway, he was responsible for this whole mess, and it burned in his gut like a red-hot phosphorous round.

***

Fort Lemand
Southern Arizona

The auditorium had what appeared to be the full complement of twenty-eight men, minus the gate guards, on hand. Two men stood at the entrance doors with AR-15s. As Cummins shuffled in behind Smith, he saw Colonel Best, dressed in a set of camouflaged BDUs, addressing the group from a podium up front. Two more guards, each wearing holstered side-arms, stood on either side of the podium. Cummins and Smith took a seat at the back. Even from a distance of about forty feet, Cummins could see that Best's face was glistening with sweat and huge circular rings of wetness encompassed each armpit. Keller was standing beside him, wearing a similar camouflaged outfit with a black baseball hat. He looked exceptionally grim. His eyes locked on Smith and Cummins as they sat. Riley, Cherrie, and Chad sat about three rows ahead of them.

"The hour of governmental tyranny is apparently upon us," Best said. "Their unwelcome unlawful presence has been observed in front of our compound. Although they have yet to make their intentions clear, we must stand ready to defend ourselves should the situation require it." He paused and licked his lips.

"We have two civilians in our midst and they will be confined to quarters immediately, for their own safety. As of now, Base Freedom is on full alert. Every man is to report to the armory and draw his weapon and ammunition. Then form up in the court yard to receive your orders for maintaining the perimeter. Remember, we, the people, are well within our Constitutional rights of assembly here and we have broken no laws. Maintain strict fire discipline and stand ready until such time that you receive the order to do otherwise." He turned his head.

"Captain Keller," Best said.

Keller stepped forward said in a loud voice, "Sergeant Cassidy, prepare to dismiss the men."

A barrel-chested man with chevrons at the corner of the podium stood and called the group to attention and then issued the order to fall out. Cummins stood and was frantically trying to figure his next move as he and Smith waited for Riley, Cherrie, and Chad to make their way to them.

"You got any ideas what's going on?" Smith asked Riley as he approached.

"None," Riley said. "Unless they fingered us for that armored car thing."

Cherrie asked what she was supposed to do in her whiny voice.

"Riley, Smith, Cummins," Keller yelled out. "Get over here."

Cummins saw Smith's brow crease as they waited for the rest of the group to filter by and then made their way up toward the front.

Why were the three of them being singled out?

This couldn't be good.

CHAPTER 11

The McNamara Ranch
Phoenix, Arizona

Wolf watched through the window as the dark sedan pulled up and parked next to the Escalade. It looked like Franker was by himself and Wolf felt slightly encouraged that the FBI agent had abided by Wolf's request to come alone. He'd taken Franker at his word when he'd said he felt he owed Wolf something and it was time to cash in if possible, although the agent looked a bit tentative walking toward the door. Wolf strode over and opened it.

"Special Agent Franker," he said, extending his hand. "Thanks for coming."

The FBI man's expression remained neutral but he shook Wolf's hand.

Wolf closed the door behind him and reintroduced

Mac and Kasey.

After Franker and McNamara shook hands, the four of them stood in a moment of awkward silence.

"I was a tad confused, Mr. Wolf," Franker said finally. "Your call was unexpected and I'm not accustomed to being told to come alone."

"Hey, call me Steve, okay." Wolf swallowed, trying to figure the best way to handle this request.

"Okay, Steve," Franker said. "What exactly do you want?"

Wolf glanced at McNamara, who nodded.

"Look," Wolf said. "I know we've been less than cooperative regarding your investigation of the Mexico thing."

Franker smiled. "You have a talent for understatement."

"Yeah," Wolf said. "And I'm willing to talk more about that. To help you with that investigation but something else has come up that's way more important."

"Oh?" Franker raised both eyebrows. The rest of his face showed an amused expression. He clearly felt he had the upper hand.

"Some of your fellow agents were here a little while ago," Wolf said.

Franker nodded. "I know."

Wolf figured as much. It would be a given that the bank robbery detail would want to gather as much info on the family of any persons of interest before interviewing them.

"My ex-husband is a suspect in an armored car robbery," Kasey said.

"I know that too, Ms. Riley," Franker said.

He was playing it cool, not offering anything in the way of information.

"The other agents mentioned they had evidence that linked him to the crime," Wolf said. "We gave them all the information we had, including two phone numbers, but they wouldn't tell us anything more."

"That's standard Bureau procedure," Franker said, giving his head a little toss. "I'm afraid I can't tell you anything about—"

"They got my grandson," McNamara said.

Franker stared at him. "Your grandson? There's an Amber Alert for missing and possibly endangered for the boy."

"He's been kidnapped," Wolf said.

"What?" Franker said. "How do you know this? From what I heard, it sounded more like a custody dispute."

Wolf mentally noted that the various teams of FBI agents had obviously been comparing notes on him, Mac, and now Kasey.

"We received a ransom call," Wolf said.

"A ransom call?" Franker's brow furrowed. "For how much?"

Wolf shook his head.

The fed frowned. "I came here in good faith because you said you had something to discuss for our mutual benefit. This cooperation you're seeking can't be a one-way street."

Wolf glanced at McNamara, who was standing there shaking his head.

"It wasn't for money," Wolf said. "Let's just say, I've got something he wants."

"He?" The FBI man heaved a theatrical sigh. "Do you have any idea who made this call?"

"Yeah. Jack Cummins. You remember him?"

Franker thought for a moment, then nodded. "He was the one we saw leaving here the night of the shooting incident. Phoenix PD stopped him and found a gun in the van he was driving."

"Right," Wolf said. "He was one of the guys that set me up in Iraq. For killing those Iraqi nationals. He was in MI."

"MI?" Franker said.

"Military Intelligence." Wolf was feeling frantic and didn't know how to explain things. He blew out a breath. "Look, you'll have to take my word for this. He's involved in this whole thing somehow. He's with Charles Riley, Kasey's ex, and they've got her son."

Franker's brow wrinkled. "I'm not following this. You're saying that the boy's biological father is holding him for ransom?"

"We're not sure how it all fits together at this point but like I said, Cummins called here with a ransom demand. He's got to be with Riley, who's wanted in connection with that robbery/murder. There's another guy named Smith who's part of it, too."

"Roger D. Smith," Franker said. "A known associate of your ex-husband, ma'am."

Wolf felt slightly encouraged that Franker had offered some information.

"Okay," he said. "We've leveled with you. What else can you tell us?"

Franker said nothing.

"Look, we got to find them," McNamara said. "You guys have the telemetry to trace those cell phones, don't you? Can't you at least give us something as to where they might be?"

Franker was still silent, staring at the floor.

"Please," Kasey said. Her tone was imploring.

"You said you owed me," Wolf said, his tone edging on desperation. "For that night of the shooting. For saving your life."

The FBI man compressed his lips, almost as if he were biting the inside of them. He took in a deep breath.

"Smith and your ex-husband are purported members of a militia group," Franker said. "They call themselves The Freedom Brigade. They've been on the Bureau's radar for some time. They're led by a disgraced army officer named Timothy Herald Best. He was drummed out of the service five years ago for smuggling and black-market issues overseas. He was a captain at the time and dropped out of sight. He's since resurfaced and started the Freedom Brigade. Promoted himself to colonel."

"I know the type," McNamara said. "One of those officers that wasn't worth a shit."

Franker nodded in agreement.

"As I mentioned," he continued. "He's been on our watch list for a while. He's set up an informal camp in an old abandoned army base down state. Calls it Base Freedom."

"What old army base?" McNamara asked. "I don't remember one down there."

"And you probably wouldn't," Franker said. "It's been closed for decades. Once was called Fort Lemand."

McNamara nodded his head slightly. "Now that rings a bell but it's a little one."

"So you think Riley might be down there?" Wolf asked.

Franker did a minute shrug, seemed to be reticent about saying more, and then relented.

"Ms. Riley," he said. "I can tell you that your ex-husband was definitely involved in that armored car robbery and murder. We found a discarded bandage at the initial crime scene and the DNA matched your ex. Then, at a secondary scene, we found a cell phone that was traced back to you."

"To me?" Kasey said.

Franker nodded.

"You purchased it, according to the store records, and it showed that you also called the number from here."

"Oh my God," Kasey said, her face scrunching up. "It's got to be the phone I gave to Chad. For him to call me every night."

Tears began to stream from her eyes.

"And you think Riley's down at this Base Freedom place now?" Wolf asked.

"We're not sure," Franker said. "We do know that in addition to finding the cell phone at the secondary crime scene, a construction site security camera recorded a U-Haul truck violating the posted speed limit in a construction work zone near this second crime scene. The truck was rented in Desolation City, near to where this Base Freedom is. And it was rented by Louis J. Keller, who is also a known militia member."

"That's got to be it," Wolf said. "Cummins is somehow involved in the militia, too."

"Cummins posted bond for himself and Roger D. Smith," Franker said. "Apparently, they met in the county lockup."

"Well, my grandson's probably being held at that place," McNamara said. "Where's it at exactly?"

Franker held up his open palms in a calming gesture.

"Mr. McNamara, you don't want to go down there, believe me."

"The hell I don't."

"Sir, let the Bureau handle things. The best thing to do, at this point, is to remain here. I'll get a team in here to monitor your phone lines and we'll wait for them to contact you."

"You expect me to sit on my hands when my grandson's life's at stake?"

Franker compressed his lips again as if he was holding something back.

Wolf sensed this and said, "What is it you're not telling us?"

It took Franker a few seconds of hesitation and consideration before he replied.

"Look," he said. "As I mentioned, the Bureau's been watching this group for a while, waiting for a chance to move in. Connecting them to this robbery/murder was all that we needed. A team of agents and SWAT are already in the process of hitting them with a search warrant."

"Do they know my grandson's in there?"

"I'll make that notification immediately, sir," Franker said and took out his cell phone. "And I will have to run these new developments by my supervisor."

Wolf, McNamara, and Kasey all exchanged looks.

Things had gone from bad to worse in one hell of a hurry.

***

Fort Lemand
Southern Arizona

Cummins watched as Riley towed his kid to the front of the auditorium against the steady flow of the thirty or so militia men who were filtering back toward the exits. The kid didn't look too happy and kept getting jostled by those passing. Finally, Riley stooped and picked him up to avoid any further problems. Cherrie and Smith were ahead of him as well and Cherrie was whispering something to him. She looked about as thrilled as the kid did. Getting the boy alone might turn out to be more of a problem than anticipated. But then again, if the five of them were able to escape the compound via that secret tunnel, the opportunity could present itself more readily. The key would be in persuading Wolf to give him the bandito in exchange for information as to where the kid was being held. It seemed doable.

They stopped at the front of the auditorium where Best still stood on the elevated platform looking down at them. Being close to the edge of the podium, they all had to look up at him. Keller and two armed guards stood off to one side.

"These two guards will escort the woman and the boy to quarters," Best said. "Where they will be confined immediately, for their own safety."

"Let's go," one of the guards said.

"Not so fast," Riley said. "I want to take my boy there myself."

"You'll do as you're ordered," Keller said.

"Daddy," Chad said. "I don't want to go nowhere. I want to stay with you."

"Easy, Chad," Riley said, still holding the boy.

"I suggest you get your son under control, Private Riley," Keller said. "We're pressed for time."

"Time?" Riley said. "It ain't gonna take no time at all for me to walk him over there, is it?"

"Nevertheless," Best said. "I need to talk to the three of you privately. Ms. Engel, if you would take charge of the child, these men will escort you to your quarters."

Cherrie looked at Smith, who appeared almost livid. She leaned forward and kissed him on the lips, then turned to Riley.

"I'll take good care of him," she said and gently removed the boy from his father's arms. "Hey, Chad, let's you and me go back to the room and play a game, okay?"

Tears streamed down the kid's face and he said,

"No. I don't want to."

"Hush, boy," Riley said. "And do what you're told. Don't you be giving Cherrie no hard time, neither. I'll be there in a bit."

This seemed to quiet the boy, at least temporarily. As they walked away with the two guards following, Cummins noticed that Best had walked over to the three steps to descend from the podium. When he got closer, Cummins could smell the crisp and pungent body odor the man was radiating. It smelled like tension mixed with fear. His eyes darted toward Keller momentarily and then Best spoke in a low tone.

"Have any of you talked to any of the other men about the procurement mission?"

Procurement mission?

Cummins almost had to laugh at the euphemism. It was more accurately a robbery and murder mission. But instead of offering his opinion, he dutifully said, "No, sir."

Best looked in turn at Riley and Smith.

Riley shook his head and Smith replied that he hadn't.

Best's severe expression didn't alter.

"So, you've told no one about the amount of money you brought here?"

Once again, Cummins replied in obedient and respectful military fashion.

Smith and Riley did likewise.

Best studied each of them as if trying to gauge their veracity. Then he nodded,

"You three are not to report to the armory to draw weapons," he said.

Smith recoiled slightly.

"Huh? Why not?"

Keller stepped forward and leaned close to Smith, their faces only an inch or so apart.

"You will use proper military protocol when addressing the colonel," he said.

Smith didn't move but Cummins saw Smith's hands clench into fists.

If the shit hits the fan too soon, Cummins thought, this thing could be a disaster.

Plus, even though he'd seen Smith in action taking on numerous foes, he wasn't so sure he could take out Keller that easily. Plus, Keller had the big Desert Eagle on his hip.

"Stand down," Best said. "Both of you. We have a common enemy to prepare for and that takes precedence."

Keller stayed where he was for a good five seconds, eyeball to eyeball with Smith, who wasn't flinching either, and then Keller took a step back.

"You will accompany us to the vault," Best said. "We will need to remove the boxes containing the recently recovered proceeds as well as anything else of significance. Said items with be transferred to the bunker for safekeeping."

Cummins thought he saw a trace of a smile appear at the edge of Smith's mouth. This was both good, and bad but it offered a way out. And he was sure Riley wasn't going to leave without taking his kid.

"Begging your pardon, sir," Cummins said, coming to attention.

He knew he didn't look much like a squared-away troop but he hoped his affected impersonation would be enough to get him a little leeway.

"What is it?" Best asked.

"My medical condition, sir," Cummins said. "I request permission for a quick personal relief, sir."

Best's lips pursed as if he were disgusted at the thought but he nodded and said, "Go ahead. Privates Riley and Smith, I grant you fifteen minutes to see your people and instruct them to remain sequestered until you come for them."

Both Smith and Riley replied with a thank you and a salute. Cummins whipped his arm up there as well to be inclusive but his mind was racing.

How in the hell could he make all this play out to his advantage?

Best returned their salutes.

Smith and Riley did an about-face and headed for the exit. Cummins split off from them toward the rear door and the latrine.

"Don't take too long in there, fat boy," Keller said as

he passed. "Or I'll come looking to see if you fell out."

Cummins bristled internally but dared not say anything. As soon as he was in the hall, he broke into a run toward the latrine. Not only did he have to puke but it was imperative that he contact Fallotti and Wolf. He had to get the ball rolling in both cases and set up his endgame strategy.

It was going to take some doing but what other choice did he have?

***

The Summerlin Hotel
Phoenix, Arizona

Soraces had just finished his conversation with an agitated Fallotti. The lawyer had received another call from that errant employee, Jack Cummins, who was claiming to be close to obtaining the bandito. When Soraces had inquired as to how credible this claim might be, the lawyer had answered with an irritated, "How the fuck should I know?"

It was then discussed that Soraces was to maintain a close surveillance on Wolf in hopes of seeing him make a move with the statue.

"Not a problem," Soraces said. "I've got my best man on him as we speak."

And he did, too, in a way. Gunther was the best but,

at this point, he was also the only man Soraces had hired. He intended to bring the other wet work guys in later, padding the payroll a bit, after they'd obtained the item. Everything would then be nicely tied up, including the money that had already been placed in Wolf's bank account—funds that he was certain Von Dien would somehow withdraw from the transfer as soon as the bandito transaction was complete. But then again, maybe not. A hundred grand to someone as rich as Von Dien was only pocket change. But Soraces was certain that the rich man would then want the loose ends of Wolf and company being tied up in a neat little bow. That might require more than just Gunther if Wolf's prowess hadn't been exaggerated.

But right now, Soraces thought, I need an update.

He pressed the button for Gunther's cell.

The big man answered on the second ring.

"I was just fixing to call you," he said.

"Give me a sit-rep," Soraces said.

"Well, the visitor in the navy-blue sedan I told you about must be a fed. After I called you, I changed up my position and used these range-finder binocks to zero in on his plate. U.S. Government tags. Looked to be a Bureau boy, if I read him correctly."

That fits, Soraces thought. They were investigating the first two cluster fucks in Mexico and the one here with the South Africans.

"So about fifteen minutes ago, the fed left," Gunther continued. "Then Wolf, McNamara, and his daughter came out carrying a couple of duffle bags of stuff, loaded them into the Escalade, and took off. And guess—"

"Where are they now?" Soraces said. "You're still with them, aren't you?"

"Like white on rice," Gunther said. "Ain't that what you said?"

Soraces laughed. Gunther always did have a flair for the metaphorical. It brought a little levity into these missions.

"Looks like they're heading for the interstate south," Gunther said.

The three of them heading south?

"Shit," Soraces said. "Okay, keep on them. I'll get in my car and catch up to you. We'll tail them in tandem."

"Sounds good," Gunther said. "But you didn't let me finish before."

"What?"

"Guess what our boy Wolf also stuck in the car?"

"Surprise me," Soraces said, mildly irritated at this game.

"A statue of that looked like that bandito thing you told me about."

The bandito ... Apparently, Wolf had little or no intention of re-contacting him regarding the transaction proposal. And with what Fallotti had told him about Cummins claiming to be close to acquiring the item, it sounded like he was on the way to make a separate deal.

But if so, Soraces thought, what could Cummins offer that could top my offer?

Maybe a written confession?

Not likely. Cummins would be setting himself up for a prison sentence.

Fallotti and Von Dien wanted Cummins eliminated, too, so this might just present an off-hand choice to get the bandito and do them both at once.

Two for the price of one...

No, he thought. It would be more lucrative to handle each one separately. Naturally, he'd include McNamara and the girl in Wolf's termination session. It would just be a matter of charging a little more for that hit. Three for the price of three.

Soraces felt a thrill run up his spine.

Was it really going to be this easy?

CHAPTER 12

Southbound Interstate 10
Southern Arizona

Wolf kept the speed at around eighty or so, occasionally creeping upward to ninety when he was approaching a cluster of vehicles, figuring the grouping would make it harder for some radar cop to zero in on him. They had to make it down to the location Cummins had specified: Desolation City. Kasey's tablet had said it was approximately an hour and fifty-five minutes away but the last part of that was on side roads. Wolf figured he could trim at least ten to fifteen off of that on the freeway with his skillful driving and given that they wouldn't have to stop for gas. McNamara always made it a point to maintain a full tank, and the traffic had thinned out considerably once they'd gotten out of the greater Phoenix area.

Mac had insisted Wolf drive and he'd spent the first thirty minutes on his phone calling an associate he knew at the Pentagon, his old army buddies, and anyone else he could think of that might know something about the abandoned Fort Lemand, the Freedom Brigade, or former army captain Timothy Herald Best. Nobody knew much about the latter two but he was able to track down a phone number for one of the guys he'd served with back in the Nam named Gus Martinez. He tried the number and it went to voice mail.

Wolf could hear the stress in McNamara' voice as he left a stumbling message:

"Gus, it's Mac. Jim McNamara, from the Hundred and First. I need a favor, ah, to talk to you. So, I'd appreciate it... Ah, please call me back ASAP. Thanks." He recited the number for his cell and then added, "It's an emergency." He set his cell phone in the cup holder in the console and sighed. "Gus was supply sergeant in our company. Resourceful as hell at finding us stuff on the sly. I think I remember him talking about some old fort in Arizona. Maybe he knows something."

Wolf was doubtful but it gave Mac something to do besides worrying about his grandson.

McNamara told Kasey to pass him the small duffle bag with the ammunition and extra magazines. She'd taken her tablet but did seem to be using it. She'd had barely said half a dozen words since they'd left. He kept catching an occasional glimpse of her in the rearview mirror her arms crossed, one hand on her forehead covering her eyes. Mac had done his best trying to get her to stay home but she was having none of that. Wolf recalled her fierce expression of defiance, the tears running down her cheeks, and she told her father in no uncertain terms that she was coming along.

A mother's love, he thought, not to mention her protective maternal instincts.

He'd stepped up and told Mac that she had a right to come along and he'd relented.

Wolf wondered if it was going to make a difference. He wondered if any of it, like going there and bringing the bandito, was going to make a difference. The call from Cummins had sounded stressed as well, with the son of a bitch instructing him to make his way to Desolation City immediately, to bring the bandito, to come alone, and not bring the cops.

Nothing else was said except, "Wait there for my call and I'll tell you more."

"Where's the boy?" Wolf asked.

"He's safe," Cummins said. "For now."

Then he'd hung up.

Another blocked number…They couldn't even try to trace it.

Wolf felt an immense frustration and the worst

part was not knowing how in the hell this had all come about. It was a still a mystery that stretched from a dirty Baghdad street, to some Incan ruins in Mexico, to some South African mercenaries holding them hostage in their own home, to here. It was a cloak of madness draped over their lives. And now, it had somehow swept up poor little Chad into the maelstrom.

Wolf felt totally responsible but knew that wasn't completely accurate. Kasey's ex was somehow involved, too. But how this all fit together was incomprehensible. It was like trying to solve one of those old Rubik's Cubes with someone timing you while holding a gun to your head.

McNamara finished topping off another magazine and grabbed a roll of duct tape out of his bag. After tearing off a long strip of tape, he stuck it on the dashboard in front of him. He then placed the two mags together with the feeding ends at opposite directions. He slid them fractionally until the edge of the one facing downward was against a measured black line on the other magazine, held them in place, and then used the duct tape to secure them in that position.

It was an old army combat method, allowing the shooter to eject the spent magazine and merely rotate the taped pack to slam the new loaded one in place. Wolf knew Mac's smaller duffel bag contained six more similarly fashioned magazines. The big duffel contained a relatively new AR-15 and an old M-16 that McNamara nicknamed "Jamming Jenny." He'd smuggled the rifle out of Vietnam by disassembling it and concealing the upper and lower receivers in two large, plaster statues of Buddha, which he had mailed home in his hold baggage.

Wolf remembered asking him how he accounted for the missing weapon when he was in-country.

"Combat loss," he said with a grin.

Ironic, Wolf thought. Plaster statutes.

Now they were in this mess because the asshole they'd sought in Mexico, Thomas Accondras, had pulled a similar stunt concealing something in a plaster statue of his own.

A mystery concealed in an enigma, wrapped in a conundrum, he thought.

"How close are we?" McNamara asked.

Before Kasey could answer, Mac's cell phone rang. He glanced at the number and then answered it.

"Hey, Gus," he said. "Thanks for calling back."

Wolf didn't know how helpful this old guy on the phone would be but, at this point, they needed all the intel they could get. This was too important.

Failure, as the saying went, was not an option.

***

Fort Lemand
Southern Arizona

Cummins excused himself to go to the latrine again. This time the excuse was real, not a subterfuge to make any more phone calls. Keller, who sat in a chair in front of the podium with Best, made another of his snarky comments.

"You spend more time in the shitter than a woman," he said.

Once again, Cummins let the remark go, despite the growing anger and resentment he felt building inside him. He had to stay in the good graces of these psychos, especially for the moment. Tagging along with Smith and Riley's escape was his only chance out of here. From there, he'd hopefully get a ride to Desolation City where he could rent a car and venture off on his own. All he'd need to do would be to steal an article of clothing from the kid… Use that as proof that he knew where the boy was, in exchange for Wolf giving him the bandito. That was if he couldn't find a way to grab the kid somehow and sneak off. But having Riley and Smith on his trail wouldn't be something he'd want to deal with either.

Anyway, at this point, it was all a moot question. He finished urinating and picked up the bucket to complete the flush but it was practically empty. Apparently, no one had replaced the water after the last usage.

Sloppy discipline, Colonel, he thought. Your Devil's Brigade is starting to fall apart.

As he walked back to the door leading to the auditorium he paused and didn't go in. Instead, he leaned forward and placed his ear against it. He heard muffled conversation, one of them Keller's unmistakable gruff tones. Twisting the knob, he pulled the door open ever so slightly and leaned forward again, trying to distinguish what was being said.

This proved impossible. All he could distinguish was a word or two.

Sighing, he pulled the door open the rest of the way and entered.

Keller cast him a sideways glance, looked at his watch, and winked.

The front door opened and one of the uniformed men hustled in, holding his rifle at port arms. He stopped in front of Best and Keller.

"Sir," the uniformed man said, sounding a bit out of breath. The guy looked young, perhaps not yet twenty.

Young and green, Cummins thought.

Not the best qualifications to hold the line in a siege. But was there going to be one? It was looking more and more like the clock was running out. Perhaps he should try to make a run for it now, try to find this secret tunnel and escape to the old ghost town.

But then what?

Riley's stupid junk car was parked there but he had no keys. It would be a matter of hiding there and perhaps trying to make his way to Desolation City after dark. But that was a good ten miles and he'd never be able to traverse that distance on foot. Not through the desert, even on his best day.

No, he had no choice but to try and find Smith and Riley.

He shuddered as his whole ransom plan began to crumble before him.

Damn this place. Damn this militia bullshit.

"Report," Keller said, standing.

"The enemy's force has advanced to within a hundred feet of the perimeter, sir," the uniformed man said. He looked scared to death. "On all sides."

On all sides?

Shit, Cummins thought. They've got us surrounded. But who are they?

He got his answer in the next moment as the uniformed man said, "They're communicating with a bullhorn, identifying themselves as the FBI."

Best got to his feet. "What are they saying?"

"That they wish to speak to you, sir. They're requesting the commander in charge."

The colonel eyed the man for several seconds.

"They asked for me by name?"

"Well, no, sir. They asked to speak to whoever's in charge."

"That's a good sign," Keller said. "Shows they want to talk rather than fight."

Cummins doubted it. It sounded like standard operating procedure before a raid. The feds probably had a full dossier on Colonel Best. They just didn't want to divulge how much they knew. Of course, they had the upper hand, too. They had the fort surrounded and totally cut off from the world. Sure, they wanted to avoid another Waco but all they had to do was wait. What were they after? Why were they here? And why now?

Did they know about the armored car robbery?

And more importantly, he thought, do they know about me?

"Said they were going to send a robot up to the front gate with a cell phone to communicate," the uniformed man said. "Do you want us to open fire on it?"

Best contemplated this and then said, "Negative. Go out there and retrieve it. But only open the gate enough for one man to go out. This might be a ruse to advance. And then bring it back here."

"On the double," Keller added.

The young uniformed guy did a rifle salute and then ran back to the exit.

"What do you think they want?" Best asked.

"If it's the feds," Keller said, "More than likely it's about one of them bank robberies. That armored car was federally insured if they were going to fill those ATMs."

"That means they probably have a search warrant."

Keller shrugged. "Guess we'll have to wait and ask 'em."

"You take the call," Best said. "Buy us some time. And be careful what you say."

"Me? I ain't no good talker." He glanced over toward Cummins. "How about him. He's a lawyer, ain't he? He should know how to bullshit 'em."

Best turned and stared at Cummins, then motioned him over.

"Do you have any experience in this sort of thing?" he asked.

Cummins knew that if he said no, which was the truth, they might just execute him on the spot. Plus, it was a way to stay in this inner circle for the time being.

"I've argued criminal cases in court," Cummins said, once again exaggerating his legal prowess substantially. "I'll do my best but you'll have to tell me what you want me to do."

"Stall," Keller said. "Buy us some time. We need to make some adjustments here."

Cummins wasn't exactly sure what that meant but he was sure it involved the money in the vault.

The colonel's next words confirmed that.

"How long do you estimate it'll take us to load and

remove the acquisitions?"

Keller shrugged. "Not that long, once we get all of us working. I gotta go get the bags."

So that's it, Cummins thought. The captain and the colonel were planning their own little back door exit. But why were they including him and the others?

To not leave any incriminating witnesses, perhaps? He remembered Keller's casual disposal of the two armored car guards.

After using us as beasts of burden, he thought, they probably line us up and shoot us.

Cummins felt the fear grip him again but he knew he couldn't show it.

Best nodded to Keller, then turned back to Cummins.

"Go get Smith and Riley," he said. "Bring them back here immediately."

"What about the woman and the child, sir?" Cummins asked.

"Leave them there," Best said. "Tell Riley and Smith it's for their safety."

That was going to make it harder to grab the kid. Plus, he doubted either Smith or Riley would try to make an escape without them and he needed those two to offset Keller and the colonel.

"Begging your pardon again, sir," Cummins said.

Both the colonel and Keller turned to glare at him

and Cummins felt the sweat burst from his pores.

"It might be advantageous," he said haltingly, "if we kept them at hand, the boy and the woman. To use as bargaining chips. The authorities might be more restrained if we can convince them that we have civilians present. Besides, this might be about the boy, for all we know."

"Horseshit," Keller said. "They ain't sending no large group equipped with a negotiator and a fucking robot delivery boy to recover some missing kid. It's got to be about the money."

"Which," Best said, "If they find here with a search warrant, will send us all up the river."

Cummins wondered if Keller had told Best about the murder of the two guards. That would up the stakes enough to fit the scenario that was now playing out.

"What you waiting on?" Keller said, his voice a growl. "Go get 'em and bring 'em back."

Best lifted his hand.

"Bring the boy and the woman, too," he said.

Keller rolled his eyes.

Cummins turned and left.

Maybe, just maybe, he thought. *The right cards were once again beginning to be dealt my way.*

***

Southbound Interstate 10
Southern Arizona

They whizzed past Desolation City and kept driving on the route that Kasey's tablet said would take them to Leesville, the now-defunct town next to the now-defunct army base. It was perhaps a ten- or fifteen-minute drive.

"Gus said they used to called it Diseaseville," McNamara said. "On account of everybody having to show up at the dispensary for penicillin shots after a weekend pass."

Wolf smirked and tried to check Kasey's reaction in the mirror. If she had one she didn't show it. Her face was pulled taut as she stared at the tablet and kept manipulating the mouse with her fingertip.

"I still can't find anything about any secret tunnel," she said. "But from what I can tell from Google Earth, the town, or what's left of it, is about half a mile from the west end of the base."

It's good the search is giving her something to do, Wolf thought, then resumed his worry about what to do with her if the fireworks started. He was sure the Mac wouldn't be at the top of his game, either, having to worry about both his grandson and his daughter.

Then again, he thought, maybe I'm underestimating him.

After all, Mac was Special Forces and had taken

out two of those South African mercenaries at the Ranch. Both Kasey and Chad had been in danger then, too. But there were a lot more intangibles to deal with now. Was Cummins armed? Was he alone? How many might be backing him up? Was this militia involved? Plus, if they had to use the tunnel to try and sneak into the fort, what kind of condition might the tunnel be in?

He'd expressed this last concern to McNamara earlier, right after the phone call with Gus.

"Gus said the army engineers did a job that would've made some VC tunnel rats proud." He frowned, then added, "Actually, we called our guys the tunnel rats."

"El Chapo, then," Wolf said. "That drug lord that had that long tunnel built to escape from prison in Mexico."

McNamara winced. "Don't mention Mexico to me." He shook his head. "You know, those poor fuckers in Nam had it pretty rough going down in those damn VC tunnels alone with nothing but a forty-five and a flashlight. They had balls, lemme tell ya. I couldn't do it, even as skinny as I was back then. I was too big."

Now we're the tunnel rats, Wolf thought. The next generation.

He listened to McNamara's reminiscence, remembering the times as a young, inexperienced GI, how the old-timers would talk about bygone missions with a certain fondness right before everybody was ready to ship out. It helped to ease the tension a bit and Wolf was sure that's what Mac was trying to do now.

"He said it was high and wide, too," McNamara continued. "Big enough and tall enough for them to drive a Jeep in it."

"A Jeep?" Wolf forced a laugh. "And the army built it? How'd they manage to accomplish that?"

"He said it was with the old man's blessing. The base commander was as crooked as a dog's hind leg and was cut in on a piece of the action. They used it for sneaking the hookers and booze in and the black-market supplies out. At that time Gus was in supply."

It sure sounded big enough, but that had been a long time ago. If it hadn't been maintained, trying to sneak in and locate Chad amongst some ongoing chaos and an edgy militia group might be problematic, even for a former Green Beret and a disgraced Airborne Ranger. Wolf also wondered what the air quality might be like in a tunnel that old even if it was still operational. And the prospects of getting into a firefight in a confined space weren't too pretty either. He wondered the extent of the federal presence there and if Franker had notified anybody about his and Mac's possible presence. Wolf had felt almost bad about ignoring the FBI man's instructions to stay put at the Ranch while he went to confer with his supervisor and bring a kidnap team to monitor the phone. But he'd deal with that later, once Chad was safe.

As much as he hated the thought of it, they had to wait until Cummins called back.

Back to being a counterpuncher, he thought.

It was getting dark now and he thought he caught a glimpse of headlights behind him but they vanished. He'd tried to check their trail periodically as they'd driven and hadn't noticed anybody following. But that didn't mean there was nobody there.

You always have to expect the unexpected, he told himself.

He felt the persistent encroachment of fatigue as he checked the rearview mirror again and saw only darkness.

***

Southbound Interstate 10
Southern Arizona

Soraces had let Gunther take the lead again on the tail and fell back. Although it still wasn't completely clear just who Wolf was going to meet, Soraces had now convinced himself it was Cummins. All the facts pointed to that conclusion. But he reminded himself that one should never assume.

It all comes to he who waits, he thought.

He recalled the many times he'd been in one of these situations and the rush never got old. His main attribute, he'd decided long ago, was patience. Letting the plan play out and not making a move too soon. It was why he excelled at chess.

No wrong moves, he thought. And always thinking a move or two ahead of the game.

His cell rang again and he answered it.

"Looks like they're getting off the expressway," Gunther said.

He was from Chicago and always said "expressway" rather than "freeway."

"They see you?" Soraces asked.

"Don't think so. I been riding without my lights for a while."

No lights ... Well, it was fairly light out with a full moon. And Gunther had brought two sets of night vision goggles in his equipment bag and was using one of them. Soraces had the second one. Gunther was nothing if not resourceful.

"Keep going past the exit," Soraces said. "Then double back. I'll pick them up now."

He pressed the accelerator to the floor, wondering when it would be prudent to make a move.

Patience, he remembered.

From what Gunther had observed back at the ranch, Wolf and McNamara were both heavily armed or at least that was the assumption. Pretty soon, he'd have the answers to that and his other questions.

Until then, he thought, ride it out.

It all comes to he who waits. He shut off his own headlights, kept the pedal to the metal, and flipped the visor down for his own night vision goggles.

CHAPTER 13

Fort Lemand
Southern Arizona

After making his way over to the billets at as fast a run as he could manage, Cummins saw Smith standing in the hallway outside his room. The man looked up at him and smiled. There was no sign of the two armed guards. Had they gone on the perimeter?

"What's up?" Smith asked. "The colonel wants us back now?"

Cummins nodded, still trying to catch his breath.

"He said to bring Cherrie and the kid, too," he managed to say.

"He did?"

Cummins nodded and held up his open palm.

"There's more," he said, a bit uncertain on how to word things. "The FBI's in front and it looks like they've got the base surrounded."

"Shit," Smith said. "How the hell they track us down so quick?"

"I don't know but right now the colonel wants us back there."

Smith's eyes narrowed to a squint. "For what?"

"Keller's going to get some bags for the money. He wants us to move the funds from the safe and put it all in the bunker."

"Does he indeed?" Smith said, grinning.

"There's more," Cummins said. "I don't think this is good. I think they might be planning to kill us once we've helped them."

"Why's that?"

Cummins shook his head. "Don't know. Just a feeling."

"You know," Smith said. "I would put it past old Lou to have some kind of escape plan in place. He always was joking about it. Maybe they seen this coming and have a car stashed in that old town someplace, same as us. You're probably right. The only thing they're planning on leaving in the bunker is our dead bodies."

Cummins felt another rush of fear and grabbed his stomach. The pressure was too great and he turned and spewed a gusher of bitter-tasting stomach bile onto the floor. He wiped his mouth and turned back to Smith, who was grinning even wider now.

"Pee-U," Smith said. "Glad you done that before we got into the tunnel."

"Sorry." Cummins tried unsuccessfully to swallow the residual stomach secretions in his mouth.

"What are we going to do about Keller and Best," he asked.

"Why you know what they say," Smith said. "Do onto others, only do it first."

He raised the left side of his loose-fitting BDU blouse and Cummins saw the handle of a blue steel semi-auto stuck in Smith's belt.

"Charlie's got one, too," Smith said. "We'll take care of them two jokers."

A shoot out in an underground bunker, Cummins thought. Can things get any worse?

***

Back Road to Leesville
Southern Arizona

Soraces slowed to a stop and waited. In his rearview mirror, he saw some movement and he turned in his seat. The green tinctured image of Gunther's car appeared in the darkness. The ambient lighting from the full moon was almost sufficient enough that he didn't need the night vision equipment. He turned back and waited, watching the disappearing twin glow of the red taillights of the Escalade in the distance. Gunther came up and got in the passenger side.

"They still up there?" Gunther asked.

"Straight ahead," Soraces said, flipping up his visor. "See those taillights?"

Gunther studied the area in front of them. "Yeah. Where the hell they going to?"

"I think I might have an idea," Soraces said. "The Agency used to use old abandoned military forts for POW training exercises, remember?"

"Wish I could forget," Gunther said.

"There was an old base around here somewhere. Right in this area."

"You think they might be going there?"

"Where else could they be going?" Soraces said. "There's absolutely nothing else out here except an old ghost town."

"Might be a good place for a meet."

"And a killing." Soraces flipped down the visor again and said, "Leave your car here. Nobody around to bother it and we'll kind of gambol about in the desert air for a while and see where our friends are going."

"Sounds good to me." Gunther flipped his visor down as well. "Let's go get us a wolf."

***

Wolf was trying to check the rearview mirror again for any signs of movement when Kasey leaned forward and occupied the space between the seats. She'd done her best to clean herself up but the black streaks of mascara down her cheeks gave her face an almost macabre look.

"How are we going to handle this?" she asked.

"*We* ain't," McNamara said. "Me and Steve are."

"Like hell," she shot back. "Chad's *my* son."

"And he's *my* grandson."

This was going nowhere. Before Kasey could retort, Wolf interceded.

"Listen," he said in a forceful tone. "Both of you, dammit. We can't afford to be arguing and fighting among ourselves. Not with Chad's life at stake."

"Stay out of this," McNamara said.

"Yeah," Kasey added. "You'd better keep your fucking mouth shut, asshole."

Wolf felt like saying, why don't you tell me how you really feel, Kasey?

But he let a few seconds of silence settle and then said, "We can't afford this emotional bickering. We've got to think about Chad's safety. What's the best plan?"

More silence enveloped the three of them and then McNamara said, "Steve's right, Kase. Let's think about this. You ain't any good with a handgun, are you?"

She said nothing.

"And," McNamara continued, "Steve and me are

trained for this kind of thing."

She compressed her lips and Wolf wondered if they'd come away bloody on the insides. She seemed to be teetering on the edge, so full of anger and emotion that she was close to the breaking point. He thought about little Chad's always-smiling face and could hardly blame her.

"Cummins doesn't know how many of us there are," he said. "And he's probably going to assume that Mac's going to be with me. That leaves you, Kasey, in a support role. Stay back and stay out of sight. Have you ever fired a pistol?"

She shook her head.

"Well," Wolf said, thinking she was going to be real liability in a fire fight. "There's a lot more to it than just pointing it and pulling the trigger so don't shoot unless you absolutely have to. Like if your target's right in front of you. And if you do shoot, don't expect him to fall down like in the movies. Point it at his chest and keep firing, but again, only if you have to."

McNamara dug into his smaller duffle bag and pulled out a Beretta 92F. He shifted in the seat, racked the slide chambering a round and flipped the safety on. He gave her a quick course in how to fire it and how to release and set the safety. Wolf hoped she was a quick study and regretted that they hadn't done this earlier when they were on the way here.

"The best way to handle this is for me to approach

Cummins alone," Wolf said. "He wants the bandito. We shouldn't give it to him unless we see that he does have Chad."

"And what if he doesn't?" she said. "What if it's all bullshit and Chad's still with Charlie in that old fort?"

"Then me and Steve will grab Cummins and make him take us back in there so we can get him."

"And me?" she asked.

"I know it's hard," Wolf said. "As hard as all hell, but the best place for you to be is with the Escalade. We may need you to pick us up and take off real quick."

"But—"

"No buts," he said. "We've all got to work together."

She closed her eyes and nodded. Tears rolled down each cheek, then she placed a hand on Wolf's shoulder.

"Steve, I'm sorry for calling you—" She hesitated, then added, "I'm such a bitch."

"No, you're not," Wolf said. "Don't worry about it. We're all rubbed raw, you most of all. Let's just concentrate on getting Chad back safe. That's all that matters."

The road dipped slightly and as they rose back upward the ruins of the dilapidated and crumpling structures seemed to spring out of the desert floor, looking like a gateway to the netherworld in the pale moonlight.

Welcome to the other side of hell, Wolf thought, and prayed they'd be able to get the boy back alive.

***

Fort Lemand
Southern Arizona

Cummins was covered with sweat as he removed another stack of currency from the safe and packed it into one of the black duffel bags. Of course, he wasn't completely sure if his sweating was due to the physicality of his movements or the immense pressure he was feeling of what was yet to come. The vault turned out to be a huge walk-in safe in the basement section of the building and it was full of stacks of money. Most of it, like the portion that they'd taken in the armed robbery of the armored truck, was in smaller denominations so it probably looked more impressive than it was and made for a more laborious loading process.

Both Smith and Riley labored beside him with Keller standing guard by the door with his Kalashnikov and the big Desert Eagle in the holster.

The thought of Smith and Riley taking him out seemed very problematic at the moment. Memories of the full-auto cycling of the AK-47 were still fresh in his mind. He heard Cherrie yelling something at the kid, who was apparently having some fun running around the basement.

Best brushed by Keller and stepped back into the

vault room.

"Jack," he said. "Those FBI men are calling back. I need you to answer it."

Cummins stood up and wiped the perspiration from his forehead.

"How about giving us a hand, then, cap?" Smith said with a wry grin. "We could use another set of hands here."

Keller stiffened and Best gave a fractional nod. The big man exhaled forcefully, put his rifle on safe, and leaned it against the wall by the door.

As Cummins straightened up and began walking out of the vault, he caught Smith giving him a quick wink.

Cummins strode over to a small wooden table where the federal cell phone lay. It continued to chime. He picked it up and pressed the button, putting it on speaker. Best stood right beside him.

"Hey, Jack," the FBI negotiator said. "It's Nick. How you doing?"

The negotiator had put things on a first-name basis in his first call and Cummins had inadvertently given him his real first name. Not that he expected anything to come of it. Not only were there a lot of Jacks in the world but the fed probably thought it was a phony anyway.

"Nick," Cummins said, "I still haven't been able to track down the boss."

"Come on, Jack," Nick said. "Don't bullshit me. I thought we were making progress here when you told me you'd find him?"

Cummins saw Best glancing back and forth between him and the vault.

He mouthed the word, "Stall," and pointed to the kid running around.

Cummins nodded.

"We are making progress," Cummins said. "And I think you should know that there are civilians inside this facility."

"There are? Who are they?"

Cummins glanced toward Best, hoping for guidance, but there was none. He decided to wing it.

"Women and children," he said. "The families of some of the members here. I know you wouldn't want anything to happen to them, would you?"

"No, no," Nick said slowly. "Of course not. How many are there?"

Best shook his head.

Cummins felt himself flush. Why didn't this idiot just take the phone and conduct this negotiation himself?

"Jack? You there?"

"I'm here."

"Not that I doubt your veracity," Nick said, "but my supervisors are leaning on me to give them an update on what's going on. If you can tell me how many women and children are in the facility, it would go a long way in helping me out."

Cummins looked back toward the vault and said, "Hold on." He motioned toward Cherrie and the kid. They both stopped and he covered the cell phone with his hand, stooping down and addressing Chad.

"Hey," he said, trying to use his most ingratiating tone. "Want to say hello to my friend, Nick?"

Chad smiled as Cummins held the phone forward.

"Hi, Nick," Chad said.

Cummins whisked the phone away and put it back to his ear.

"There," he said. "See? There are about a dozen or so inside here. I'm trying to work with Colonel Best to set up a release to get them out of harm's way. But we have to have your assurance that you won't move on us unexpectedly. For the sake of the women and the kids."

"Jack, I give you my word. The last thing we want is anybody getting hurt."

"Fine," Cummins said. "Now give me some time. I'll call back in half an hour."

He pressed the button and set the phone back onto the table. It had a special setting that prevented him from calling out to any number except Nick's. But hopefully, after that little bit of gamesmanship, he'd bought them some time. He'd said half an hour so they should have at least fifteen or twenty minutes.

Cummins looked at Best for approval but the other man frowned.

"Why did you tell them my name?" he asked.

Cummins felt the question was absurd. Did he actually think the feds would be ignorant of who was running this show? But Cummins knew he couldn't exactly say that.

"Sorry, sir," he said.

Best stared at him, glanced at his watch, then placed his hand on Cummins's shoulder, easing him back toward the vault.

"Don't be troubled," Best said. "Let's just finish getting this stuff loaded."

When they got inside they saw that the others had finished emptying in the safe. Five large duffel bags sat on the floor stuffed to capacity.

"Ready for transport, sir," Keller said.

Best nodded and went to what appeared to be a huge wooden platform mounted against the cement wall on heavy steel rails. He removed a set of keys from his pocket and slipped one into a heavy-duty security padlock. Once he'd disengaged the lock from the hasp, he pushed the wooden platform to the right, revealing a sloping ramp that descended into the darkness. Best reached over and flipped a light switch and a set of fluorescent lights above the ramp lit up. Additionally, at the sloping base of the ramp, a seemingly unending series of spaced overhead lights blinked on, exposing a long tunnel. Four golf carts sat side-by-side with cords running to a charging post that ran to an outlet on the wall.

Thank God for the colonel's well-maintained generators, Cummins thought.

This was it ... The escape tunnel.

And that meant that it was almost show time.

Cummins knew the next few minutes meant life and death and he didn't even have a weapon.

"Get those duffle bags loaded onto the carts," Best said.

"You mean we're going somewhere, Best?" Smith said, his voice taking on a mocking tone.

"Watch your mouth, Smith," Keller said. "That's the colonel you're talking to."

Smith held his hands up and shook them in theatrically exaggerated fashion.

Keller stepped forward, balling up his fists, and Smith skipped closer executing a jumping kick that caught the bigger man in the chest. He fell backwards.

Best reached down and withdrew his sidearm but Riley popped out of the door, a semi-automatic pistol in his extended right hand.

Riley's gun exploded, seeming to shoot a flame at least half a foot from the barrel.

The back portion of Best's head exploded like a melon hit by a baseball bat. As he did a pirouette to the floor Cummins caught sight of a small, black hole next to the ersatz colonel's right eye.

The gun's thunder in the enclosed space had left Cummins temporarily deaf. He saw Cherrie's lips peel back in a silent scream and an expression of surprise on the kid's face with his mouth gaping open.

Everything seemed to be occurring in slow motion.

Riley stepped out of the vault, framed in the doorway. Suddenly he jerked forward like he'd been kicked in the back, the pistol tumbling from his hands as his fingers fluttered against the front of his blouse. He took two halting steps forward, twisting a bit to look behind him. Cummins, who was frozen in place, saw Keller standing behind Riley, the huge handgun in a two-handed grip, a trail of smoke rising from the muzzle.

Then Smith fired his gun and Keller rolled forward and fell to the floor. Smith ran forward and kicked Keller's gun to the far side of the room, grabbed the Kalashnikov, and knelt beside Riley. Cummins stumbled forward on unsteady legs, like a drunk sideling up to the bar for last call.

His hearing came back in tiny increments and he heard Chad yelling, "Daddy, daddy."

Smith looked up and said something to Cherrie that sounded like, "Give him one of your pills."

Cummins turned and saw Cherrie grabbing the kid and pulling him away as she opened her purse. He looked back to Smith and Riley.

"He dead?" Cummins asked. His own voice sounded distant, indistinct.

Smith's mouth twisted into a frown and he nodded and began going through Riley's pockets. He found what appeared to be a set of car keys, stuffed them into his lower blouse pocket, and then picked up Riley's gun, jamming it into his belt. Standing, he did the same with his own weapon and then ran to the array of duffel bags.

"Come on, Jack," he said. "We got to load these on the carts and get outta here."

His voice still sounded like it was being yelled down a tunnel.

***

Defunct City of Leesville
Southern Arizona

They were operating on the assumption that if Cummins was with Smith and Riley, they were all still in the fort. Since Cummins's last call had been over two and a half hours ago, Wolf also assumed that if they planned to go to Desolation City, they'd be coming here to Leesville first, via the tunnel. And they'd probably be coming soon. Wolf had received and not answered three calls from Franker, who left a series of progressively angry voice mails berating Wolf for what the agent termed violating their "mutual understanding agreement and endangered the situation." Wolf felt slightly amused by Franker's roundabout circumlocution but he also knew that once this was over he would have to get with the FBI man and try to set things straight, even if it meant being more forthcoming about what had actually happened down in Mexico. But if he could capture Cummins and drag him along, he could force his former lieutenant to give the FBI man some real answers.

Answers ... Those would be nice. Wolf had inadvertently gotten into this mess back in Iraq and had been stumbling around like a drunk, punching at shadows ever since. It was clear that the scope of it was way beyond his capabilities of handling it and he needed help ... Governmental help ... The FBI. His only condition for total cooperation would be to keep Mac out of it.

Not much to look forward to, he thought. But all that now paled in comparison to getting Chad back safe.

That was his main and only focus now.

With the information from Gus about the tunnel, they were able to narrow their search down to an approximated area on the eastern edge of the town. Wolf shut off his lights and drove slowly past crumbling houses, a dilapidated wooden framed church, a variety of smaller buildings along a walkway, and several brick buildings that had weathered the blowing winds better than their wooden compatriots. A slight wind had stirred up and Wolf hoped it would possibly bring some relief to the still oppressive heat, but no such luck. The air was hot and dry, like a breeze from hell.

El viento del diablo, Wolf thought. The devil's wind.

Other than an occasional sporadic rustle, the place was blanketed with an ominous silence.

The fort lay in the distance, beyond the glow of the FBI floodlights that lit up the area like a traveling carnival. The FBI had arrived and the siege had begun. Knowing the federal agent's penchant for slow-speed negotiations, things were no doubt proceeding at a snail's pace.

But would it last long enough for them to find the tunnel and perhaps enter the compound and locate Chad?

He assessed the distance to the glowing lights again. If the tunnel was still intact, it would be a hell of a jaunt through what was most likely a precise killing zone. Their adversaries wouldn't even have to aim. He thought about Mac's story about the tunnel rats in Nam.

At least we've got more than just eight rounds from a .45 to throw back at them, he thought.

But they couldn't afford to let it get to that point.

Wolf parked the Escalade out of sight at the end

of the block and they got out to do the rest of the searching on foot. Wolf took point with the AR-15 and McNamara came after him on the opposite side carrying his Jammin' Jenny M-16. Wolf knew that the nickname was an intentional misnomer. The early versions of the rifle did have a tendency to jam in the muddy rice paddies of Vietnam but Mac treated the weapon with respect and reverence, making sure the bolt was never without a light coating of oil and the parts all lubricated. It wouldn't jam in a thousand years.

Better make that a thousand rounds, he thought with a smile. Keep it light, keep it loose, keep it ready.

Kasey, despite Mac's admonishment to "Stay with the car," trailed along behind them. Wolf hoped she'd inherited enough of Mac's combat instinct to take cover if the shooting started. He didn't even want to think about the prospect of McNamara possibly losing his grandson and his daughter in this op.

McNamara emitted a low whistle and Wolf stopped.

Mac had flattened against a wall and motioned toward the twenty-foot gap between two of the still-standing brick buildings. Wolf glanced toward Kasey, who was advancing rapidly toward her father. Moving across the street, Wolf intercepted her and whispered.

"Easy. Abrupt movement will give you away.

Her eyes widened, and she nodded.

They came up behind McNamara who gestured with his thumb.

"There's a car in between the buildings," he said. "Covered with camouflaged netting."

Wolf told Kasey to stay where she was and to get down.

He scanned the rooftops across the street and saw no solid perches where someone could take up a sniper's position.

McNamara crouched and did a quick peek around the side of the building.

"Don't see no trip wires," he said. "But that don't mean there ain't none."

Wolf waited for McNamara to make the first move, advancing around with a quick, but cautious deftness until he got to the camouflaged vehicle. After doing another check they determined that the car, a Dodge Caravan, was empty.

"Look familiar?" McNamara asked.

Wolf nodded. It was Charles Riley's car.

"Guess we're in the right place," McNamara said. "He must've stashed the car here thinking he could slip out through the tunnel."

Wolf was thinking the same thing.

McNamara bent down and pulled a knife out of his boot. After flicking open the blade, he jammed it into the soft rubber sidewall. As he stood the air hissed out in a slow, but steady stream.

"I really hope to hell I get a chance to even things out with that son of a bitch," McNamara said.

Wolf nodded, thinking he'd settle for just breaking even and getting Chad. He was sure Mac would too, but he understood a father's frustration.

And a grandfather's as well, he thought.

Mac pierced a second tire.

They went out and briefed Kasey, whose eyes widened, looking glossy with tears in the moonlight.

"Does that mean he's bringing Chad here?" she asked.

"Hopefully," Wolf said.

They resumed their search and Wolf traversed the street once more.

He passed the rickety church with many of the boards missing from the side and front. It somehow reminded him of a star hockey player's gap-toothed smile that he'd seen at a USO show a few years back. They'd brought a group of celebrities, singers, movie stars, sports figures over to Afghanistan as a morale booster for the troops. Wolf remembered thinking with all the money the guy must be making, he should have gotten his teeth fixed. He later heard that hockey players didn't make all that much compared to other professional sports. Then he thought again about seeing all those professional players kneeling for the National Anthem and figured they were making way too much as it was.

The church's large wooden cross had tumbled from its perch on the front area of the roof and was now imbedded in the sandy earth in front of the structure.

An upside-down cross ... Was that emblematic of something?

An upside-down flag meant distress. Perhaps the church symbol meant something very bad was about to happen ... something without goodness and mercy.

Every sound, every movement seemed heightened and magnified.

A tumbleweed skittered past him. The moon shone so brightly that he didn't even need the flashlight that he carried with him in his left hand. His right rested on the hard, plastic pistol grip of the rifle.

Movement on the side of the building—

He stopped and in an instant realized it was a lizard of some sort.

They'd had large spiders in Iraq that used to skitter about in odd places. This walk was starting to remind him of the Sandbox. The night patrols on his first tour were the worst. You never knew who or what was waiting for you behind one of those doors you were sent to break down.

He came to the last building on the block, a huge three-storied affair, and wondered if it had been a hotel or office building in the town's heyday. Glancing over to check on Mac, Wolf saw him wave an, "I'm okay."

Wolf rotated some more and spotted Kasey, walking along as cautiously as she could, the flashlight in one hand, the Beretta in the other.

He hoped she wouldn't end up firing it and questioned Mac's decision to give her a weapon in the first place. But this was her kid that they were after.

A mother's love, he thought. There's no holding her back.

Then something else caught his eye: a cigarette butt lying on the cracked and dusty sidewalk in front of a solid-looking wooden door. And not just any cigarette butt... He switched on the mini-mag flashlight and shone the powerful beam over the distinctive, then red and blue rings that encircled the base at the top end of the filter.

Uptown Blues Menthol, he thought. For those with sophisticated tastes.

CHAPTER 14

Fort Lemand
Southern Arizona

Cummins left the FBI cell phone on the floor next to the vault. He figured the thing might have some kind of tracking device inside it and didn't want to risk bringing it along. He and Smith managed to carry all of the duffel bags to the golf carts, with Smith carting three and Cummins two. Cherrie held both arms around the struggling kid, who was screaming in an almost hysterical manner.

Smith glared at her.

"You give him one of them damn pills?" he asked.

"Yeah," she said. "Had to shove it down his throat. The little bastard bit my finger, but, shit, I hope he's okay."

Cummins wondered how soon the tranquilizer

would kick in and what the effect would be. He got the answer to the first question as they were starting up the carts. The kid's breathing slowed and the screaming stopped. He was still crying and his breathing seemed labored.

Another advantage falling into my lap, Cummins thought.

He didn't have to deliver the kid unharmed to Wolf, only keep him alive enough to hand off in a trade. At this point, he'd most likely have to cut Smith in on the deal but would he go for it? But the hillbilly queen might balk at the prospect of leaving the little son a bitch. Perhaps he was bringing out her maternal side.

Smith jammed the AK-47 under the top duffel bag and jumped into the driver's seat. Cherrie, still holding the now quiescent kid, squeezed into the seat next to him.

Taking up most of the seat in his cart, Cummins adjusted his bulk to a degree of comfort and shifted into gear. He'd driven one a few times and didn't have to familiarize himself with the controls. Smith seemed to be adept as well and he took off down the ramp. Cummins was secretly glad that Riley wasn't in the equation anymore. Getting him to give up his kid would have been a difficult obstacle that had been fortuitously eliminated.

Yeah, he thought. With a couple more breaks, things will definitely fall my way.

He followed Smith down the ramp and into the tunnel.

The walls, floor, and ceiling were smooth concrete and the periodic lights seemed sturdily affixed, for the most part. The long, heavy-duty electrical cord sagged lugubriously in a few places but all things considered, the passageway was in pretty good shape. The top speed of the carts was about 5 miles per hour and there was only an occasional bump in the flooring. The tunnel veered slightly to the left and then straightened out again. Cummins felt it getting harder to breathe and he couldn't shake the feeling of something gritty in his mouth. The air seemed dusty and exceptionally foul. The possibility of some kind of noxious underground gas occurred to him, but he dismissed the idea.

This was fucking Arizona, not Iraq or Afghanistan. The only thing lurking in this tunnel was the miniscule sand particles that had seeped inside over the course of several decades.

After what seemed like an eternity but couldn't have been more than ten or twelve minutes, he saw a more substantial brightness ahead. Smith slowed slightly and they pulled into a wider area with another ramp, this one winding around in an inclining hairpin curve that led upward to a flat platform and an overhead door. It had to be the loading dock that Smith had mentioned. A Ford Windstar van was parked in the flat area by the overhead door.

The colonel and Keller's escape vehicle, no doubt.

Smith must have gotten the same impression. He jumped out of the golf cart and said, "Them fuckers was planning on leaving all the rest of us high and dry."

Cummins shut his cart down and slid off of the seat. "I wonder if the keys are in it?" he said.

"Wouldn't do us no good," Smith said. "We ain't got keys for the overhead. I shoulda checked their pockets more but who knows when them FBI motherfuckers will come barreling in."

Cummins estimated that they still had a slight margin of time. He glanced at Chad, whose head was now slumped over to the side. His eyes were closed and his breathing looked shallow.

"How's the kid?" Cummins asked.

Cherrie brushed some of the boy's hair back from his forehead and held her hand there.

"I hope I didn't give him too much," she said. "One of them pills usually knocks me out pretty good but I'm a lot bigger than him."

Not to mention the systematic tolerance factor, Cummins thought, but once again kept his mouth shut. There was room for all four of them in Riley's old Caravan and once they were safely in Desolation City, they could divide up the loot and he could rent a car. If they gave up the kid to him, fine. If not, he could try cutting them in on the trade with

Wolf, or maybe convince them to drop the kid at a hospital. At this point, he was both a bargaining chip and a liability.

"I don't got no keys for that door, neither," Smith said, gesturing toward a solid metal door at the top of a six-foot stairway. "It's got a deadbolt and leads to the inside of the old whorehouse. Remember?"

Cummins did recall seeing it on their earlier trip.

"So what are we gonna do?" he asked.

Smith pulled out the AK-47 and set it on the driver's seat of the cart. He then grabbed the bags and motioned for Cummins and Cherrie to accompany him over to a ladder that was built into the wall adjacent to the stairway leading up to the metal door. Cummins grabbed the two duffel bags and followed him. Smith dropped the bags down at the base of the ladder and looked upward.

"See that lever there?" he asked. "On the trap door."

Cummins looked up and saw a handle attached to a framework of levers.

He nodded.

"Climb up there and pull them latches back," Smith said. Then pull and then push on that lever and it'll open the hatch. Got it?"

Cummins did. It seemed relatively simple, the hardest part being trying to get his heavy frame up the ladder and through the hatch. He climbed upward and when he got to the top, tried his best to push back the securing latches, but they seemed frozen in place.

"They won't budge," he said.

"Shit," Smith said, scaling the ladder. He swung up next to Cummins, clinging with a seeming prehensility to the side of the ladder and banging the slide of Riley's weapon against the knobs of the hasps to force them back. The pungency of his sweat was highly noticeable in the close proximity of their bodies. Cummins felt a revulsion welling up from his stomach again but it subsided.

Smith grabbed the lever and pulled, then shoved it upward. The hatch of the trap door sprang open.

"Go on up through there," Smith said. "And here." He handed Cummins Riley's weapon. "Take this. Charlie ain't got no need for it no more."

Cummins grabbed the gun and edged up through the opening. It was dark inside and he wished he had a flashlight. As he worked his belly through the opening and then his legs, he fell over onto his side and panted. Smith's head appeared in the opening, lighted from below.

"Here," he said. "Take these."

Smith disappeared and the end of one of the duffel bags came up through the opening. Cummins grabbed it and set it aside. He heard the sounds of Smith descending and then ascending the ladder again and another bag was thrust up through the opening. Cummins set that one aside too, and Smith paused, his head visible once again.

"Jack, take these keys. Go get Charlie's car and pull it around to the other side of the building by that big door. I'll get the other bags up here and help Cherrie and the kid."

He handed Cummins a set of car keys.

For a brief moment, Cummins considered aimed the pistol at Smith's head and pulling the trigger. It would be an easy, can't miss shot. That would leave him an unencumbered path to grab the kid and maybe even Cherrie, and take off. But there were complications. He would have to catch them both, although the kid still seemed out of it, and then carry or force them up the ladder, not to mention carrying all of those five heavy duffel bags to the car. Jamming the gun into the front left side of his belt where he could get to it with a cross-draw, he set aside any thought of dissolving their partnership.

No, for the time being anyway, he and the hillbilly king were still buddies.

Cummins accepted the keys and got to his feet. He picked up the two bags and started moving as cautiously as he could toward the front entrance, recalling the door to the outside they had to push open leading to the outside but it had already been removed. Had they left it that way?

He couldn't remember. The moonlight streamed through the vacant door frame as well as through the empty portals where the windows had once been.

He made his way toward the door, his boots making gritty, crunching sounds as he walked along the wooden floor.

He went through the door to the outside and the street, hoping to catch a cool breeze but instead the wind was hot and dusty. Cummins looked around to try and get his bearings.

Where did they leave that damn car?

Then something caught his eye… Something in the middle of the street about fifteen feet away with nothing else around it.

Cummins staggered forward, the image not quite distinct in the moonlight.

It was about a foot and a half tall and was suddenly illuminated by a flashlight beam.

The smiling, mustachioed face under the Mexican sombrero seemed to be staring back at him with a mocking insouciance.

The bandito.

Wolf was here.

Cummins turned to run back into the building but Wolf emerged from the shadows on the side, pointing a big Glock pistol.

"Cummins," he said. "Don't fucking move."

***

Wolf moved forward and ripped the gun from Cummins's beltline. After snapping on the safety, he stuck it in his own belt, off to the side, then grabbed the fat man's ear and tugged him back into the shadows, holding the barrel of the Glock to Cummins's temple.

"Where's Chad?"

"Shoot me and you'll never see him," Cummins said. He felt the vomit roiling in his gut again. "I'm sorry, I have to throw up."

With that, he spewed forth a gusher of puke. Wolf stepped back just as a figure burst through the window, his one hand striking Wolf's head, the other seizing his gun hand. The momentum carried them both forward and into the street, Wolf landing hard on his side and his opponent landing on top. It was Roger D. Smith, from the trailer park.

Wolf felt the Glock slip from his hand as a series of punches struck his abdomen and worked downward seeming intent on striking his groin. He kicked with his legs and managed to flip his body to the left. Smith was bringing up a gun, a blue steel semi-auto, and Wolf grabbed it with both of his hands.

Smith tried to twist away but Wolf managed to wrench the pistol out of the man's grip. The sweat on the weapon made it impossible to hold, and it went skittering away as Wolf's Glock had. Rising, Wolf caught a glimpse of Cummins running past them. He grabbed the bandito and trundled off at a jiggling run.

He called out to Mac, who rushed past him yelling, "She's got Chad."

In the split second Wolf took to see a woman jumping through one of the vacant windows and running while clutching something to her chest—a tiny human body, he realized it was Chad. The running woman was Cherrie with an I E.

Kasey shot by him running full tilt after her dad.

Then the spinning kick caught him in the gut. Stumbling backwards, Wolf tried to take a breath but his opponent shot forward with another jumping kick.

This time Wolf was ready and blocked it, countering with a quick punch to the other man's side. He landed as nimble as a cat.

Looks like the gang's all here, he thought, and raised his hands into a guard position.

"Oh," Smith said. "You wanna fight?"

He grinned and assumed what appeared to be a karate *kumite* stance.

Wolf's breathing was coming in ragged gasps. Just as he was hoping that Mac and Kasey had caught Cherrie, Smith danced forward and shot out a backfist. Wolf blocked the blow, brushing it away with his right hand and shooting out a quick jab with his left. The jab caught Smith flush on the mouth and his lower lip opened up and sent a stream of blood down his chin. Grinning, Smith licked at the wound and moved forward again, this time flipping up a double round-house kick to Wolf's abdomen and then his head. The body blow made Wolf drop his guard slightly and the second kick bounced off his right temple.

The black spots swarmed in his eyes for a second, then vanished. Wolf danced back a few steps and when Smith's leg dropped as he completed the kick, Wolf thrust a front kick into Smith's exposed left side. His lips curled back exposing crimson-covered teeth. As he straightened up, Wolf moved forward, as lithely as a ballet dancer, and sent a double jab into the other man's face. One of the telephone pole jabs smashed into Smith's nose, causing a new torrent of blood. He seemed to blink twice and Wolf came across with a straight right that sent Smith staggering back and then to his knees, dropping down toward the street.

Wolf searched in vain for that extra shot of adrenaline that would allow his sleep-deprived body to follow up but felt a few seconds too slow.

A few seconds was all it took for Smith to recover, exhibit another sly, bloody grin, and stoop down to pick up one of the fallen pistols.

"You're pretty good," he said and pointed the gun at Wolf's chest. "Ain't sure I can beat ya."

Wolf's anticipation of the round ripping through his body went unfulfilled. Instead, the distinctive, loud, piercing sound of an automatic rifle set on full auto thundered through the otherwise silent night air.

Was it Mac's Jammin' Jenny?

No, he realized. It was a Kalashnikov.

He'd heard that sound too many times on the other side of the world to mistake it.

Smith's body arched forward and twisted in a gyrating whirl, his face registering a grimace with the striking of each round.

Wolf hit the dirt.

A big man in camo BDUs stumbled out through the open doorway holding an AK-47, red blood staining the front and side of his blouse. His mouth drooped open and he seemed to be gasping for air, the same as Wolf. The man's eyes glowed with a look of madness. He placed his left hand on the door jamb for support and raised the rifle, redirecting the muzzle at Wolf.

The equally familiar zipping pops of an M-16 rang out at an oblique angle from Wolf's left side and the AK-47 drooped as the man in the doorway tumbled forward.

McNamara ran up, a wisp of smoke still filtering from the end of his rifle's barrel. He flattened against the wall and peered through the window frame. Wolf stooped down and grabbed his weapon, then ran forward and plucked the one out of Smith's hands. The other man's vacuous eyes stared unblinking from his expressionless face.

"Any more of them?" McNamara asked.

Wolf moved to the window and shook his head.

"Don't know," he said.

"What about Cummins?" McNamara said.

"He took off," Wolf said. With the bandito, he added silently.

"Well, go after the son of a bitch," McNamara said. "I'm good here."

"Let's clear this building first," Wolf said, thinking this new one had probably come through the tunnel. "You never leave a residual force on your flank."

Mac grinned.

***

Cummins ran between the buildings, holding the bandito close to his chest and hardly believing how perfectly things had turned out for him.

Well, not too perfectly, he thought. He still had to get the hell out of here but from the sound of the gunshots, he'd be able to pull it off if he could find that damn car. Keller's sudden reemergence had given him the break he needed to escape the kill zone and the fire fight would keep any of them from following him, at least for the moment. He kept trundling forward, each breath feeling like it was littered with razor blades.

And suddenly there it was: the Caravan.

He ran the remaining steps and tore at the camouflaged netting with his free hand.

It came away easily and he shifted the precious bandito to his left hand and pulled out the car keys.

His foot bumped into something as he moved around toward the driver's door and he saw the flat tires—both the left front and left rear.

Tears came to his eyes as he thought how close he'd come to making it all work. It would have all been so perfect.

Straightening up, his mind raced, trying to figure out his next option. There was always another option.

Wolf had to have come here in a car. If he could find it and somehow get it started ... Maybe the keys were in it ...

Maybe he could just hide here or bury the bandito and surrender when the FBI eventually came. He'd call and tell Fallotti that he had the statue hidden and if they got him out of jail and gave him a reward, he'd tell them where it was.

Would they go for it?

They had to. It was the only option he had left but in the meantime, he had to find a good hiding place for both of them, him and the bandito.

Cummins dashed through the building to the next street. He heard no more sounds of gunshots, which meant that they were either dead or coming for him.

A sudden flood of light blinded him for a moment and then he saw that it was a car's headlights. The silhouette of a big man appeared at the edge of one of the beams. He raised his arm and Cummins saw that he was holding a gun.

The jig was up. He was caught.

"You from the FBI?" he asked.

"Wrong agency," the man said.

"Wait," Cummins said, pausing and starting to strip off the neoprene brace with the money-belt inside. "I've got money."

The next second he felt the round pierce his gut before he heard the noise.

***

The sound of the gunshot told Wolf that it was on the next block, right down from where they'd seen Riley's vehicle. He moved quickly through the piles of debris and saw the Caravan, the netting partially ripped off.

He moved past the vehicle and up to the edge of the building. A big black guy holding a gun stood in the center of the street standing over a fallen Cummins. Next to him, a white guy with feathered back blond hair stood next to a bronze Blazer holding something. Wolf looked closer and saw that it was the bandito statue and the white guy was Richard Soraces. Cummins was on his back, his arms and legs moving like a big crab that had been upended on the beach. The black guy leveled the pistol at him and fired another round. Cummins jerked and then lay still. As the black guy stooped down and started to undo something from Cummins's supine form, Wolf brought his weapon up and acquired a sight picture on the black man's chest.

"Don't move," he shouted. "You're surrounded."

The black man froze but didn't drop his weapon.

"Wolf?" Soraces said. "That you?"

"The FBI's got the area surrounded," Wolf said. It was a total bluff but he hoped the lawyer and his associate would buy it.

"I think not," Soraces said. He ducked down out of sight and the black guy's pistol exploded with a muzzle flash.

Wolf squeezed off two rounds and saw the black guy fall.

The Blazer accelerated backwards down the street, its lights extinguishing as it went.

Wolf thought about firing in that direction but didn't.

No sense shooting at someone you can't see, he thought, and began moving up on an oblique path toward the fallen assailant.

Keeping his weapon trained on the fallen man, Wolf stepped close enough to catch a glimpse of one open, glazed eye. He kicked the black man's gun away and knelt to check him, pressing his finger against the man's exposed eyeball.

There was no reaction.

He shoved the dead man off Cummins, who was also obviously dead. Something dark and long was in the black man's hands.

Wolf studied it and saw it was a neoprene back brace of some sort but there was something protruding out of it made of brown leather. After managing to pull the back brace free, Wolf saw it contained a leather money-belt. He unzipped one of the pockets and saw a thick bundle of greenbacks, all hundreds.

McNamara appeared at his side, holding the M-16 and shining his flashlight down on the two bodies.

"You get Chad?" Wolf asked.

McNamara nodded. "He's okay."

Wolf felt a flood of relief. "Thank God."

"Who's the guy that took off in the Blazer?" McNamara asked.

"That lawyer, Soraces," Wolf said, momentarily wondering if they could go after him in the Escalade. But what would be the point? And they now had Chad with them.

"That Cummins?" McNamara motioned toward the bloated corpse.

"Yeah."

"Who's the other dude?"

Wolf shook his head.

Down at the intersection, the Escalade drove past and McNamara waggled his flashlight. The vehicle jerked to a stop, backed up, turned, and drove down to them.

"It's Kasey," McNamara said. "We got Chad and

that Cherrie gal in the Caddie. She's hog tied."

Kasey honked the horn. McNamara waved.

The beam of his flashlight swept over the money belt and Mac whistled.

"Looks like whoever that dude was, he was rich."

"This was on Cummins." Wolf said.

"Shit, then it's yours then."

"I don't know about that."

"I do." McNamara stooped down and grabbed the belt. "We gotta get Chad to the hospital," he said.

Wolf stood up quickly. "I thought you said he was all right?"

"He is, but he's unconscious." McNamara's clenched jaw twitched. "That stupid broad said she give him one of her sleeping pills to quiet him down. Seems he saw his daddy buy the farm back in the fort."

"Shit," Wolf said, wondering what effect that would have on Chad. He'd been through so much already ... But kids were resilient. He handed his gun to McNamara. "You go ahead. I'll stay here and call the FBI."

"You think you oughta do that?"

"Somebody's got to," Wolf said. "And we're going to have to explain some things anyway."

McNamara made a slight jerking motion with his head. "I don't know."

"I'm through running," Wolf said. "And I gave Franker my word."

McNamara stared at him.

"Don't worry," Wolf said. "I'll keep you out of it as much as I can. Tell them you and I came here because Cummins called with the ransom demand. We exchanged the bandito for Chad and the bad guys shot it out with each other. I'll tell them you're at the hospital."

"This is sounding an awfully lot like Mexico. Think they'll buy it?"

"What choice do we have?" Wolf clapped him on the shoulder. "But I suggest you look around for a good, temporary place to stash all the weapons real quick, especially Jammin' Jenny."

"Hell, if need be, I can still dig a pretty good foxhole, and I got my entrenching tool in the Caddie," Mac patted his rifle. "I ain't gonna let nothing happen to this old gal."

Kasey honked again, twice this time, and McNamara turned and ran to the Escalade.

Wolf watched as they drove away and then walked over to the side of the street. He sat down on the curb, wishing he had something to wipe the sweat and blood off his face and hands. As he took out his cell phone he felt the exhaustion creeping over him once more and longed to be anyplace but here.

But they'd saved Chad and that was all that mattered.

Now, it was time to call Special Agent Franker.

CHAPTER 15

Pima County Jail
Tucson, Arizona

72 hours later

Wolf walked out of the county jail lockup wearing the orange uniform they given him during his brief 72-hour stay. Although he hadn't been given a chance to shower, the deputies had allowed him to wash his face and hands. The food hadn't been that bad either and compared to four years at Leavenworth, this place was a snap. He saw two cars parked by the curb. One was the Escalade with Mac, Kasey, and Chad all waving. The other was the familiar navy-blue sedan with the U.S. Government plates. Special Agent Franker got out of the passenger side of that one and walked over to him.

"Got a few minutes to go for a little walk?" Franker asked.

"If we walk fast," Wolf said. "And if you don't mind the way I smell. I haven't showered in about four days."

Franker smiled. "I'll try to stay upwind."

They fell into step together, walking side-by-side at a slow pace.

"That girl give anything up?" Wolf asked.

"Cherrie, with an I E?" The FBI man smiled. "Started singing like a canary. Claimed to have been an innocent victim brought along by Smith and his partner Riley. Claimed she cooperated out of fear for her own safety and to protect the kid. Basically corroborated your account of the shootout in the town but said that your buddy McNamara had a rifle that we still haven't recovered from the scene. You wouldn't happen to know anything about that, would you?"

Combat loss, Wolf thought. "What did Mac say about that?"

"Not much. He lawyered-up, too."

"How'd the siege of Fort Lemand turn out?" he asked.

"Over before it started," Franker said. "As soon as the militia guys found Colonel Best's body, they folded up like a Japanese lantern."

"Been a while since I saw one of those."

"Yeah, me too." Franker sighed. "You know, I really

expected more out of you. You promised to come clean with me for helping you and then all you did was lawyer-up in there."

"Not true," Wolf said. "I called you and gave you the location of the dead bodies and the stolen bank loot, didn't I? And I stood by until your SWAT team arrived and arrested me."

"True, and we appreciate that. But there's still a lot of unanswered questions about all this."

"And maybe someday," Wolf said, "when I have all the answers, I'll give them to you."

Franker snorted a laugh. "Yeah, right. I won't be holding my breath on that."

"It's never a good idea to hold your breath," Wolf said and stopped.

The Escalade came to a jolting halt.

Wolf started to turn, then paused and held his open palm out toward Franker.

"Until the next time," he said. "And thanks."

Franker canted his head and gazed down at Wolf's hand, then shook it.

"See you around, Wolf," he said and headed back toward his sedan. "Stay in touch."

Wolf got into the front passenger seat. Chad waved a welcome from his car seat with both hands and Kasey reached forward and gave Wolf's shoulder a squeeze.

"How you doing, little guy?" Wolf said.

"I'm good," Chad said.

"He's fine," Kasey added.

Wolf smiled and nodded. He shifted around in the seat and fastened his seat belt.

"So we got to go dig up Miss Jenny?" he asked.

"Nah," McNamara said. "After I dropped these two off at the ER, I went down the street and rented myself a car with a solid looking trunk. I then parked the rental in the hospital lot with Miss Jenny and her friends inside. Left them there for the duration."

Wolf grunted an approval. "Where'd you find that lawyer?"

"Ms. Dolly recommended him," McNamara said. "He do all right by you?"

"The guy was great. We prepared a general statement and read that, then he told me to clam up, which I did. He threatened to go to court with a habeas corpus and they had to let me go without any charges."

"Kept my you-know-what out of the ringer, too," McNamara said with a laugh. "Of course, we haven't got his bill yet, but I ain't worried. You want to know how much was in that damn money-belt?"

"Surprise me later," Wolf said. "Right now all I want to do is get home and stand under a hot shower for a couple of hours."

"And speaking of lawyers," Kasey said. "There's no sign of that Soraces guy at Bailey and Lugget anymore. Seems he was only temporarily employed there."

"I gave his name to the feds," Wolf said. "And I'm sure his employer, Mr. Von Dien, was less than pleased when he found that his bandito contained nothing but solid plaster." He snorted a laugh. "I'll bet it was reminiscent of that scene in *The Maltese Falcon*, minus Bogey of course."

McNamara turned up the air-conditioning and hit the gas as they got onto the northbound entrance ramp of the freeway.

Wolf leaned back and closed his eyes. He'd had plenty of time to ruminate on the situation over the past 72 hours and plan his next move and there was one thing he knew. There was a video out there that could clear him, and come hell or high water, he was going to find it. And as for Von Dien, it was time to stop dodging his attacks.

Wolf was tired of being the stalked. It was time to do some hunting of his own.

"As long as it takes," he said aloud.

Wolf rotated his head and saw Mac glancing at him out of the corner of his eye and looking like he could read his thoughts.

"How far?" McNamara asked.

"All the way," Wolf answered.

"Damn straight."

A LOOK AT: DEVIL'S ADVOCATE

WILL REDEMPTION EVER COME?

That's the question former Army Ranger Steve Wolf keeps asking since he served time for a war crime he didn't commit.

Wolf has been struggling to rebuild his life and ultimately clear his name, and when a path to doing just that materializes, Wolf finds himself being stalked by shadow-like foes who seem to know his every move. Unbeknownst to Wolf, his adversaries are being funded by the same wealthy sociopath who set Wolf up for the false war crime charges back in Iraq, and this rich man will stop at nothing to obtain a priceless artifact and see Wolf destroyed.

Following this trail to possible salvation, Wolf and his friend and mentor, Jim McNamara, find themselves facing a brutal gang of bikers as well as a group of highly proficient rogue CIA-trained killers.

In a desperate struggle to save an innocent life and seize his last chance at redemption, Wolf must face overwhelming odds in a battle against the powerful forces that have tormented him for so long.

AVAILABLE FEBRUARY 2021

ABOUT THE AUTHOR

A decorated police officer in the south suburbs of Chicago, Michael A. Black worked for over thirty-two years in various capacities including patrol supervisor, SWAT team leader, investigations and tactical operations before retiring in April of 2011.

He has a Bachelor of Arts degree in English from Northern Illinois University and a Master of Fine Arts in Fiction Writing from Columbia College, Chicago. In 2010 he was awarded the Cook County Medal of Merit by Cook County Sheriff Tom Dart.

Black wrote his first short story in the sixth grade, and credits his then teacher for instilling him with determination to keep writing when she told him never to try writing again.

www.MichaelABlack.com.